THE MONKEY
AND CHAIN OF LIFE

BY:

Nadereh Oweissi

THE MONKEY AND CHAIN OF LIFE

BY: Nadereh Oweissi
Translated By: Sara Kent
Edited by: Sarah Ravani

First Edition- 2012

I S B N: 978-0615775289

Novel

"The Monkey and chain of life, is an amalgam of Iranian culture and politics.

This mixture of fiction and nonfiction gives an amazing story of an Iranian girl named Azadeh that accidentally got involved with Afghani drug Traficant in Iran. To find a way out, she had to make many decisions. But she bravely chose the road less traveled.

This story portrays a picture of the people in my country, Iran.

I have attempted to find a way among the homicides, accidents, deaths, and ill fortunes to put my thoughts together. The story depicts effort and perseverance in the face of life's challenges, all expressed in simple diction. Even when imagination is at work, the story has reflections of underlying truth and reality."

CONTENTS

CHAPTER ONE

Azadeh looked pale. Frightened and motionless she was looking at the darkness in the garden. She was watching the shapeless shadows, which were moving through the trees.

She was working as a nurse at a hospital for the past fourteen years. The hospital used to be a castle a long time ago during the Qajar dynasty. She had heard strange stories from the patients during this time. The ghosts were looking for something in their old rooms, rooms that, at some point in time, belonged to women from Naseriddeen Shah's 'haramsara" (residence of wives and concubines). Perhaps they could even hear the sound of the Shah's cane hitting the floor. These stories would not surprise her any more because she knew they were created by the patient's imaginations that were fabricated by the movements of the little boughs in the garden at nights. This was the first time that she was actually taking her patients' imaginations seriously. The shadows seemed to be like ghosts. This autumn night had a strange taste to her. Her gut was telling her something bad was about to happen. She took her gaze off the darkness and threw her wimpy body on her chair by the desk. It was such a long night! It seemed to her there was no end to it. She took a magazine out of her desk in hopes of distracting herself by looking at the pictures.

She heard some footsteps. It was Maryam, her coworker, with coffee mugs in her hands. Azadeh took the coffees from her and said: "Maryam come! Look outside. Tell me, do you see what I see? I mean, the shadows." Maryam, who couldn't believe hearing what was coming out of her mouth, looked into her hazel eyes, which in her long and pale face were filled with fear, and asked; "Shadows? You mean, you see them too," as she continued to press her face onto the window and look into the garden. Azadeh was staring at her like a frightened child. Maryam looked at her mischievously and said, "Are you crazy? What ghosts? Are you okay?" Azadeh said, "I don't think I was dreaming, I really saw some shadows in between the trees," Maryam laughed. "Let go of this nonsense Azadeh, you're crazy." Azadeh responded, "Well, I don't know. Maybe you're right. Maybe it was just a dog or a fox in the dark. But still, I don't feel alright and I am very worried. I have to call on Hamed to make sure the boys are fine." Maryam wrinkled her eyebrows, narrowed her dark eyes and said, "Put the phone down! It's past midnight. You're worried over nothing! The kids are fine. Do not call and wake them up at this hour over nothing!" Azadeh put the phone down and said, "I have a weird feeling, I have never felt like this before. I hope I can make it to the morning." Maryam shook her head and impatiently asked, "Why? What has changed? This is the same garden you have been looking at for the past fourteen years, seeing shadows are not new either. Why are you doing this to yourself? Have your coffee, it will calm you down." Maryam was kind with a smiling face. Azadeh said, "I'm happy to have you as my friend." With a smile Maryam replied:" Of course, you have to be happy, who else is going to listen to this nonsense at this hour of the night?"

Azadeh responded, "I guess, you are right. Talking to you makes me calm. The nights that you are not here, these walls close on me."

Maryam was content with her reply. She liked that Azadeh liked her too. Within a few months they both were on the verge of turning forty. Their life stories were almost the same. They were both divorcees with the same worries as mothers away from their children. Maryam took the empty mugs to the kitchen and then, went into the ward to check on the patients. She was worried about Azadeh. What was going on with her? It was strange that after fourteen years, she was still not accustomed to people dying. It must be the leftovers from yesterday's nervous breakdown. As she was about to turn away from the hallway, she turned her head to make sure Azadeh was not on the phone.

Azadeh was supposed to write a report on a patient for his doctor, but she could not do it. Her brain was not cooperating with her. She threw the pen on the desk. There were strange noises along with the howling of the wind. It sounded like an army was running on the roof. This was not hallucination. These noises are not my dreams! There must be something happening on the roof. She got up to get

Maryam, but she froze in her place. A throng of shadows, which in low light looked like a dark cloud, were coming toward her. Azadeh confused and scared sat on her chair. Her heart was racing. She covered her face with her hands. She was too frightened to look. She could not think. She was about to jump and run when the shadows became too close to her. The noises sounded closer. Someone touched her shoulder. She jumped with a scream. She opened her eyes and saw faces lined up in front of her staring at her. There were two women dressed in the black Chador (The lower-up from head to toe), two men in Pasdar (slamic guard) uniforms and the night watch Mr. Hassan.

She took a deep breath and put her hand on her beating heart. Her eyes were fixated on the faces. She could not stand up and instead, fell on the chair. An icy smile came to her lips and said, "You guys scared me. For a moment I thought you were ghosts coming toward me. You know, there's a history of ghosts and spirits in this building and tonight we were quite involved with these illusions. I have to tell you, your presence in here is unusual too. Certainly you are not here to visit a patient at this hour of the night."

Two of the Pasdars were females. One of them said; "You guessed it, we are not here for a casual visit. We have orders to arrest you. Get over here with your arms up in the air."

-"I don't understand? Me? I'm being arrested?"

Azadeh looked at the hospital guard with disbelief. He shrugged his shoulders to indicate his total ignorance about what was going on. Azadeh said to him, "Maybe you brought them here by mistake." She then took her gaze off him and turned to the Pasdars. "Who are you guys really looking for? Obviously, there's a mistake!" The same female Pasdar said, "No, there's no mistake. We know exactly whom we have to arrest. What are you waiting for? Arms in the air and get over here, otherwise we have to use force." Azadeh, as though trying to ignore the fact that they really were after her, calmly said, "You must be joking, right? Please leave and do not waste my time." The female Pasdar took her by the wrist and said, "We are not joking with anybody." Azadeh, now scared, with a trembling voice said: "Why and for what? It's my right to know my charges, isn't it?"

-"They will let you know in the jail."

-"Jail? What are you talking about? What prison?"

Azadeh tried to grab the phone. She was thinking of calling her uncle. She had to warn him. A hand forcefully grabbed the phone from her and slammed it on the receiver. Then they grabbed her wrists, pulled her and handcuffed her. A voice commanded her to go with them. Azadeh, startled by this sudden action, screamed and protested. The night guard, silent, rigid and suspicious was staring at her. Azadeh yelled at him to get help and call someone, but the guard did not move. He did not want to miss a minute of this show. Azadeh, confused and surprised, was looking at the women who were emptying the contents of her desk drawer and her pockets. Her cell phone, a pack of cigarettes, a lighter and everything else, which belonged to her, were all confiscated.

She surrendered now. She did not know what wrong she had done to the government, which resulted in her going to prison. The patients were awakened by her screams. Those who could walk and get up from their beds were now in the hallway, maybe there was another case of exorcism?

Maryam heard the noises too. She was in the break room taking a broken nap. Thinking that a patient was in pain, she hurried to the hallway to quiet them with a painkiller or something. What's going on in here? She saw a few patients going towards the end of the hallway. Her stomach churned. Something must have happened to Azadeh. She saw her in between the black wings of the women's chadors coming toward her along with two big bearded Pasdars.

Maryam confused and frozen in her place looked into Azadeh's face and asked, " What's going on Azadeh? Where are they taking you?"

-"I wish I knew, wait till morning, do not wake my mother. It's better to talk to Sepideh only."

They put Azadeh in the back seat of the patrol car. She was trapped in between the two women. Two fat butt cheeks were pressing her between them. She was suffocating. Her wrists in pain from the tight handcuffs were burning. She said to the women, I cannot run away, how am I going to run away, move over! But there was no reaction from them. They were quiet and only looking in front of them. The car, as if traveling with the wind, was splitting the night in a hasty run.

Her mind was fast at work. She was looking for

something that she must have done wrong. Then the face of that young guy in the park came t o her. Maybe he is the reason, is he caught? They must have seen me giving him my jacket. That's it. That's why they are arresting me.

Azadeh was born in Vanak village and continued to live there on the fifth floor of a six story building in a small apartment overlooking a small public park with a beautiful view.

She took walks in that park every once in a while. She loved walking. Walking on the pebbles and hearing their little song under her feet always sounded amusing to her ears. On one of her walks, Azadeh met a young man, who at a first glance seemed like a crazy person. The way he dressed suggested he was mad. He had no shirt on, had tie and a green shawl wrapped around his head like a turban. His jeans were torn up. Azadeh smiled and passed him. The guy, pointing to his clothes, said that he was confused by all the unharmonious events and felt like he had been looted. He mostly blamed the Arabs for this looting. To him, the government was like an Arab. But that quiet Tâe-à-Tâe had become a scream and he had exploded by sharing everything on his mind about the government.

His destiny was clear. The government agents had heard him. They came after him to teach him a lesson. The guy had run away. Right at that moment, Azadeh had called him to get her jacket to change his appearance. The guy put it on while running away. Azadeh saw him buttoning up his jacket, and walking slowly and calmly by the guards. They were looking for the naked guy in the crowd!

Thinking about the guy didn't last long since it was useless. Let's say they came after me because of that incident, but why now? After six months? And in the middle of the night at my work? If they were after me then they knew my address. They could have come to arrest me at my home, I would have been more helpless there than my workplace.

Now she started to feel less worried. It seemed more logical to her that this whole thing was a mistaken identity case. It was not unheard of these mistakes happening within the country. They would arrest someone, keep them for a few weeks or even a month, and then conclude it was all a mistake and let them go.

The car's windows were tinted. Her eyes could only see darkness and she couldn't figure out where in town they were. She only knew they were taking her to a distant place, but distant in comparison to where? She had no idea.

Suddenly the car halted to a sudden stop. They threw a thick rag over her head, which covered her head all the way to her chest. One had to be blinded to ensure they did not see anything. She was shoulder to shoulder between the women and was walking step by step with them. She could hear them giving her directions, "there are stairs here, climb up six steps and then three here, bend your head now up, that's it. Go on." Azadeh followed all their directions since she was unfamiliar with this maze of a building. A door opened on its hinges. The woman said to take three steps ahead. She did not follow that order.

-"Where is this place? Which prison?"

-"Go in and you'll find out later!"

She took only one step when the door shut closed behind her with an old cracking noise.

She took the rag off her face with a rage and threw it away. It was all dark, there was no light to allow her to see anything. She sat down instinctively since she didn't know what was around her, maybe a hole, nails or bars. She wanted to stay still, but could not help it. She had to use her sense of touch to get a feeling of this place that felt like a dungeon. Cautiously she started to slide down on the floor until she could touch a wall. She then turned around and leaned on it. It seemed to her this place was a basement with no windows and ventilation. The smell of moldy air hit her nostrils. She was cold. Her fingers were stuck on her short and dark hair underneath the headscarf. She started thinking. Pasdars, the young guy and the ghosts, were running through her head. She had to find that rag to cover her legs with it. She pulled her body off the wall and started to slide her way back to find the rag. She found it and a childish smile came across her lips.

An hour passed and she could hardly tolerate the heavy air in the dungeon. She was getting scared. What if they don't come for her, I'll die in this dungeon. She jumped up and with tiny steps felt her way through the walls. She had felt three of the walls and on the fourth wall her fingers touched an iron gate. Azadeh started banging on the doors nonstop with her handcuffed hands. Nothing. God please send someone. Do not let me die here. She started crying. Then she thought she heard a footstep. She wiped her tears away. The sound of footsteps came closer and stopped at the door. The door opened and a weak light flashed into her eyes. Now, Azadeh could see in front of her feet. Without any hesitation she threw herself outside. She was hyperventilating.

These two women were not the same ones she had seen before. One of them asked her, "What is it? Do have a heart problem?"

- "No, but there's no air in here, I was suffocating. It's so easy to die in here."

- "No you won't die, don't make a big deal out of it."

- "Are you mad? I told you there is no air in there. I was dying."

- "Go in, two more hours won't kill you."

Despite her anger, Azadeh knew it wasn't in her best interest to fight with the guards. These were nobodies and she did not have the patience to hear nonsense from them too. One of the guards who was silent and seemed to be younger said, "Maybe it's better to transfer her into another cell." The other guard said they had to get permission from Hadji Khanoum and she was not there yet. "Go in, we'll be back to get you soon."

- "No way, not even for a second am I going back into that cell. I'll die in there." The younger guard suggested they take her with them and if Hadji Khanoum wasn't there then they would bring her back.

Azadeh was walking in between them and with open

eyes she looked at her surroundings. They passed a short hallway. Azadeh reached a room with its walls covered by posters of mullahs. Hadji Khanoum was sitting behind a wide desk. She was playing with her rosary beads. She seemed to be in her sixties. Her arched eyebrows were joined together by deep frown lines. Her glasses had a big frame. Her eyes behind the glasses seemed as big as a cow's eyes. Her expression underneath her puffed eyelids seemed naughty and bitter and that could bring fear into people's guts. Azadeh was frightened and tried to not look at her directly.

The woman realized that her appearance had intimidated Azadeh. She felt good and tried to blow up like a blowfish. Her chins puffed up underneath her veil. She ordered the guard standing next to her to open Azadeh's handcuffs. "We'll take care of her right now." Azadeh looked at her swollen wrists and as she was cursing the woman silently, she sat in front of her as she had been ordered to. The phone rang and the woman started talking on the phone. This gave Azadeh a chance to think and calm herself down. She looked out the windows. The blinds were halfway drawn. All she could see were walls and windows with iron bars on them.

The woman was talking on the phone but at the same time she was analyzing Azadeh. Azadeh was calm with her legs crossed and was looking out the window. It seemed to her that Azadeh wouldn't be an easy person to deal with. She was not like the others. She was not shaking, nor was her gaze to the floor. She was not chewing on her fingernails and was not crying either. Even the fear, which Hadji Khanoum had seen in Azadeh a few minutes ago was now gone. Azadeh was involuntarily listening to Hadgi's conversation on the phone. They were discussing charity food for Ramadan, the holy month of fasting. She was giving them instructions on how to put it together. Finally she finished her talk and as she leaned her fat body on the desk she said; "I'm sure you know why you're here."

Azadeh replied with a smile, "No, I don't."

-" Really, so you're saying you don't know why you're here?"

-" Of course not, please enlighten me."

The woman leaned back, looked down at the desk and said;" You're making it hard, so you don't want to talk."

-" Talk? Tell me why I'm here I promise I'll talk, I'll become a chatterbox for you."

The woman was experienced. She had encountered prisoners like her too many times before. She must do the same thing again; ignore her to show that her demeanor didn't affect her a bit.

She puffed up a little more and threw the rosaries around her wrist. With the same huffing voice she said, "Listen carefully girl; we don't want to take your deposition now. Wait for a while and think. Your fate is in your own hands. You can wise up and tell the truth to lighten up your sentence, or spend the rest of your life here and get tortured."

Azadeh pulled herself up to the level of Hadji's eyes. Her facial muscles tensed up. There was a big question in her wide eyes.

-"Truth, what truth! What are you talking about? What am I supposed to say? Are you sure you haven't made a mistake and arrested me instead of someone else?"

Hadji was great at her job, she made a gesture of laughing, moved her fat body in her seat and as she was turning the rosary beads she said," You know what sister; silence in solitary is not that bad, especially for a person like you. Maybe there, fear of God will come to your heart and you will get wise, then you will help yourself and us."

Solitary prison was a fearful word, which hit Azadeh like a bullet. She felt like fire, her eyeballs were burning, fire was even in her voice, "Do you even know what you're talking about? What am I accused of? You can't imprison me without indicting me first! I know there are no laws but it's not like you can do whatever you want either. You have to tell me why am I arrested, it's my right to know."

The woman's look was accusing. As if she was saying it's useless, don't pretend! We will catch you. Azadeh clearly got the message. She banged her fist on the desk, "God is my witness I don't know anything, I swear to all things holy, I have no idea why I'm in this God forsaken place, you guys are all crazy, crazy!" Hadji was certain of her control over her, yet Azadeh's fearlessness did not agree with her and she wanted to slap her in the face. But the mask of aloofness she had on, made her ignore her anger and she just said, "Shut the hell up. I don't see any use in this; take her back to her cell."

Azadeh screamed and cursed with all the energy that was left in her body. She fought to free herself from the guards who were dragging her toward the cell. Fearless, she was throwing punches in the air in all directions. She heard the guard's ouches and something fell on the floor. Hadgi Khanoum jumped from her seat to the middle of the room; she pushed hard against the floor and commanded the guards to handcuff this rebel woman

Azadeh, beaten and exhausted, was dragging her body in between the two women guards through the long corridors. The small cells were jammed together, a pale light was coming through a small crack in the ceiling, and the noise of crying, screaming and foul language was overpowering.

At the end of the corridor a door opened, a hand freed her hands and another hand pushed her into the cell. The cell was as small as a chicken coup with a window close to the ceiling. Through the iron bars that shielded the window, a handful of sky showed through. There was a camel colored blanket and pillow on a small bed on the cement floor.

A vague smile, which showed her sorrow and disbelief, formed on her face. This hole smells like death. She laid down on the bed, put her hands under her head and looked up at the small sky and listened to the raindrops hitting the glass on the window.

Was she to believe that she had done something wrong and broken the law? But, what? What had she done? She was wracking her brain out. Hadji Khanoum had asked her to reveal a truth. Her thoughts again went to the young guy in the park, but what could she know that she was supposed to reveal? Pasdars had heard the guy and known about him, he was not an underground activist, otherwise he would not have been making those comments in public. Then the truth must be elsewhere. She didn't belong to any opposition, nor did she have a high-ranking position of authority, which might have made someone angry at her. She was only a nurse with a meager salary and was hardly making ends meet. She would whisper her dreams to herself so that no one could hear them. She didn't know how long she was staring at the rain, but her eyes were starting to burn. She turned to face the wall. The wall was covered with names etched into it, Shahla, Maliheh, Fatima, and others. Where are you now Shahla or Fatima?

Her entire body was craving for a cigarette. Her mouth was dry. How was she to endure this and stay calm? How was she going to find a way out?

The night was limping into the room. She was twisted in the middle with cramps in her stomach. She had to go to the rest room. A very weak light was lighting the cell. The glass covering the light seemed like a dead turtle pinned on to the ceiling, smoked and black. Azadeh could not tolerate it any longer and was pounding on the door with her fists. But it seemed like she was the only one who could hear her pounding. She crawled back into her bed and brought her knees to her chest. Then started cursing everyone and anyone who came to her mind. The loudspeakers started the Azan (the calling to prayers for moslems). In a few minutes there were footsteps at her door and the key in the lock turned. She saw two guards at the door. One of them was holding a bowl of food, with a spoon and a piece of bread. Azadeh abruptly put her scarf on her head, "Take me to restroom, I can't hold it anymore." The guard put the bowl down and said, "Then, hurry up and cover up your hair."

Azadeh barked at her, "You're a woman! Is my hair exciting you?"

They took her through the maze of corridors as they held on to her tightly. She was bent over in pain. She was praying to God that she could make it to the restroom. In the bathroom she saw other women standing next to the sink. They were standing side by side washing up for the morning prayers. There was no sign of life in their faces. Their eyes were sunken. Their bodies, hanging underneath the gray uniform, looked like a puppet. From their appearance she figured they must be addicts, and was only out of fear of the guards that they were pretending to be God abiding citizens and washed up for the prayers and whispered nonsense in Arabic. Although they were standing side by side there was no conversation going on. There was no noise other than the water running. There was nothing to say, they were just waiting for something without knowing what it was. Azadeh was surprised at this silence. She was more surprised at herself for not having any interest to start a conversation with them. Not even asking them questions about the whereabouts of the prison. It was hardly possible that they knew the answer.

It was cold in the cell. She was shivering. Everything was

too light and not appropriate for the weather, the blanket, pillow and the mattress. She even thought the walls were too thin. When she saw the highly decorative plastered ceiling in the interrogation room, she knew it wasn't a conventional prison building; it must have been one of the mansions of the rich, which was confiscated by the revolutionary guards at the time of revolution. She thought to herself; where are you now to see what has happened to your beautiful mansions and flower gardens, now they are turned into prisons with crows nesting on the trees and roofs.

As she was looking out to the sky, she started to review her life, counting her sins, sifting and weighing them. These sins were not really sins, but in this upside down labyrinth where nothing was in its place and evil was ruling, she had to look for a sin. But what could have she done or said that was so offending? If only she knew she could calm down and bear her punishment.

She started by going through the opportunistic chameleons, who changed their colors according to benefits of the time. There were those who would come to the hospital as patients, complaining of the tyrannical government to find a sympathizing ear and would then report them to the authorities. So many times people would lose their jobs by sympathizing with these chameleons. But she was always aware of them and had never said anything discriminating. Although her heart was heavy, she would put a smile on her face and go to the praying room to listen to the preacher woman, who would come from time to time to lecture the nurses. The woman preached empty words, which would never go to heart for they were only condemning words suggesting that only the preacher was right in her faith and only she truly believed in the causes of the revolution. Azadeh wished she had not sympathized with the revolution and had regretted it many times.

Azadeh continued searching in her mind and could not find anything. She thought she must have done something that she could not remember. Small sins don't stick to mind. Even if that was the case, if they could twist an arm and ask for a lot of money, then why prison! More than that, they were asking for a revelation of the truth. What truth? What is it they are looking for? What is this game of cat and mouse they are playing? Why don't they just tell her of her conviction?

Around her everything was confusing. She could not comprehend the meaning of what they were saying. Her brain was numb and her head heavy. It was fall with short days, but to her the day lingered endlessly. She had nothing to do but stare at the door and wait. Night passed and the day came. A sleepless night with no results, nothing would take a true shape in her mind.

A guard came with a cup of tea and a piece of bread with some cheese on it. She was hungry and thirsty. Tea was cold and she gulped it down in a few sips. She ate the bread and cheese in small pieces to kill time. That too was done, now what! She got up, stretched her arms and legs, but since the cell was too small her twisted body fell on the bed. Night came again, she was getting depressed. The nights would take her to a land with no sleep and no peace of mind. Her

mood was indescribable. She wanted to cry and she did that..
The loud speakers announced the Azan again. Since it didn't
seem sincere, it was depressing rather than soothing. At that
moment she felt that she didn't like God anymore, as if His
love was broken apart and fallen out of her heart. But a deep
superstitious fear was warning her; what are you doing? Get
your God together and put His love in your heart. Trust in
Him and wait. She pulled herself up to heavens and clung on
to God, she took the shepherd into her heart and whispered
to herself the old poem of Mowlavi[1] to calm down;

I'll make your shoes, comb your hair

Kiss your hands, caress your legs

In the nighttime make your bed

Yesterday she had heard from a guard that the prisoners
are released before noon. So, with every footstep at her door
her heart skipped a beat with hope. But with every bowl in
the guard's hands she knew she should spend another night
and day in the prison. It was noon and lunchtime. The door
opened and a smiling guard came in. They had brought
lunch. She wanted to complain that the soup smelled like
rotten sewage, but did not say anything. What good would
complaining do for her except ruin the good mood of the
guard and make her mad too? Forcing herself, she put a
spoonful of the soup in her mouth but spat it out with disgust,
what the hell is this poison? She moved the soup aside and
started to chew on the rock-hard bread. It would take a lot of

---

1- 13th century persian - Muslim poet known to English - speaking people as Rumi.

energy to chew on that. She shook her dress to clean it from breadcrumbs and slid under the blanket. Wishing for a deep sleep she closed her eyes, but her brain was restless and sleep was not able to enter. She was dozing off when suddenly her boys' voices came to her in a dream. She sat up and stared into the dark. What a nice dream! Her tears rolled down her face. She remembered the sad days after her divorce, all of those hard days were in the past now. All the anxieties that overwhelmed her then were gone. Now she was at ease with herself and her new life. Her life was nowhere near as glamorous as before, but she was comfortable and stress didn't keep her up anymore. She was finally at ease and could sleep without having to worry about saving the disaster she called her marriage. She had come to terms with her loneliness and accepted that her happiness should not depend on the warmth of a man's body in her bed.

She would spend Friday[2] afternoons with her two sons. She would go to Hamed's house in a melancholy mood to pick them up, then she would take them to the park or to the movies, buy them ice-cream and snacks, and tell them to be nice to their step-mom Zohreh, and to always say thank you after dinner. She would then kiss them goodbye and remind them about homework and going to bed early. For her, this had become a routine in the past four years. Everyday was the same as yesterday. Deep down, she was pleased with this arrangement that Hamed, her ex-husband, had given her. According to the Islamic law she was not allowed to see her kids more than once a week. But Hamed had ignored that law. She was their mother, after all, and should have been

---

2- In Iran Friday is the weekend.

involved with her children's lives as much as she could be. She was allowed to go to his house whenever she wanted to talk about her kids with him.

Hamed had been remarried for three years. He married his Jewish secretary, Zohreh. Hamed's new wife loved the boys and would take care of them as her own kids; Azadeh was lucky in this respect, her children were in good hands. Zohreh was a big-framed woman, her olive skin shined and her dark eyes had a sparkle of green in them. She would easily laugh and cry with the same ease. She had lost all her family members, but she had a lot of friends and they replaced the loss of her family. She loved Azadeh and her family too; Zohreh had found new mother and sisters in her family for herself.

Azadeh remembered that stormy day. It was the first time she met Zohreh. Zohreh had come to her house with puffy, red eyes from crying. She had just visited her mother's grave and on the way, she had also visited her tree. However, alas the tree was cut.

Azadeh had asked her, what was she talking about, what tree?

-"My cherry tree. We were going to escape the country. My dad had already gone. He had gone to Israel to arrange for our immigration, but a bomb had exploded in his hotel. The government did not let us bring his body back here. He is buried there in Haifa. My dad had always known he was not a welcomed guest over there, but he went and ended up dying over there. Then there came Jacob. He was not in love with me, but married me for my money. He conned my mom and lost her money in risky investments. When my mom died, I divorced him. My dad had planted a cherry tree in our backyard when I was born. He named it after me, Nissa's tree. I have loved the tree since it is the only thing I had from my dad. The tree and I grew up together. I played house underneath it and in the summertime, underneath it's shadow I would read books. In my dad's memory I would visit it every now and then. I did not need to have them open the door for me to see it. It was so tall now that it was visible over the walls. I was just happy to see it happy and growing. Today though, the door was open and I saw the inside of the backyard. My tree was stacked up in a corner. It was all chopped up."

Seeing her in that condition that day, had made Azadeh worried for her sons' well- beings. She was asking herself, how could a girl this sensitive fall in love with Hamed? Has she made this commitment with open eyes? Could she take good care of her sons and make them ready for the future life? Or will she live in the past and cry for her tree?

Azadeh remembered the day that Nissa was supposed to convert to Islam and take the name "Zohreh." That day, Zohreh had called her to be ready the next morning, "Put your prettiest dress on, I want to take you to a holy ceremony, there's a party in the Heavens for me!"

Azadeh who hadn't forgotten the cherry tree said, "Party in heavens? What do you have going on there?"

-"Angels! All the angels are supposed to take me to God

Himself in a special ceremony. Last night I dreamed of Satan. He was so mad. He was jumping up and down on the fire and drinking whiskey. Well, he had to be mad, the dirty Jew is going to become the holy Muslim!"

There was a flash of lightning and Azadeh could hear the thunder. The thunder shook her. Ahhh, just as she was falling asleep! The sleep that she was yearning for so badly! She was hoping the sleep would never leave her eyes. She was struggling to fall asleep again when the cell door opened. What now?! The light fell over her body. She saw two women. The one in front had a flashlight. The light slid from her and fell on the window. Then, they left silently. A show in darkness! What for? It's impossible to escape from this window. The storm must have broken a window somewhere.

She tried to go back to sleep, but her mind was wide-awake and her eyes could see underneath the closed lids. They were keeping watch. Azadeh's mind went back to Zohreh, her heart was with her that night. She remembered the day at the clergy's office. When she was sitting quietly and the clergy was watching her in silence while playing with his beard, both waiting for Nissa (Nissa is a jewish name and people who convert into Islam have to pick a Moslem name). The clergy would occasionally look up and pretend that he wasn't looking. Zohreh arrived, accompanied by Hamed and his mom. She looked pale and weak. Disappointment was apparent from her demeanor.

The clergy opened the book and started reading something in Arabic. Zohreh repeated the unknown words after him. She was Muslim now. Hamed's mom said, "You are not a Jew nor Nissa anymore, we have chosen Zohreh as your Muslim name. Come and have a cookie, let's celebrate." She had a box of cookies with her for this occasion. The clergy also congratulated her and guaranteed a good place for her in Heaven.(Muslims cannot marry non-Muslims, so the non-Muslim party has to convert before marrying a Muslim)

Zohreh was quiet. Azadeh wanted to tell the clergy to shut up, but didn't dare, so she just kept it to herself and thought, was this way of converting really worth anything? Couldn't he see the sadness in his helpless lover's eyes? Maybe he did, but he just ignored it since in this God pleasing act there shouldn't be any questions or observing eyes!

She threw her angry look at Hamed instead. He must have promised everything and showed a lot of money to this thirty year old girl to make her fall in love with him. Then she looked at the clergy again who was now drunk from his good act and a broad smile had spread across his face. Azadeh became angrier.

She didn't believe in "shall's" and "shall not's." She took her look off of them and left for her mother's to relieve her angry thoughts.

Her mom, although, not very educated, was very observant of what was happening around her and had a clear reasoning for everything. Every now and then, she would pick up a book to find logical answers to her questions. That day she encouraged her daughter by saying that it had always been like this, God is forgotten, people just blow their own horns and think that they are right.

That day, Azadeh calmed her nerves down by drinking wine. The wine had been made in her uncle's basement, a small homemade winery. After big wineries were shut down, basement wineries were opened to quench ever-increasing people's thirst for drinking wine.

Noon had passed and it was Azan. The sky was cloudy and the rain was still lingering from yesterday. Sleeplessness and anxiety had made Azadeh sick. Half asleep, dazed and entangled in a broken sleep, her temple was pounding and she was moaning in pain.

She turned her head when the cell door opened. It was lunchtime, but there was no bowl in the guard's hands. It was a new guard with an angry and dirty face. She must be from the south, Azadeh murmured to herself. The guard said, "Come on out and cover your hair, Hadgi has summoned you." As Azadeh got up, she felt herself get dizzy. She sat down and threw up whatever was left in her stomach. She wanted to fix herself up, but there was nothing to do about her look. She covered her mouth with her veil and followed the guard.

The interrogator was a relatively young man with a short beard and he was wearing a gray suit. His devotion to praying was apparent in his posture. His shoulders were rolled in with his neck bending over. It seemed like he has given up on the earthly existence and was anxiously waiting the afterlife where he would be rewarded by God himself for all the good deeds he had done on this earth.

The guard ordered her to sit down on the chair facing him. She greeted him as Hadji threw the pen in his hand on the desk and replied with an elongated syllable. The reply sounded like a cat's purring from deep down in his throat and brought a smile to Azadeh's face. Show off! What if he's really an Arab?!

Hadgi seemed tired. In order to not waste time, the guard skipped introductions and proceeded to that matter at hand since many prisoners were waiting to meet with him. The guards were going to interrogate prisoners only in hope of drawing a confession out of them. He pulled a picture from a drawer on his right and put it in front of Azadeh. He then slowly asked her; "Do you know him?"

Azadeh glanced at the picture and thought there's nothing left from this miserable person to be recognized. She was going to say that she didn't know him when the face looked familiar to her. Her eyes grew sharper and fixated on his face. Then she recognized him. That was her neighbor, Ahmad, who had a frightened expression in the picture. Surprised, she said, "Yes, I know him. He's my neighbor and he lives on the top floor of my apartment building. What about him?"

A lifeless smile opened Hadgi's narrow lips. Azadeh didn't understand the reason for this smile. Although, her neighbor didn't seem that important to her, she still couldn't figure out why they had kept her in prison for what her neighbor must have done. Her lips were going to move to say something, but she stopped herself. Hadgi asked, "Does your neighbor live alone?"

-"I don't know. Maybe. I haven't seen his wife or kids yet."

-"How long have you known him?'

_"It must be about two years."

-"Do you know what he does for a living?"

-"No, why should I know? Why are you asking me these questions? If he has done anything wrong it's none of my business. Why did you bring me here?"

Azadeh got up thinking that it's over. "OK, now you know who it is. Why are you waiting then, you didn't have to keep me all this time! If you had shown me the picture that very first day, I would have told you who he was and where he lived. Now you know the truth, please order them to take me home." She then got up and went toward the door, but stopped before walking through it.

The tense atmosphere in the room turned to strange when suddenly, the whole room burst into laughter. Everybody was laughing and she didn't know what she had said to have amused them this much. The female guard, whose face was as red as beets with laughter, took her hand and sat her down. Azadeh looked up and threw her anger at Hadgi. She thought, I didn't know people like him could laugh too! Hadgi, while still laughing said, "Where do you think you're going?"

-" Home, of course. You took me in the middle of the night from my work and brought me here to see if I know this guy? Well I told you what I know, so why don't you let me go? First, show me the exit, then laugh as much as you want."

-" Don't fake insanity. You know very well why you're here. Quit playing games. It will only make your case worse."

-" Games? It's you who are playing games with me. I still don't know why you have arrested me. If Ahmad has committed a crime it's not my fault, why are you punishing me?"

Hadgi turned the jade ring in his finger with a nervous gesture. It seemed like he was losing his patience. But he kept his appearance as calm as possible and said, "Then you know that the person in this picture is a criminal and what his crime is. Now tell us about yourself, who else you were working with?"

Hadgi then put on his jacket and looked at Azadeh through his glasses. His calm style in interrogation was usually effective, but in Azadeh's red face he couldn't see anything else except anger and glaring eyes. Hadgi couldn't wait anymore. He could see that the prisoner was in full control. With a calm voice he said; "OK, it's alright if you don't want to talk, but you should know you're the only one who will suffer. We will open your mouth. In here even a rooster will lay eggs if we want it to."

Azadeh's voice could hardly come out of her mouth. She said, "What crime? What crime is this that I am involved in?

If I don't know about the crime, how do you expect me to talk about it? Dammit! Say something."

Hadgi's face became so bitter that it was impossible to look at him. His tone of voice could turn the dead in their graves.

-"You imbecile woman, do you know what you have done? Your sin is so big that there is no repenting for it. Even death is not a just punishment for your actions. You have destroyed lives, killed innocent children, you spread corruption throughout the society."

Azadeh started coughing. A dry cough that scratched her throat and made it burn. When she stopped, she cried out; "Please stop it. For God's sake stop it. My ears are full of this nonsense. If you don't want to tell me, at least let me hire a lawyer, maybe he can tell me what you are talking about."

-"You know damn well what we're talking about. Don't stall, tell us who else was involved with this scoundrel!"

Rage took over Azadeh's body, she was shaking, even her lips and cheeks were shaking. She screamed, "What do you want from me? What has he done that I was a part of? This guy was only a neighbor, as any other neighbor in my building. I have only seen him occassionally in the elevator. There's no other connection between us. Are you implying I had an affair with him?"

Hadgi snorted, there was doubt in his eyes. He turned the pen with his fingers and started tapping the pen on the desk.

He was thinking, was it better to be patient and continue with the interrogation, or tell her about her crime and if she then failed to cooperate, use the whip and pliers. His phone started ringing. What he heard on the phone cleared his thoughts. He hung up and very gently, which was in total contrast to his mood a second ago, said, "My sister, why do you play dumb? Why all this nonsense! We found ten kilos of heroine in your house. You know why you're here. It's better that you quit this game otherwise your punishment will be worse."

Azadeh stopped shivering. Her body quivers were replaced with a bitter paralysis. It was as if all her joints were falling apart. Her legs and her arms were hanging motionless by her body. Her head fell back and her eyelids closed without her control. She could hear Hadgi saying, "Sister, open your eyes, we have a few questions for you." But her mind was so far away that she couldn't come back. Hadgi continued talking, he was used to these reactions. He was patient now. Azadeh pulled her head and with every bit of strength, she opened her eyes. Hadgi was standing in front of her with a glass of water in his hand. She took the glass and drank it all. Under Hadgi's stern gaze, she looked down and stared at her hands. Jumbles of thoughts were circling her mind. In the deepest corners, she was searching for an enemy. Who could have done this to her? Who's the enemy? Who wants to get rid of me by destroying me? Where has this poisonous fungus erupted? Something came to her mind and bit her like a snake. She got up and with a doubtful look, she turned to Hadji, "Now I know why I'm here. It's not fair! I know who is blowing on this fire, that bastard is still after my mom's house. He thinks I will let him get his hands on my mother's house? I'll kill him! You are all lying. Heroine in my home? It's a set up. I know everything. You are all wrong, I won't let him get my mother's house. Even if you kill me, I still won't let that happen. I won't let you guys set foot in her house, you thieves, thieves, thieves!" The cry burst in her throat and her tears started to roll down her face as her sobbing filled the room.

Her mother's house was in Vanak village. The building was a fixer upper being more than 70 years old. But the land was priceless, a lot of people were after that prime real estate, it was perfect for building a high rise. Her mom had turned down all the offers, this house to her was as dear as her children and she couldn't bear the thought of parting with it. It was left by her father and was filled with memories of her youth and childhood.

Among those whose offers were denied by her mother, Simin, was a powerful Mullah who wouldn't give up. He had even started a rumor that their street was on some city plan that required demolishing the street and her house.

Hadji's face drew together and his eyebrows twisted in a knot. He cursed underneath his breath. Now, it was his turn to defend himself and his colleagues. He put his glasses on the desk and said, "Do you even know what you're talking about? Who's after your mother's house? You're talking nonsense. Where do you get these ideas from? This is all espionage, these godless people making rumors about us.

The country has laws; our government is a just one. What has your mother done to deserve repossession of her house? Is she against God and His people? Now be quiet and answer my questions."

Azadeh pulled her veil down and thought, the fucking son of a bitch talks like he is an innocent child and has no idea of what's going on. She didn't answer Hadgi's questions. She heard her family's history from Hadgi's mouth and found out that they know everything that has happened to them and only want her acknowledgment as proof. Hadgi closed the folder and ordered the guards to take her back. Two female guards took her by the arms and led her to another room, which served as a finger printing, lab and photo room. The guards took her urine and blood samples, finger printed her and took her picture and within minutes, they took her back to her jail cell.

Azadeh was overwhelmed and confused. She couldn't think of any other reason, but her mother's house. It didn't make sense to link Ahmad to all this. Why would they involve him? She was about to believe the heroine story, but who would plant that in her apartment and who would have such a big grudge against her? Maybe it was the ancient grudges coming from life that were haunting her. For the past twenty years, she had been carrying her grief in the deepest chambers of her heart and had never said anything about her father to anyone in fear that it would cause problems for both her mother and her. Her mother's pleadings were always ringing in her ears like church bells. When she was crying over her husband's death, she had told Azadeh and

Sepideh that they were the only reasons for her to keep living and warned them not to give anyone any reason to take them away from her. Azadeh could feel the true meaning of her words now after all those years. The memories of her dad and his bravery, like his grief, must be buried in their chest. Her dad was a journalist, with a sharp tongue that would target any injustice. When Shah was overthrown he had become a hero. But after a year or so, he didn't feel right in the revolution that he had helped form. He didn't belong to this new system. Disappointed he drew back and aimed his pen against the new rulers. Her father was mostly angry at himself. He blamed himself for partaking in the revolution and helping establish the system that now served as full-grown government. As an intellectual, he transformed his image from a suit and tie to growing a full beard and wearing revolutionary attire over night. He did this just to protest against the westernization of the society without thinking about the outcomes of the alternative which was the Arabization. But, when he finally realized the results of his mistake, it was too late, despite his confession once he was behind bars. After six years in prison, they told Azadeh that he had died after a massive heart attack. But Simin, his wife, never believed this story and had told them that their dad was much stronger than that. He was a very brave man and at his age she didn't believe he had just died from a heart attack.

Thinking about her mom made her heartache. Simin was a very sensitive woman, who not only, had her own share of sufferings, but was also sensitive to other's needs as well. She would sit in the kitchen for hours and while staring at the smoke from her cigarette, she would think about others or imagine her dreams had come true. She had worked hard all her life. A monotonous job that she had grown accustomed to and it seemed impossible for her to think of herself as a separate entity from her typewriter. Simin had retired just six years ago and had spent forty years typing her way through life to support her family. Although she never earned much, she still managed to make a modest life for herself and her daughters, and even grant her deceased husband's wish. A wish that until recently had been a forbidden pleasure and punished by whip lashing. However, this threat did not stop Simin and she hired a famous musician to teach her younger daughter , Sepideh, to play the Tar(Tar is a musical instrument which is used mostly in the eastern countries indifferent forms to play the traditional music of these regions). The anxious sound of the Tar was always heard from their basement. Those were memorable times that even after sixteen years Sepideh couldn't forget. Her mom would watch and signal them if the revolutionary guards would show up and if that were the case, the teacher would run away through the roof. Sepideh was 24 with a petite frame and her hazel eyes resembled her mother's. She kept to herself and rarely spoke. Her adolescent years were spent during the suppression times. Her energy and enthusiasm was always set off by the front she kept. Her ever-vanishing smiles weren't a reflection of her true feelings on the inside. She was her uncle's secretary and was always occupied with her work and music.

Azadeh wrapped the blanket around her and was thinking of her neighbor, Ahmad. He was a quiet man.

Neighbors were always gossiping about him. He seemed like a total stranger by avoiding anyone's eye contact and never striking conservation with people. All the neighbors hated his black leather jacket. The janitor hated his guts because he was the ass throwing his cigarette butts everywhere and still refused to pay him a penny as a tip. Azadeh thought, now I know you were busy with your dirty work. You were so preoccupied in your own shit that you could not even look us in the eye. You were scared of talking to us fearing we would find out about your mess. But why, you scum? Why did you tie your life to mine? Where is it all coming from? I can imagine you in my home looking for a hiding place for your heroine. Oh God! Why did I not think of this before?

Thinking of this she banged on her head, cursed Ahmad, you fucking bastard, you homeless vagabond, why didn't I find out about your schemes, you pitiful excuse of a human. If I find you, I know what to do with you. I'll kill you; I'll cut you into pieces. Why did you do this to me, I'm innocent! Why don't you take the blame, you can pay them up and buy your life. But what about me, I don't have a penny or know anyone powerful in this government…

Just thinking of him in her apartment when she wasn't there and maybe having some of his stoned friends on her furniture made her skin crawl. She felt so sick that her head started pounding. She started feeling sorry for herself when suddenly she thought that she couldn't have missed ten kilos of heroine in her tiny apartment. She didn't even have much furniture where Ahmad could have hid his drugs under. That same day, Azadeh was supposed to work the graveyard shift and she had just cleaned the apartment thoroughly. Not a single space was left untouched. Her mind was exhausted, but she had to search through it again. Oh God, you must have brought it in my apartment during those few hours that I was gone. Can I prove my innocence and make these bearded people accept what I believe now? Her mind now was full of Ahmad's name. She could not think of anyone or anything else.

She was thirsty and it was getting unbearable. Her mouth was dry and her tongue felt like a piece of dead wood. She could not figure out her body. She was warm and cold at the same time. Her face was hot and wet from a feverish sweat, yet she also was cold and shivering. Her body temperature was escalating with passing seconds. They brought her dinner. She drank her water in one gulp and ate a little bit of the rice. Shortly after dinner, the lights were out. Tonight, like all the other nights she was sleepless because she was thinking of Ahmad, her sick body, hatred of her present situation and fear of tomorrow. She was worried about herself. She felt like dying, as if she was dragging her own corpse to the cemetery. Frightened of her situation and the constant feeling of hopelessness made her hate herself. What's wrong with you woman? You know damn well that you're innocent. This should be reason enough for you to calm down and stop thinking nonsense. They have found heroine at your house and they are doing their job, so, instead of sitting here thinking about your own death, think about a solution and make a plan to prove to these stupid's that you are innocent. She laid her body on the mattress but could not sleep. Ahmad was still dominating her mind. More hopeless than before, she couldn't help but think that if they do not believe her, then what can she do? Their language was the language of money, which she had none.

Hadje Sayed Mehdi wants money too. That dirty scroundrel has been freeloading all his life. Of course he would never put himself in danger to save her for free!

Hadji Sayed Mahdi was a clergy who was the middleman between the city officials and her uncle's construction company. For a large fee, he would get building permits for her uncle. He liked her uncle and had provided some kind of leeway for his construction company to operate. Azadeh began to think of her two innocent sons. Thinking of them made her heart tighten with sadness. It was only a few days since she had seen them, but it seemed like years to her and her heart was yearning for them. Each moment felt like a century. The possibility of seeing her loved ones again seemed like an impossible dream to Azadeh. If only she could hear their voices on the phone, then maybe this difficult time would be a little more bearable.

With an anxious mind, her eyelids started to slowly drift shut. She was both asleep and awake. Suddenly, her eyes burst open and she looked around. A cold sweat was on her face and her veil was stuck to her neck. Frightened, she continued to turn around, shook her hands, held her head in her hands tightly and wiped the sweat off. Thinking about what she saw in that twilight zone made her sick to her stomach. In her nightmare she saw herself dead and her head wasn't on her body. It was hanging from the ceiling and she could see her headless body on the bed from there. Her brain was ordering her to put the head over the body, but the body wouldn't obey it. The people in black came in and took the body with them. She sat down and held the hard pillow tightly. She looked up at the dark skies. She felt sleepy but was scared to fall asleep. She got up and walked around her tiny cell. It was a miserable wait and she was begging God to bring the sun up as fast as possible. The rays of the cold, early morning sun crawled into the cell and the demons of her nightmare were hidden. Now, she could finally close her eyes and fall asleep, but she was interrupted. The door opened and there was the same guard waiting to take her to the restroom. She let the water run over her feverish face. It was mandatory to wash up for the morning prayers. So far, she had excused herself from attending the prayers by pretending to have her monthly period. She did know how to say the prayers and couldn't pretend to be pious. She did not take long in the washroom and hurried back to her cell to get some sleep. Rather than eating her piece of bread, she succumbed to a deep slumber. The sleep, which had escaped her for three nights was now engulfing her. Sleep felt like a heavy rock taking her down the deep ocean. But something was shaking her vigorously to bring her back. Get up, let's go. Azadeh tried to ignore it but the shaking got worse and she finally opened her eyes and sat on the bed.

"Are you deaf? I said get up

Now the cell was completely bright with sunlight. She looked up and said, "Last night was a shitty night." The guard took half a step back and said, "You will have many similar nights, cover your hair and hurry up." Azadeh, yawning put her shoes on and started walking. She was sleepy and they took her through the same confused maze of corridors to the same room they had taken her the first night. The clergy this time was a middle-aged man with an expensive pair of glasses on his face, which had no enthusiasm or expression. If he wasn't wearing a turban his existence could be ignored. Azadeh said hello and sat down. She couldn't help her yawning and her eyes were watering. She closed her eyes and dropped her head down. She thought she was falling asleep. The clergy stared at her with a slanted look and said, "It's your choice if you want to answer the questions with closed eyes. We only expect the right answers from your mouth, although we already know the answers." Azadeh brought the veil down to her eyes, and slowly said, "I'm happy that you know the truth, please bless me with it too. "So you want to stick to your words that you don't know anything about the heroine?"

Azadeh thought, here we go again, God damn you all. The clergy said;,"No sister, there's no use denying it. Ahmad has already confessed. He said you were his accomplice in drug trafficking. If you're wise enough you will tell us about the rest of the gang and reduce your punishment."

Azadeh laughed bitterly. It stretched her lips and made them burn. She wet her lips with her tongue. "The son of a bitch." Then she said out loud "If you want to get his gang you have to put pressure on him not on me. I have no idea about these drugs. That bastard had planted them in my apartment." Azadeh was calm and together. She knotted her fingers together and put them under her chin with her elbows on the table not too far from the clergy's face. In her delirious state it seemed to her that the whole thing was like a movie that she was watching. Her demeanor didn't set well with the clergy. He got mad and said that he couldn't stand her disrespectful behavior, she should sit up straight, confess and get it all over with. Azadeh put her hands down and said, "Just get over with it? If I confess will you let me go?"

The clergy turned his eyes towards the window and said, "At least you won't go back into solitary." Azadeh laughed and said, "If I have to be in prison I'd rather be in the solitary." She was a no nonsense woman and the clergy was not used to dealing with this type of person. He was thinking of how he could break her spirits and make her beg. It seemed like a very difficult task, through his entire service he had rarely seen people like her. If he was hundred percent sure of her involvement then he would know how to treat her, but there was doubt and she could be completely innocent. He put on a false bitter façade and started drilling her with fearful and psychological threats. He went so far that not only woke her up and agitated, but got him pretty agitated as well. All of his body was shaking, his voice, his eyes and his shoulders. Even his short beard was standing up in his thin long face.

Azadeh couldn't take it any longer. What could she have done? For what reason should she be tortured and threatened? Why should she be denied the right to see her loved ones and had to stay in prison? Now she wasn't sitting anymore, she was standing up and screaming. The words were like un-stoppable bullets falling down on the clergy.

She was so agitated that she didn't care for anything. At this point, she was blaming all the religious figures, she could only see the turbans that took her father from them and lashed her sister. They put bitterness in their life and took the innocence from their souls. She had never rebelled in her life. She was used to enduring her pains in silence, but now fearless and persistent she was pouring out everything that was buried deep down inside her and took her happiness away from her. She pushed away the hands that were trying to keep her in her seat. Her voice got silent in a deep breath and then she sat. The guards in the room got worried and were staring at her in amazement. They were thinking that this poor woman shouldn't have lashed out her mouth like that; only God can help her now. She didn't know what would happen to her then and didn't care about it either. The clergy turned his head toward her with with a sad calm, insincere look. It seemed like it was beneath him to show any emotions or say anything. He pulled his cloak to his knees and took his glasses off. With one hand he scratched his eyes into his eye socket and with the other hand motioned to take her out of the room. She was calm now. She had no secrets any more. Even her dad's secret was out now. The swamp of hatred was drained and her soul was relaxed. She felt better and the fever left her body. In reality she was still feverish, but she wanted to free her relaxed brain from the worries of body. A few days had passed. The nightly delirium and nightmares of a dark punishment had made her fearful and nervous. She wasn't thinking of freedom anymore and was waiting for her horrible punishment. She was shaken by the thought of lashing and could already imagine the painful burning of lashes. She was still wearing the white scrubs of the hospital. They were so dirty and stinky that the stench was burning her nostrils. That morning she woke up with a strange feeling that she will never see the outside and will end up with the same fate as her dad. She was the daughter of a traitor to the revolution! An ungrateful traitor, who closed his eyes to the just causes of the revolution and all the holy men who helped achieve it. A lost man with a lost cause, who only had regurgitated the words of freedom and revolution without really putting his heart into them! Not only that, he was not even taking part in sharing the benevolent feast of victory! In that way he was detaching himself even further from his former freedom fighter friends. He should have accepted his share and pretended to enjoy it just to show his faithfulness to those people.

Azadeh, hopeless and disappointed, was drowning herself with the memories of her sons, mother and sister. Although she felt better after her harsh encounter with the clergy, she still knew it was a mistake and that it wasn't the time or the place to settle old grudges. Now she was seeing the faces of her beloveds and was regretting her irrational rage now. It wasn't just herself that she should have been concerned with. There was her family and kids as well. In this game she felt she was the loser and had risked the lives of her loved ones. When one feels helpless with nowhere to go, one will look to the heavens hoping for a miracle to happen. She held her hands under her head and was looking up to the skies, "If your heart is pure God will show His face and send the angels to your help and there will be rays of hope in your heart." There was a very faint light peeking through dark clouds. She was so mesmerized by it that she tore apart the dark clouds with her eyes. The light seemed brighter to her eyes, as if it was coming lower and lower. She thought to herself, oh God, this is a sign from you. Maybe there's an angel coming to warm up my frozen heart. She busied herself with the thoughts of angelic help and was giving herself hope. When the cell door opened and a guard brought in her lunch, she asked her if she could smell the stench from her clothes.

-"Ya, you smell like a dead dog, your scrubs, weren't they white? Now you look like a chimney sweeper."

-"Do you know what they'll do to me?

_"How should I know? They don't keep you guys in solitary confinement for long."

- "What do you mean? Where do they take us?"

-Well, if you're on death row that's obvious, the end is right here, if not then you'll be transferred to another prison and you'll rot there for a long time."

- "Then you're telling me this is temporary jail?

- "Yes, what were you thinking? Did you think you're going to be here and party on us? No, you have to work and pay for your food.

Azadeh began thinking, well I was working! Didn't she know it's our money that pays for her salary and all the Islamic schools?

The guard was gone and left a deep fear in Azadeh's heart. She was the angel of death giving her the death message. She thought of her dad again. She saw the similarity between their fates. Now she believed his death has happened as it had been told to her. She could see his frightened eyes looking from behind the bars. When his death sentence was not reversed and she saw how the shadow of death had made his eyes colorless. That day she felt so sorry for him, without really feeling the depth of his pain. She was mad at her dad and didn't understand the reasons for his actions that led to his imprisonment. She found it useless to feel sorry for his fate, but nonetheless she loved him very much. He still seemed like a hero in her eyes, who was fearless and would do anything for his beliefs.

She imagined his stubborn face, a stern face and the hate that would pour out of his mouth when he was talking about his beliefs. It seemed like he was enjoying his house arrest and out-lawed pen. With every pounding of punishment hammer, he would feel relieved from the shame he felt for his past participation in the new government.

But Azadeh, without any involvement with his cause was caught in a minute of fury and now she must spend the rest of her life paying for that moment.

Her life and death seemed so worthless to her. She was crying with regret when the cell door opened. She wasn't expecting anyone so soon. She got scared and with frightened eyes looked at the guard. This one was new. She was different than the rest of them. She was a very tall and heavyset woman. Her sunburned face smelled like the southern sun. Her veil was hanging from her head, she was neither a woman nor a man. She seemed sexless. Azadeh, as agile as a mouse, slid her body from the bed and stood up. She thought the end was there. The angel of death had come. She was so mad at herself that she started to curse herself. The guard hesitated at the doorframe to see the fear in Azadeh's eyes. Then she moved away and said,"Come on."

- "Why?"

The question seemed so irrelevant that she tried to correct herself, "Where do you want to take me?"

-"To a place where you would mind God."

Azadeh covered her mouth with her hand and with a crying voice said, "Well, if you sure are going to torture me, how many lashes?"

The guard with a calm voice said, "Well then, you think God's lashes will bring reason to your head."

Azadeh thought, God damn this lash that God gave you guys. As she was leaving the cell she said; "I never thought this would ever happen to me, I wish you would give me some time."

- "Time for what?"

- "Well everything has a price."

The woman stared at her, "You are beyond that."

Azadeh took it as she won't be left with nails or teeth.

Her heart started to beat faster. She could hear it in her ears. In a few minutes she was taken to a big, well-lit room. She looked around the room. She was expecting to see the whip or hot iron or the pliers to pull out nails or the electric shock belt. But there was nothing except for a few praying rugs rolled against the wall. Then she thought she smelled the stench of death. She had heard from her dad that they would pray for the prisoner's soul before execution. She didn't know why she was thinking of death so much. She knew there were a few steps before her sentencing and she had to go through them first. She wanted to say something but her voice wouldn't come out of her throat. Her tongue was numb and her brain with the thought of grave was going crazy. She felt like a drowning person helplessly searching for a log. She started thinking of everybody she knew, her dad's old friends, those who were silent to salvage their own lives. But they couldn't help her either, they were in trouble from both sides and their words didn't mean anything to anyone. Although they were well off, but not that generous to spend money to save her.

Her last resort was to sell her mother's house and give the money to the judge. Send Hadji Mehdi to interfere and repented. She was thinking of all these when the guard called out,

"Do you know why you're here?" Azadeh came to herself and wiped her sweaty forehead with her hand and said, "Yes I know, this is the end. I'm here for the prayer before death.

"That's right, pray if you're worthy, God will accept your prayers, I'll pray for you too."

"At least, let me call my family. Why don't you let me get a lawyer? Whatever the costs, I'll pay. Take me to Hadji, let me talk to him or at least say goodbye to my loved ones."

The woman stared at her. "Goodbye, why goodbye? Are you going anywhere or do you want to commit suicide?"

Azadeh wiped her nose and stared back at her. "Commit suicide? Why should I commit suicide? Are you guys planning to kill me like the others, then tell the public that I have killed myself?"

The guard got mad and shouted, "What are you talking about? Who told you we're going to kill you? Why are you thinking this way? All we want to do is to talk to you, we want to advise you, and show you how wrong your actions were. Maybe you will see and help us catch the criminals. If you help us, you won't stay here for long."

Azadeh felt ecstatic. For the first time life with all the hardships felt so precious to her. At the same time she was confused and didn't know how come they are going so easy with her. So her harsh words didn't bother Hadji that much. He wasn't sensitive to her insults. She was so wrong in taking his rage seriously by making an enemy out of him in her mind. She felt sorry for herself. The sexless woman now seemed feminine and even pretty to her. Even her beady eyes seemed big and beautiful. At that moment she loved everyone. The shadow of death on her face was gone. Her short and stumpy fingers looked like the hands of angels and even her movements seemed sexy to her. She felt so ecstatic that even a cockroach would have looked like a beautiful butterfly. Although she was enjoying this new feeling, at the same time she felt sad that her words didn't mean anything to anyone and that she wasn't taken seriously. She laughed with the woman.

"I never thought they would leave me alone. Then everything I said is gone like the spit from my mouth? So the real problem is still about heroine?"

"Of course it is still about heroine! I heard you have made a lot of noise. Everybody does that. You're the same as the rest. Well then, don't listen to these rumors anymore. These are the propaganda of the anti-revolutionary spread to discourage people. As you can see, the person who gets tortured or killed brings that to himself. These people, even after a few years in prison, do the same things again once they're out. I'm gonna leave you alone to think about what I just said. You don't wanna stay here forever, do you? I heard you have two kids. Think about them. God will forgive you and show you the right way."

Azadeh shook her head impatiently and said, "To what should I confess? What sin? Believe me, I have nothing to say. I'm confused. I'm telling you Ahmad had planted heroine in my house. I have never had this shit in my house." The guard closed the door and sat next to her. She shook her head and looked at the ceiling. She called out to God to help her. "Lord, show me a way to bring these sinful people around to your ways." Azadeh looked up at the ceiling and smiled. The guard looked at her in silence.

Azadeh didn't know what she had done to make the guard angry at her and why those beady eyes are giving her the look. She stopped smiling, and stared at the woman. She was asking with her eyes, what? Have I said something that I shouldn't have? The guard pulled herself closer to her. Her warm breath hit Azadeh in the face. Her look was bitter. With even more bitter voice she said, "Listen bitch, we are wasting our time on you. You rotten, faithless people with no conscience have no place in God's eyes. I'm wondering how you could still be a nurse. Maybe it was just a front. There's no change in your ways, you don't appreciate the opportunities we provided for you. Well, it's your choice. Hell's doors are open to you. Get up! Let's take you back to the cell where you belong."

Azadeh was so startled by her words that she couldn't even find the strength to breathe. She could bear the situation until her innocence was established, but the guard's insults and accusations were too much for her. She thought, 'the bitch accuses me of being rotten and unconscientious so easily. She got so angry that she could hardly keep her hands from jumping at the guard's throat. The only thing that kept her in control was the glimpse of her revolver hanging from her waist. She got up with all her anger in her voice, screamed, "Why do you accuse me of this? My guilt in this matter is not proven yet. So you can't just open your dirty mouth and insult me. You are the rotten one! You are the one with no conscience! That's why you can accuse people so easily, and disrespect their integrity!"

She was amazed and angry at the same time. How

come the guard was not barking back at her? It even seemed to sound like she was laughing. Right at that moment, the door flew open, a middle-aged woman rushed in and yelled at the guard.

"What's going on in here? Why are you two screaming so much?" The guard didn't say anything. She pulled the sides of her veil together and straightened it on her head, and left. Azadeh felt that this woman must have a higher rank than the other one and was about to start complaining about the other guard's behavior, but she couldn't say anything. Her tears started rolling down her face and she began a bitter cry. The woman with a nice tone said that the other guard was new and didn't know how to handle the prisoners yet.

"Did you curse her?"

"No, I didn't say anything. I don't know why all of a sudden she got mad and told me whatever that was really suiting her to me."

"Well, I've told her before that she should be careful in the way she treats the prisoners. Now, don't worry, I won't let her be around you anymore. Let me see, are you an addict?"

"Well, I was, but you guys made me quit. It must be two weeks since I had my last cigarette."

"Okay then. Prison wasn't all that bad for you, after all. Have you seen the addicts in the restrooms?"

"Yeah, I see them everyday."

"Today, we gave a body back to her family. Not everybody

can go through withdrawal. In fact, it's too late for them."

Azadeh asked, "Are all of these prisoners here for addiction, or they're dealers too?"

"No dear, addiction now isn't such a big crime. It's impossible to imprison half of the population. Our goal is to expand the rehab centers and capture the dealers." Azadeh said, "I never thought these miserable people could be dealers."

"Well, you're not thinking like an addict. If you were like them and needed your fix bad enough, you would do anything for it too." The guard seemed reasonable to Azadeh. The same woman brought her lunch that day to her cell. It was a good lunch. This was the first time that the guard would actually come in the cell. Her voice was simple and sincere, and her eyes were kind. In Azadeh's eyes, she had no connection to the prison and prisoners. The guard sat down with her to have a cup of tea. She sat next to Azadeh on the bed and asked her how many times they had taken her for questioning. Azadeh, while spooning her rice, said "Once. I'm sure my family has hired an attorney for me, but I haven't heard anything yet. Only God knows what will happen to me."

The woman said, "Don't worry, everything is going to be alright. People like you, won't stay long in the prison. The Lord will open several doors to you."

Azadeh thought, "I only see one door and that door costs a lot of money. The guard patted Azadeh on the shoulder and said, "You're a good woman. From what I understand,

you're a nurse. That's a good career. God likes nurses."
Azadeh, with a sarcastic tone, replied, "That's why I'm still
doing it." The woman in the praying room said the same
thing. The woman laughed, "Take it easy. Well, tell me
about yourself. What does your husband do for a living?
How many kids do you have?"

Azadeh's face brightened up for a second. Thinking
about bearded clergies and lashing, and death penalty had
taken a toll on her soul and it was nice to rid her mind from
these dark thoughts for a short while and think about normal
life again. She said, "I'm divorced, but my ex-husband is
still a good part of my life. Well, my sons are partly his and
I can't just ignore that fact." The woman scratched her head
and asked, "Well, why did you divorce him then?"

"We were too different. I was the one who asked for
divorce."

"Why?"

"We couldn't get along."

The guard asked, "Who's fault was it?" Azadeh said
with a smile,

"Neither of us. We were two different people and paid
our dues for making that mistake too."

"Is it a long time since your divorce?"

"Yes."

"Do you have the custody for the kids?"

"No, but I'm not worried about them. Their stepmom is nice." The woman looked at her with pity.

"Well, then life shouldn't be that easy for you."

"No it's not, especially now that I am too worried about my mom. I don't know how she's dealing with this stress and her sick heart. My only wish now is to hear her voice on the phone." Thinking of her mom brought tears into her eyes. At that moment she forgot that she's a prisoner and her listener is a prison guard. She wanted to talk and was talking about herself with no hesitation. Whatever she told Hadji in a rage, now she was saying to her calmly, and was criticizing the government. It felt good to talk freely. She was telling her that her job was not satisfying to her, what she really wanted to do was acting and theater. It was always a far-fetched dream. She was afraid of rejection, she knew acting wouldn't give her the wings to fly away. She dismissed that dream altogether and made herself go through nursing. It was a job that during these hard times could at least pay her rent.

The guard put her hand on her shoulder and sympathized with her. When she was leaving she said, "Sister, I will pray for you. Fear no one but Allah. He is forgiving. We are here to serve God, and have a responsibility towards him. Counseling and advising to his order is our main job here. You are different than the rest of prisoners. My instincts are telling me this. I want to help you, if you want."

Azadeh wasn't listening to her. She was thinking of her mom, and was hoping to hear from her with this woman's help. She said, "I want nothing more than your help. I feel that you have believed me and know that I'm innocent." The woman sighed and nodded. "Well, what can I say? The truth will come out. I told you that I will pray for you."

"Can I ask you for something?"

"What? What is it?"

Azadeh looked at her in silence. She was hesitant. She felt the guard would never do her any favors. The guard saw that hesitation in her eyes. She said,

"Are they giving you enough food? I can have them give you more bread."

"No, that's not my concern. I'm worried for my mom. She has heart disease. I wish I could get some news about her health. Maybe you can help me."

The guard was confused. Did she want to use her to get in contact with members of the gang? She said with a gentle tone, "Okay, I will call your mom, it's not a bad idea. I will do this, but you have to do something for me."

"What?"

"Trust me, and think of me as your sister."

"Of course, if I didn't feel that way, I would have never asked you for such a favor. I trusted you from the first glance. I'm not a talkative person, but I just wanted to talk to you. I'm not scared of anything anymore."

The woman smiled and said, "Well done. Talking is

good, you have to say whatever is bothering you." She stood up. "I'll get a piece of paper."

"But my mom's number should be in my file."

"Well, it might be, but I have no access to your file." The guard left and Azadeh felt very happy. This woman in these dark times threw a warm light into her heart. Maybe she was that angel that she saw in the sky. Well now she could contact the outside world, the world that she had been disconnected from for the past fifteen days. Maybe she could get some good news as well. Then her only problem would be waiting.

The woman came back with a piece of paper.

CHAPTER TWO

The wait was killing Azadeh. What if the woman was deceiving her and she would never come back? The more she waited, the more she was feeling deceived, a fool to believe, who poured her heart out for a nosy woman. She should have known that she was after all a prisoner and the woman was her guard, who could not be on her side. She wished she could believe all this and stop waiting for the door to open.

The sun was setting and a few stars appeared in the sky. Azadeh was in struggle with herself. She wanted to crush the hope in her mind and calm herself down, but she couldn't. She couldn't help staring at the door. A few footsteps were heard. She sat down, and at the same time she was ashamed of her doubts. But when the footsteps faded, her heart felt heavy, and she cursed the woman. The light outside started blinking and finally died out. She said to herself, well now I won't see that damn angel anymore. She was starving. Her stomach was growling and she remembered she didn't have dinner that night. She spat on the floor and smiled. Well then, that sun-dried bitch had punished her and took her lentil soup and olives away from her. What a pitiful punishment. She was exhausted and was longing for the weightless feeling of the twilight zone. That was where she could stop thinking.

Molawna came to her and calmed her soul. Attar came and sang to her of love. Hafiz came and gave her a cup of wine. But all of these were useless, since the demons of captivity and the gnarling of her stomach was holding her down and it pressed her to the cold floor. The Morning Prayer summons woke her up. As soon as she opened her eyes, the woman and the useless hope came back to her. She told herself the woman had no reason to make her wait if she didn't want to call her mom. She could have said it straight to her face, that she couldn't break the prison's regulations. She must have been busy. For sure, she would show up in a few minutes. She was calming her mind with these words and didn't want to discourage herself. A guard came by and took her to the restroom. She didn't spend much time in there, washed up in a hurry, and went back to her cell so she wouldn't miss the woman. Yesterday she washed her neck and face with her veil, but thinking of washing her clothes again, made her freeze. Since she didn't have any spare clothing, she would have to put them on wet if she washed them. She got her breakfast and fell on her bed. She didn't understand why she had her shoes on, so she freed her feet from them and pulled her knees into her chest. After one hour, her eyes grew tired. Too much staring at the iron door had made them itchy. She took the praying rug that the woman had brought her yesterday and started to examine it. There were rows of golden palm trees painted on it. She remembered the sick woman who was singing for her roommates. She rolled the praying rug and thought about the Zay Coffee House. A fortuneteller had recited this poem for her there:

The faithless have made me old. I should find a faithful love.

If I can't find a faithful one, then I should die

Next to the one's tomb.

Azadeh, with a faint hope in her heart, was counting the minutes and waiting. A sleepy sun appeared in the sky and threw a very faint light on the wall. Azadeh got up and stood in the heatless light. A key turned in the lock. She started laughing and felt so happy to see the woman. She took her hand into her own hands and anxiously asked,

"My mom, is she okay? Did you tell her I'm okay?"

The woman pulled her hand away and put it on her shoulder and said, "Calm down, calm down, of course she's well."

"Did you talk to her or my sister?"

"I don't know, I think it was your mom. I told her that you're fine. She says she's okay too and you should seek help from God."

"Well, what else? Did she say anything about the

lawyer?"

"See my dear, I can't get into details. I did what you asked me to, your mom's okay and is praying for you. You wanted this, right?"

Azadeh said, "That's right, forgive me. I am so thankful to you. I was so stupid. You know, I thought you would never come back."

"Of course, we will never forget people like you. As I told you before, we will help you. You must have been too nervous to sleep last night, huh?"

"Yes, the covers are too thin. I'm really skinny too, cold bothers me." She was hoping to get another blanket. She was thinking that the guard is her friend and wants to protect her. But the woman didn't go anywhere and pretended that she didn't hear anything. Azadeh gave up on the blankets. The woman was kind enough to break the rules and did something far more valuable for her. She shouldn't push her luck. She actually wondered if the woman felt offended.

The woman said, "Dear, did you know that the sleepless nights are the best times for praying? Especially if it is combined with crying. Crying in the early morning will cleanse the soul. It will wash away the sins and enlighten the heart. God is kind, and loves his creatures, especially those who repent. A few months ago there was a young inmate here. She was lulled into prostitution and drug trafficking. But she repented, and found her way back to God. Do you know what we did with her?"

Azadeh instantly said, "Hung her?"

The woman laughed, "It seems you are ignorant to God's ways. As much as his punishments are hard, his forgiveness is easy. He wouldn't throw away a repentant, just as he forgave that whore."

Azadeh was curious to know if the woman was still alive or executed. She asked,

"God forgave her where? On earth or in heaven?"

"No dear, here on earth. A few days ago, after her repentance, she was free to go. We all prayed for her and asked God to accept her."

"That easy? She repented and went home?"

"Well, there was a small fee involved. The alms that she hadn't paid all her life."

Azadeh laughed cautiously. This story didn't seem right to her. If it was true, then who were all those who were getting executed every day? It was too farfetched to believe that government would be so easy on the drug dealers. Nevertheless, she must let the woman think that she had believed her story. She said with a sorry tone,

"I wish I was guilty like that woman so I could confess. When it's so easy to get rid of all the charges, one must be really stupid not to take advantage of this holy opportunity."

The guard said "That's true, the wise person would not reject God's helping hand. God has given you this opportunity to rescue yourself and change your path." She turned and took Azadeh's hands in hers. There was no sincerity in her face; there was a trace of impatience and anger. She said, "Listen girl, give your heart to God as I said before. Think of me as your sister, my heart is like a safe full of secrets. Trust in me and let me help you. Your situation is very dangerous. There's no use in denying. You are too involved. Come along and give others names. You are a wise woman. God will forgive you and show you the right path." She got up and leaned against the door. Her head was tilted to one side, she was looking sideways at Azadeh. She was thinking to herself, open up your mouth, prisons are full. "We don't have time to deal with you. You are lucky we have been this patient with you so far."

Azadeh was pale and sad in disbelief. She was feeling extremely disappointed. Her nauseous look was vomiting onto the woman's face. What a useless hope. She had never believed in her, only had played her to get information from her. She was mad at herself. Now she could only see her as the embodiment of perversion, a witch with a sly smile, and a big fat mole on her chin, which she was playing with. Azadeh laid back on the bed and hid her head under the blanket. The woman came closer and pulled the blanket away and said,

"You have a long time to sleep. Sit up, this is the last chance."

Azadeh grunted and turned away. The woman said,

"You haven't heard me, it seems. Believe me, no one

would help you except for us. Why don't you trust me?"
The word trust pierced Azadeh's heart like a dagger. She
sat up and threw the cup of tea madly towards the woman.

"Aren't you ashamed to talk about trust to me? Leave me
alone, you lying whore!" The cup didn't hit the woman, but
the tea was thrown on the door. The woman was shocked
for a moment, then came towards her and smacked her hard
on the face, then left the cell without saying a word.

Azadeh was so consumed in her anger that she didn't
even notice the light in the room. Her face was hot and
burning where the woman's hand had hit her. She hadn't
slept the whole night with expectation and now she was really
mad at herself. She was a complete idiot and had played the
fool in this cunning game. She was a naive woman, who got
excited with the slightest words of kindness, a gullible fool
who in her simplicity, had believed the woman had actually
called her mother out of sympathy. Azadeh knew that the
woman was doing her job and realy didn't hate her. But at
the same time, she couldn't calm down. She was wondering
what the woman would report to Hadji and what would
be waiting in store for her. She could have only made her
case worse and the punishment heavier. She was thinking
this time she could not find a way out of the system. She
was envisioning the tall walls of the prison behind which she
would spend the rest of her life. For a second she wished she
didn't have anyone to wait for her.

The sun was about to set. With her hands under her
head, her tears were rolling down her face and onto her
neck. Behind her tears, in the dim light of the cell, she saw

a spider that was hanging from the ceiling like a bell and she couldn't figure out how it got in through the closed windows. She always hated spiders. But then, she didn't want to get rid of it, in her isolation it was her only companion. She stared at it until the dark curtain of night covered the ceiling and hid the spider. Sleep filled her eyes. She closed them to sleep, but she took the spider with her into her dreams. Frightened, she woke up and looked at the ceiling. In the light of the dim lamp she saw it climbing down the wall. She got up, took the paper cup, and waited for it to come down. As soon as its legs touched the floor, she put the cup over it. She then said,

"Excuse me, I know the wind's touch has blown away your nest, but if I wasn't in this miserable situation, I would have let you make more webs around the desert of this cell. For now, please stay there and let me sleep without fear."

It was morning when she woke up. She turned around and saw the cup, thinking that the spider might have been suffocated in there made her sad. She turned the cup, but in her amazement, she didn't find the spider there. How could it flee? She looked at the ceiling and saw it hanging from it. She started laughing. Its escape was a puzzle to her. The day was dark and so was her mind. Darkness was integrated in her thoughts and she couldn't figure out day from night and had lost track of time. Her body was in pain and her mind lazy and helpless. When there is no hope for the future, one thinks about the past. Till now, she had a different feeling. There was a "happiness" feeling from which she didn't have a fair share. But now that word seemed like a false hope. Now she wasn't thinking of that absolute happiness anymore. It was enough for her to get out of here and see her sons grow up. In the misery that filled her brain, other's lives came to her mind. The kind of lives, who at their weakest point, had lost any faith in God and their days and nights were spent in the game of death.

"Make a beggar out of me and I'll be at your door forever." Faces were coming to her mind one after another, each with a painful story. That skinny guy who would sell his blood for a dime, or that woman who would sell her kidney to make bail money for her husband. A nervous pain was slowly coming to her stomach. She should calm down and rid herself from the painful lives. With this hope she closed her eyes, her mind went to her sons. Their joyful laughter was sounding in her ears. She thought of the joy in their eyes when they were making fun of the sloppy goalie of the other team in their soccer games. A faint smile came to her lips and left. She went to the Prairie of No Worries and saw the sparrows on the trees. She picked the red flowers that would grow in the backyard of her mom's house. She wanted to give them to her mom. The thought of her mom waiting for her in that backyard made her sad, and she left the prairie of no worries. They brought her dinner, but she had no interest in looking at the black veiled woman. She saw them as snakes that would come one by one and bit her in different ways. She took a spoon ful of her soup in her mouth and thought about her mom's kitchen with aromas of food in it. She liked her mom's cooking and she would always inhale whatever she was cooking for her. The homey atmosphere of her mother's kichen always made her calm and safe. She felt so secure in there that she never wanted to leave that house. When she was a little girl, she could feel the security and harmony, and she was happy in that shell. Memories of the far away times in the past were now coming back to her in great detail. She remembered when she was fourteen and was spending the day at her grandmother's house. She called her grandmother Bibi. That hot summer day, Bibi's neighbor's son had kissed her in the backyard, but Bibi had caught them. The boy fled and Azadeh was crying. Bibi told her,

"Have you got no shame? Go get my hookah pipe, I want to talk to you." Azadeh put the hookah pipe on the bench under the grapevines in front of Bibi. Bibi puffed into the pipe and told her not to talk to that loser boy. It was a few years now since Bibi had been gone, but to Azadeh she was still alive and she loved her all the same. She made a picture frame of Bibi's scarf and had all the pictures of her loved ones on that frame on the wall. To Azadeh, Bibi's house was the most beautiful house in the world. The vast rooms, windows with colored glass as tall as the wall. The reflection of the sun performed a light show in the windows. In the living room, the plastered birds on the ceiling would catch her attention. There was a fireplace and on the mantle there was a chandelier lamp and a carved copper hawk. What happened? Again screaming and shouting. She got up and put her ear on the cell's wall and said out loud,

"What are you doing in there? You are making it harder for yourself. You can't stop the boot beating on your body by just cursing. Stay quiet, and don't do as I did or you will end up like me." The woman next door got quiet. She couldn't figure out if she actually listened to her or if the beating made her quiet. She didn't know the prisoner next door on the charges. But, she was aware of the guards' treatment of the prisoners, which had turned from ugly to dirty and it made her sick to her stomach. It took her a while to get over the woman and find the string of her thoughts. She could examine her path in life by remembering her past. She went back to the time when she had met Hamed for the first time. It was her graduation day from nursing school and she was celebrating with some of her friends. Hamed didn't quite fit the picture of the "man of her dreams." That man had a distinguished face and even by thinking of him Azadeh could feel excited, ecstatic, and sad all at the same time. This felt so real that she could feel his breathing in the bed next to her. But that day, she didn't know why she responded to the inviting looks of Hamed, who didn't resemble "him" at all. Hamed wasn't tall and skinny, neither had a wide forehead. His hair wasn't straight and he didn't have the deep, penetrating look. His jaw wasn't what Azadeh imagined either. Azadeh loved creative and artistic hands. Hamed had owned a car dealership, which he had expanded into several branches. He had a good sense of humor, but mostly on the cheap side. He didn't know the meaning of pessimism. When he couldn't do something for someone, he would keep them around by empty talks and false hopes. His generosity and at times excessive generosity had kept him in a long circle of friends, which would fill his spare time. Amongst them were a few women too, but later on, when Hamed would come home drunk, Azadeh knew her husband must have spent the night at their houses. In his drunkard state, he would confess to his betrayal and the next day would beg her for forgiveness with teary eyes. Hamed, careless, was busy in his world. That world was not acceptable to Azadeh anymore. Azadeh questioned and judged herself several times, considering her sons too. She wanted to know where she was heading. The picture she saw would have her as a bystander in her married life. Finally, after ten years she told Hamed that she knew her words were landing on a deaf ear and she couldn't change him into her ideal man and asked for a divorce.

It was the first day after twenty days in jail, that there was no guard at her door right after morning Azan. The cell was completely lit by sunshine and it must have been mid-day. She was surprised and then she remembered what the older guard had told her. She thought to herself, this was the end. She could picture the big jails rooms with older prisoners who had spent years in there. Guards who had seen it all and were as mean as a snake, with big huge bodies and brains as small as a bird, their faces hard with anger and dirty life. Azadeh wanted to stand up and memorize her small figure so that after years in prison she could remember the way she was now. She looked at herself, and then looked around. First she started laughing, and then sat down and cried bitterly. Suddenly, the door opened; there was no food in the guard's hands. She said,

"Come on. If you want, I can take you to the restroom first."

Azadeh thought, well then no one could do anything for

me. She put her shoes on, and started to put on her veil. She was doing everything slowly to buy some time. She was now satisfied to be left alone in this small cell. The guard was looking at her surprised.

"What the hell are you doing? Maybe you don't want to leave here. Did you have too much fun in here?"

Azadeh threw out her shaking body and followed the guards into the room that they had taken her the first day. Behind the desk, she saw the same clergy who had made her so mad that she lost control and said whatever she wasn't supposed to. She almost collapsed into the chair and said hello to him. The clergy, with an expressionless face, looked at her and then continued writing something. There was complete silence in the room, as if no one was in the mood to even breathe loudly. The two guards standing on either side of him were motionless as a tree and were looking out the window. Azadeh was anxiously moving in her seat.

"You mean bastard! If you hadn't made me that mad I wouldn't be here now. Now do whatever you have to do and do not write so much nonsense."

Finally, Hadji looked up. There was an icy smile on his face with a satisfied look. He closed the file and recited from Quran and felt his face from his forehead to the tip of his beard. Then he opened a drawer and pulled out a plastic bag. Azadeh saw her own rings and watch in the bag. A big lump came to her throat. It was true. They were going to transfer her to another prison and make her rot there. Hadji laughed at the mortified expression on her face and looked at the two guards. Then he gave her a pen. Azadeh saw the amusement on his face and thought, 'You blood sucking fascist, you finally won. I wish I could smack you in the mouth and wipe out the smudge of a smile on your face.' Hadji pushed the file towards her and said,

"You're lucky, your innocence is proven. Sign down here, you're free to go." Something dropped in Azadeh's stomach. Did she hear correctly? Was she free? Maybe she was dreaming.

"You mean, I'm really free Hadji?"

Hadji nodded several times. All of a sudden all of the sadness went away and Azadeh started crying in joy. Her heart was filled with happiness and she saw the clergy in a different light. Now she could trust him and that joy showed in her eyes, which she turned towards Hadji. Hadji liked it and smiled. Azadeh didn't wait any longer to find out what had happened and who had caused all this trouble for her.

Her uncle, Sohrob and her sister were waiting for her outside. She ran to the exit door. She was so happy that she felt weightless. She was flying. She sat next to Sepideh in the back seat. She felt as if she had conquered the peak of a mountain. It felt so good not to be afraid anymore. She took her sister's hands in hers and said,

"If I knew I would be there for only twenty days, I wouldn't have taken it that hard. What tricks life plays on us."

Sepideh looked at her with sad eyes and said, "We

thought the same. I had a dream of you being really old. It was amazing that mom had the same dream, you being old with grey hair and no teeth."

Azadeh laughed and said, "It's amazing, I had the same dream several times." Her uncle, who looked in the rear-view mirror, had the same dream, but he didn't say anything. Azadeh rolled the window down to feel the cold air on her cheeks. Her uncle said,

"It's all over now. Take the owl of unhappiness out of your soul now and fill it out with the polluted air."

Azadeh said with a smile, "It's gone. But it will come back into our lungs!" There was so much commotion going on at her mom's house. Azadeh saw relatives whom she hadn't seen for years. She saw a few of her dad's friends too. The same Don Quixots who stayed out and sent her dad ahead. Now, seeing Azadeh had given them an excuse to get together again and argue over the same old ideas for hours, the same ideas they kept repeating for more than twenty years now.

Simin was looking at them with a judgmental look, "Instead of opening your mouths, open your minds and eyes. She was almost praying to God for them to leave. Finally, one of them said the last word and the rest applauded him.

"Well, what did you think? We did what we did, there's no use fussing over it. Now all these talks about socialism and democracy are just dreams. There's no room for democracy in this country. People want a dictator. They want someone to control them. It doesn't make any difference to them if this Shah has a golden crown or yards of white linen as a turban.

Those guys were gone and Azadeh finally found a moment to hug her kids and calm her heavy heart. The boys' image of prison was whatever they saw in American movies. Tall walls with barbwires, a courtyard filled with prisoners with a guard watching them while pointing a gun at them. Now they were asking questions with a tone mixed with curiosity and concern.

"Mom, is the women's prison the same as men's? Did you guys fight like in men's prisons? Were you scared of the guard? Was it dark in there? Were there a lot of cockroaches? How about rats? Were you scared? Did you scream?"

Their grandma was sitting there and looking at them with an admiring look, not believing what she was seeing. She had been hurt so much before that now everything would concern her. She had lost the hope of her daughter's freedom and had imagined a fate like her husband's for her. Since she had wasted a lot of time, energy and money to free her husband with no avail, she didn't really think that she would see Azadeh again sitting in her bath towel and kissing her sons.

Azadeh looked at her mom who was taking off her hat exposing her gray her wrapped in a bun. With love she remembered the warning that she had given them years ago, "Don't let them take you two away from me too." Now she could feel those warnings deeply in her mom's face. Her mom's hair was all gray now. She was slouching and there were a few new wrinkles around her mouth, making her look a few years older. Zohreh gave a glass of milk to Azadeh and sat next to her. Happy and sad feelings were intertwined inside her. Her mouth was smiling and her eyes crying. She put her arms around Azadeh's neck and said,

"Girl, we were worried sick about you. I didn't know what to say to Keyvan and Kaveh, and how to calm them. Well, if you were planning on going to jail, why didn't you tell me to pour water behind you and pray" (An Iranian custom to pour water behind a traveler to wish them safe trip)

Azadeh laughed heartily and looked at her kind eyes and kissed her on the cheeks. Then she said, "My dear Zohreh, the last twenty days felt like a century to me. But I was always thinking about you. You have no idea what a big blessing is your existence in our lives. The only calming thought I had was you being with my sons."

Sepideh prepared a small snack on the table with scrambled eggs and honey tea.

"Sis, come here and eat. Put some meat on your bones. You don't look healthy."

Azadeh took her hand in hers and said, "I'll eat, but let me look at you first." She felt her face with her hand and continued, "Don't let these wrinkles stay on your face. You should buy the best moisturizers."

Their mom said, "Don't you worry about her, your presence has already brought life into her face."

The doorbell rang and it was Hamed. It seemed like he didn't have anything to say. He stood in the middle of the room and with a smile on his face, was looking at Azadeh. At the same time he was twisting his silver mustache. Azadeh knew this gesture very well and knew it meant he was still very much disturbed by the events. Azadeh looked at him with gratiying eyes and said,

"I know you went through a lot for me. I have no idea what you've done, but it couldn't have been easy. I thought they would never let me go. Well, tell me what exactly have you done for me? From what I heard, there was no lawyer involved either."

Sepideh laughed and said, "No, we didn't hire any lawyers. We put the fee for the attorney in an envelope along with the keys to a new Mercedes and gave it to Hadji."

Hamed laughed too and took his cigarette out of Simin's packet and lit it. His laugh and the way he looked at Azadeh was clearly saying to her that he was really lonely and that it was more important to him to see his sons happy again in their mom's arms and he would happily pay any price for that. Azadeh thought to herself, what does this man want in his life? He had me with his sons and he was looking around. Now, what does this mean? Hamed gave the half finished cigarette to Azadeh and took his two-year-old daughter in his arms and said,

"Well kids, it's time for us to leave. I have a lot to do. You had better stay here and relax. I'll bring the kids back again on Friday."

The boys kissed their mom. Azadeh took them to the car and followed the car with her eyes until it disappeared. Dark clouds covered the sun and the crows were jumping nervously from one branch to another. All of a sudden, the clouds broke apart and started crying with raindrops that fell on Azadeh's teary face. Azadeh spent the night at her mom's and slept in a warm, cozy bed, but couldn't quite sleep the whole night. All night long she was asking herself, what was it all about? Why were they insisting on my guilt and then all of a sudden I was found innocent? Now she was thinking about Ahmad's role in all this with doubt. If he planted the heroine in her house that night he must have removed it the same night because he knew well that she would go back home from her work and see the package. She was asking herself, why? Why would he plant it in her house only for a few hours? He didn't know if police were to raid his house that night. If he knew, he wouldn't have stayed there to be arrested.

When she smelled the aroma of fresh bread, she pulled herself out of the warm blankets and went to the kitchen. Her mom was setting the table for breakfast. She kissed her on the face and started dialing her uncle's house. Her mom said,

"Who are you calling at this hour?"

"See mom, it doesn't sound right to me. I have to talk to Uncle Sohrab. I can't believe that Ahmad has planted the heroine in my house."

"Why my dear? It must be the unconscionable act of that

boy, otherwise why would they think you were his partner in this crime?"

"No mom, it doesn't make sense. I think uncle didn't stay here yesterday so that I wouldn't ask him any questions."

Simin put a few boiled eggs and hot bread on the table and said,

"My dear, what difference does it make now? Don't think about this and let it go. Come sit by me, let me look at you. I couldn't believe last night that you were in your old room."

Azadeh got up, "Mom, how about if I asked uncle to stop by before he goes to work? I can't wait any longer. It feels like I'm on hot coal." She only calmed down when her uncle said he would stop by in an hour. She put the phone down and rushed to Sepideh's room. She pulled the curtains and said,

"Rise and shine." Sepideh opened her eyes and saw the newly risen sun.

"I just fell asleep. It seems you are used to the morning alarms of prison."

"Mom's awake and breakfast is ready. Get up, get up!"

Sepideh got up and said, "Poor mom, she must have been too excited to sleep."

Azadeh opened her closet. "Uncle is coming to help me. This Ahmad has made me so confused." Azadeh took a dress and put it on and looked at herself in the mirror. She saw a woman whose face was older now, under the stress, and there was something in her eyes that made them so strange to her. She had lost so much weight and the dress was hanging from her body. The doorbell rang and she opened it to her uncle. She took his hand and as she was walking with fast steps, she was dragging him through the backyard into the house. Her uncle smiled,

"I see you feel better."

"No uncle, I won't feel better until I can figure this out. I can't understand what has happened. I just want to know, why would Ahmad or any other son of a bitch, have done this and made so much trouble for me?"

Uncle said, "My dear, why do you confuse yourself? These are all his doings. Maybe he didn't mean for any harm to you. It seems like he got all confused and lost his cool."

"Why, why confused?"

"It's all my theory. Maybe he saw the police from the eyehole."

"Well, you better talk! I know everything and now we are going to discuss it. That son of a gun didn't tell Hadji why he put the heroine inside my house. I have to change the locks on my house today."

Uncle shook his head in disagreement. "Why?"

"Well, maybe he has made copies of the key and passed them around to other low lives like himself."

"No, he didn't have the key to your house and he didn't set foot in there either."

"Are you kidding me? He has been found guilty, and now you're telling me that he didn't set foot in my house? Did he drill a big hole into the ceiling?"

"Oh, I see, they haven't told you anything."

"No, they haven't. Maybe they wanted to, but they left too soon."

"See, my dear, that brainless twit had thrown the package from his balcony to yours. Fortunately or unfortunately, the police who were watching him had seen him when he did this stupid act and thought that you must be involved with him. So they came after you."

Azadeh got up and took a long breath and shook her head in anger.

" That son of a bitch, Ahmad! He put me in such a mess! But uncle, still it doesn't make sense that the prison people got so much money from us."

"You don't understand. In this country they always charge the innocent people with something to get money. Leave it alone! In your case, they actually had something on you. We had to buy your innocence or you would have stayed there for a few years."

Azadeh looked guiltily and said, "You mean you paid them all that much because I showed my rage?"

"well that's an understatement! Assaulting a guard? Cursing, insulting the holy people? On top of all that, you had a few wine bottles in your home too, that was a big sin."

Azadeh grunted, "Holy people! It seems the bitch finally got the upper hand." Azadeh looked up and saw her mom looking out the window. She said out loud, "Mom, I had nothing to give you but trouble."

Her mom said, "Don't even think it, thank God your uncle and I had some savings to give them. Hamed was so helpful and generous too."

Azadeh's heart was aching from all this. She went into the backyard to breathe in some fresh air. Her uncle followed her and as he was leaving he said, "Go to your home, it must be a mess."

CHAPTER THREE

Azadeh couldn't believe what she was seeing. She grunted, "Only God's hand can punish you, this is not a search, it's destruction. God, oh God take this ruthlessness away." With difficulty she pulled the broken parts of furniture away. She put the insides of the TV back in there and as she was putting the fillings of the couch away, she stared at the torn green flower patterns. She was murmuring to herself; "what a pity, Bibi forgive me for not being able to take care of your keepsake." She went to her bedroom, which was as bad as the rest of the apartment. She stood in the middle of the room and was thinking where she should start when the doorbell rang. She looked into the eyehole. It was her neighbor. In her state of mind she didn't want to see anyone. She was sad and wanted to be alone. Slowly she walked away from the door, but she tripped over a broken table and fell down. Door bell started ringing nonstop. She got up and started massaging her painful elbow cursing everybody, then she opened the door.

The neighbor woman saw the upside down apartment and Azadeh's miserable state at the same time. Startled she asked, "What has happened here? Was it a burglary?" She didn't wait for Azadeh to invite her in, she asked, "Do the police know?"

-"Yes they know."

-"Sons of bitches, why have they done this to your home?"

"I don't know, maybe they were after hidden treasure in my furniture."

"Do you hide your jewelry in the pots?"

Azadeh realized that they didn't know anything about her arrest. In a few sentences, she made up a story and led her to the door. But the woman was stuttering and turned around and sat in the middle of the room. Curiosity was killing her. She couldn't leave without getting any information.

"No, that's not right. Tell me everything. If you don't want anyone to know, that's okay. My mouth is shut. Mum's the word. Well now, tell me everything."

Azadeh saw there was no way out and the woman wouldn't leave her alone until she found everything out. She sat next to her and told her everything. The woman left with the deepest sorrow, but as Azadeh expected, instead of going to her apartment, the neighbor took the elevator to go downstairs and tell the story with many exaggerations to all the neighboring women.

Azadeh went to the balcony and with sorrow, looked at the iron railing of the upstairs balcony, which belonged to Ahmad. Her heart filled with sadness, she screamed,

"You scoundrel! Stupid, crazy! See what you have done to us!" Some windows opened and heads stuck out, saying,

"What the hell is your problem? Shut up!"

Azadeh went inside and continued her cries behind closed doors. As she was madly talking outloud, she started picking up her clothes from the floor. Thinking about what her mother had to endure was bothering her. She had lost her life's savings overnight, over something stupid that this guy had done out of desperation. She was getting angrier as she was thinking about it. She could see his face and something was telling her that it's not the last time they would meet. She would see him again and get her mom's money from him. She couldn't figure it out, how and when, but this was the only consolation she had. She put on rubber gloves and started cleaning up her apartment like a mad woman.

Winter was about to come and nature was getting ready for hibernation, but in Azadeh's soul, something was waking up. She could feel the change and couldn't think of going back to her old lifestyle. Her usual habits and routines seemed so insignificant now. When visiting her friends, she was feeling restless and couldn't stand the usual jokes and now she would rather spend all her time at her mom's. They had long talks, lit a cigarette, and with a glass of wine, they would listen to Sepideh playing her Tar. There was an indescribable connection between them, as if there was no other world around them any longer.

That Friday, Azadeh had spent all afternoon with her boys in the park, she bought a few books for them, and had tried to talk to them. But boys are boys. They don't want to talk to their mom; they'd rather play around. Azadeh could see with sorrow that her maternal instincts were fading. It was about an hour since she dropped the boys at their father's and could see from the window that the movers would be putting Ahmad's stuff in a pickup truck. She was reviewing the past. Although she was mad at him, she didn't mean any harm to him either. Who was to be blamed? Was everything Ahmad's fault or was he the loser in this game.

Sun was pulling away the pale rays and was going to hide behind the mountains. It was a depressing time. Crows noisily were going back to their nests in the trees. Azadeh didn't want to go back to her nest. Dirty hands had touched it and she couldn't feel homey in there. She had cleaned it up over the past few weeks and replaced the broken furniture, but it still didn't feel the same as before. She stayed in the balcony until there was no one in the streets. She felt hungry, but didn't have any desire to cook. She knew dinner would end up being low fat yogurt and scrambled eggs. She picked up the book she had bought that day. It was supposed to have all the answers to her problems. She read only a few lines when she heard the doorbell ringing. Who could it be? She wasn't expecting anyone and the nosey neighbor was on a trip. She got up and looked into the eyehole. There was an old lady she didn't know.

"Yes?"

"Hello dear, are you Azadeh?"

"Yes!"

"Oh dear, I'm coming here from Quom(one of the holy cities in Iran that is the burial place to the daughter of Imam Hossein the grandchild of the prophet Mohammad, it is holy to the Shiit Moslems) to see my son, but he's not home yet. I waited by his door for a few hours, but he hasn't come home. The lady next door told me to come down here. Do you know where he might be?"

Azadeh was really surprised when she heard Ahmad's name. Never in her wildest dreams did she think she would meet his mother. She was confused and didn't know what to say. Should she say no and get rid of her? Or invite her in and tell her the whole story? All of a sudden she got scared. She felt Ahmad's presence shadowing over her life. Maybe the drug dealers have sent this woman here to get some news. Thinking of these dark thoughts made her face look dark too. With a cold and angry tone she said,

"I have no idea where he could be. You had better wait for him upstairs." She slammed the door on her but continued watching her through the hole. Ahmad's mom didn't want to go. God damn it, I have to call the police now!

The doorbell rang again.

"What? Leave before I call the police!"

Ahmad's mom, surprised, took a step back. In a low tone, she said,

"My dear lady, have I done something to offend you? Why police? That's okay if you can't help me. I'll just go upstairs. God willing, he will show up." Her tone was so low and desperate that it calmed Azadeh down. She started studying her face from her eyes, then to her nose, and ended on her pointy chin. Her son looked exactly like her. Now she new for sure that she was Ahmad's mother, but she still couldn't say anything about him and she couldn't figure out the reason. Was it because she was cautious? Or was it because she didn't want to hurt this old woman?

Ahmad's mother, filled with exhaustion, said goodbye and turned towards the elevator. Azadeh rested her head on the doorframe, and looking at her with pity, Azadeh wished she had never shown up there. She was trying to forget all the bad memories and now this woman had shown up and stirred everything up. The old woman's face clearly portrayed her exhaustion and her lips were shivering from the cold. Azadeh was struggling with herself. On one hand, she couldn't ignore her wretched state, and on the other hand, she didn't want Ahmad's mother inside her apartment. The elevator doors squeaked open. Azadeh cursed the upstairs neighbor and reluctantly said,

"Wait, it's better if you waited here."

Ahmad's mom, waiting for this invitation, came in with a smile on her face and a small traveling bag under her veil.

"May God bless your life, I was dying in the cold. I have rheumatism. Cold floors make all my bones achy. It took me a while to find this place. At first, I went to another building, but there was no one named Ahmad there. Do you have any men in your house?"

Azadeh said bitterly,

"No, there's no man. You can take off your veil." She pointed to the couch, "You can sit down." She went to the kitchen to brew hot tea. Ahmad's mom took her veil off and put it on her bag, sighed and said,

"God bless you dear," and then said it louder so Azadeh could hear her. "God bless your kids, but kids are a lot of trouble."

Azadeh came back with a cigarette on her lips. She was mad at herself. She puffed the smoke into Ahmad's mom's face, then she felt she had to say something.

"So, you are really his mother?"

"Well, of course deary, why would I lie? I've come all the way from Quom. It's been a while, I haven't heard from him. I was worried sick, you know. He always calls, at least once a month no matter what. But now it's been a couple of months that I haven't heard from him. I told my daughter, I have to go to Tehran. Maybe, God forbid, something has happened to him. Well sweetie what can I do, I'm his mom, but I don't know anyone here. Tell me the truth honey, is he okay? Will he come back home tonight?"

Azadeh didn't say anything. She went back to the kitchen to bring tea. She was confused and was still struggling with herself. She didn't know what to do with this woman. Azadeh was convinced there were no tricks, but she still didn't know what to say. She wasn't even sure where Ahmad was. Maybe he's in prison or maybe he's executed. And she couldn't say any of this to his mother. What would she do with this innocent woman? Would she just play ignorant and send her home? All of a sudden she thought of something, something that would fulfill her wish as well. Her face lit up. This woman was her key to see Ahmad again. Something was telling her that Ahmad was still alive. She had to look for him, and if necessary, go to all the prisons, even the scariest one, Shoorabad.

Ahmad's mom was confused. Why did the upstairs neighbor send her to this woman, and what was her relation to Ahmad? How come this woman knew about Ahmad's whereabouts and now she was denying it? Although, Ahmad's mother was happy to be in a warm place, Azadeh's bitter mood was making her bitter too. She was thinking if anyone needs anything from this woman, then God help them, she's so tough. She started praying outloud and asked God to send Ahmad home as soon as possible so she could leave and never see this woman again.

Azadeh heard her praying.

"Oh God's prophet, help me and send Ahmad home soon."

Azadeh came back with teacups. "So you don't know anyone here?"

"No my dear, I have no one. If only I knew someone, I wouldn't be here. God willing, Ahmad will come soon, and

I won't be bothering you anymore. He didn't say anything to you about his plans tonight?"

Azadeh was amazed at herself as to why she couldn't bring herself to say, "listen woman, your son is in prison, and caused a lot of touble for me too". But instead she asked her if she was cold and needed a jacket.

Ahmad's mom said, "No, I have a jacket in my bag." She opened her bag and took out a green jacket and a box of candies, specialties from Quom. She gave the box of candies to Azadeh. Although she said out loud that she would be honored if Azadeh accepted this small gift, she was thinking, take this, hopefully they will make you more pleasant and sweet. There was a slight accent in her way of talking.

Azadeh said, "It seems like you are from Kermanshah." (from Kermanshah in the west of Iran which is part of Kurdistan)

Ahmad's mom said with a sigh, "Yes, originally I am a Kurd, but it's been fifty years since I've moved to Quom. My late husband came to do his civil duty in there. When he was done, we got married and he brought me to Quom. Well dear, this was my destiny. You can't fight it, God wanted me to live in a place that was totally strange to me."

Azadeh thought to herself I know how your life is, the past should not have been much easier.

Ahmad's mom put the empty cup in the tray and asked for the restroom. It was praying time and she wanted to wash up before her prayer.

Azadeh pointed to the bathroom.

Ahmad's mom took out the praying stone out of her pocket and looked at Azadeh's feet with shoes on. She thought, this woman must not be the praying type, otherwise, she would not be wearing the same shoes in the house as in the bathroom. Therefore, the whole house must be filthy and unsuitable for praying.

Azadeh went into the kitchen to make soup. She put whatever she found in the refrigerator into a pot and went back to the room. Once Ahmad's mother was done praying, she began to recite her rosaries and asked God to cure all the sick people. She slid her hands over her face and then put her praying stone back into her pocket and said,

"It's been so long since I have prayed with Saint Zahra that I forgot the Mohammad's Prayers. My husband used to say, 'You are in Zahra's town now, and you have to live with her.' Well, that's exactly what happened to me. I was thirteen when I got married, they wouldn't let me go anywhere except for Saint Zahra's shrine. Sweetie, I cried so much by that tomb. Well, you know I was too lonely, he wasn't kind to me, and my only condolences in life were my kids. I bore six, but only three survived; as you know, there weren't as many medical facilities as there are today. A simple cold could have killed a child. But maybe even God didn't want me to have all my kids. My Hamid was killed in the war when he was only sixteen. I have a daughter named Fatima. She married her cousin. Well, that didn't end up very well either."

Azadeh was quiet, but she wasn't really listening to her. She was thinking, how could she start telling her about Ahmad. She heard her asking,

"Do you have a mosque here?"

"Oh, several. You haven't told me your name yet. Should I call you 'Ahmad's mom?' "

"Dear, you can call me anything you want. My real name is Goli, but my mother in law called me Roghieh. She said, 'your name is not respectable. It means flower and in our town, no one would ever call a respectable girl by that name. A respectful name should be religious.' She was a lier, her own name was Narges, you know, the flower! She was just jealous."

"Well, I'll call you Goli."

"I like that, dear, it reminds me of my childhood when my mom called me by my name."

Azadeh laughed, "My name is Azadeh, just Azadeh."

Goli wet her dry lips with her tongue, "Dear, I'm going to go upstairs, maybe Ahmad's back. He doesn't have a phone number, otherwise I would call him from here. And you say you don't know when he will come back?'

Azadeh started towards the kitchen and Goli looked at her, standing in the dim light by the stove, and all of a sudden, her heart skipped a beat. She must be his fiancée!

That's why she's not saying anything, and as soon as she hears his name, she turns white like she has just seen a ghost. The old spinster! And imagine, she wanted to call the cops on me too! A lump came to her throat. What kind of a son do I have? Is this the kind of respect he shows me? Couldn't he trust me enough to consult me before getting engaged to this ugly, bony girl? Goli got up, went to the kitchen to tell her future daughter-in-law how her son was disrespectful towards her, but suddenly, she burst into tears and started crying loudly.

Azadeh looked at her, surprised. "What's wrong Goli, what happened?"

"Nothing. I hope you too have a long, happy life together."

Azadeh started laughing. She put the lid on the pot, and sat next to her, took Goli's hands in hers, and said, "Did you really think I'm his wife? No my dear, he's still waiting for you to choose a good wife for him, a good girl from your own hometown."

Goli wiped her tears with her veil and went back to the room. She stared at the patterns on the carpet, and realized that her heart had lied to her. This tall, bony, ugly girl with a boy's haircut and jeans wasn't going to be her daughter-in-law. All the sadness went away from her face and with a smile she pinched Azadeh's cheeks and said,

"Well, I wish I could have a girl of your stature. As my daughter-in-law. You are the best." The lying was evident through her tone, which made Azadeh laugh. She went back to set the table for dinner. The way Goli talked and her manner, especially those motherly tears and her long, toothless face, made Azadeh take pity on her and instantly, her attitude towards Goli changesd. (As if Goli was not related to Ahmad, and she couldn't blame her for his faults or even complain to her about them. Now, Azadeh was concerned that tomorrow she would have to work and wouldn't be able to help Goli find her son. On the other hand, she couldn't see it in her to be able to find Ahmad on her own in this huge city. Cautiously, she started thinking of Sepideh. This would be a big favor to ask from her. The memories were bitter and spending time at a police department or prison were not a suitable place for Sepideh to dig around. But she had to ask her. She went to her bedroom and dialed her mother's phone number. Azadeh's mother reacted the way that Azadeh expected her to and was ready for it. Her mother began yelling at her.

"Are you out of your mind? How could you take her in your house? What else can happen to you to make you open your eyes? Get rid of her as soon as possible! For once in your life, listen to me and don't feel sorry for her. If anything happens to you, my heart won't take it this time. It's all on you now, don't waste your breath on me either."

After her mom, it was Sepideh's turn.

"What's going on there? What's his mom doing in your apartment? Didn't you have enough? Did you already forget what you went through? Get rid of her as soon as possible, and give mother some peace of mind. You know very well she's worried sick now."

"I know, but I can't throw her out at this hour of night. If we can get some information about Ahmad tomorrow, it's a big help to this worried mother. I can't take the day off tomorrow, but you can. Come here and take her to the police and give his information. He must be in one of these prisons. Maybe he's executed."

Sepideh started laughing, "Are you kidding me? You want me to go around prisons to look for Ahmad? Stop this joke right now! What I can do for her, is to get her a taxi tomorrow morning, and give the driver the address to the bus terminal so she can get back to her town."

Azadeh put the phone down and believed her family had a point. This wasn't only her problem. She was worried for her mother, she knew now that her mother wouldn't be able to sleep and would probably finish a pack of cigarettes that night, calling her every five minutes to make sure she's still alive and Ahmad's mom hadn't killed her. She wanted to call her mother again to make her believe that this old lady is not trouble, but she knew it was useless. She knew not until her mother met Goli and talked to her, it would be useless otherwise. So she decided to take Goli to her mother's house the next morning before going to work.

Azadeh threw a blanket on Goli's shoulders and said, "Let's have dinner."

Goli shyly said, "Thank you, deary. I don't know what you have cooked but it smells great and has already made me hungry. May God give you more, I have caused you too much trouble." She followed Azadeh into the kitchen, she figured that Azadeh lived alone. She almost asked her if she was single, but then she changed her mind and said,

"Don't you want to wait for your man?"

Azadeh, thinking about her plans for tomorrow, replied, "I'm not married. It's been a few years since I've been divorced.

Goli said, "It's a shame dear, I'll go check on Ahmad, maybe he's back."

Azadeh, ignoring what she had just said, gave her a bowl of soup and pulled a chair out for her.

Goli thought, maybe she's acting this way because she doesn't have any kids of her own.

Azadeh saw the hurt in her face, but knew if she said anything now, she wouldn't be able to eat her dinner. So she just said, "Goli I don't think he'll show up tonight. Have your dinner and don't worry, you can spend the night here."

"Well, okay, if he doesn't come back, there's still a long time until bedtime. I'll just check one more time." She left her soup on the table, put on her veil, and went out.

Azadeh, thinking about what she was about to tell her, was trying to make her sentences as soft and cheerful as possible. In a minute, Goli came back and said, justifyingly, "Well, he's single, he won't stay home alone. God help him to fall in love and end these lonely nights. Single life is enough. He's almost forty now, I have a few candidates in mind, but whenever I talk to him, he just laughs at me.

He says, 'children are trouble and they make you old.' I'm always worried sick over him, you know, he's the only one left from four sons. What about you dear? Are you like my daughter Fati, sterile?"

Azadeh laughed, "No, I have two sons. Their pictures are over there in that room."

Goli looked at the pictures and admired them, all of a sudden her face changed and became filled with hurt and sadness. "Did he choose another wife over you?"

"No, it's been four years since I've been divorced. He married a very good woman two years ago. We are friends now."

Goli pulled her eyebrows together in astonishment and said, "How could you be friends with the other woman? Are you joking?"

"No, I'm telling you the truth, she's a good woman and loves my sons just the same as her own little daughter. Also, she's not the other woman."

"That's right, you said that. My mind's busy with Ahmad, you know, Sedigheh hated my kids. Karbalai, my goddamn late husband married again. Well, what could I do? Men are like roosters, they don't pass on any hens. As soon as they hear them, their crown stands up, don't you agree?"

Azadeh laughed so hard until tears started coming down her eyes. Goli laughed too, but suddenly she became quiet and her face got sad. Now, Azadeh knew that Goli would sigh right before telling a sad story. Azadeh got a hold of her self and said,

"I bet you they brought a new bride to your house on a camel."

"Camel? Why camel dear? Karbalai rented a car." She sighed and put her hands over her eyes, she was cursing Karbalai. It was all his fault. She shouldn't have to depend on her son for her livelihood after his death. Karbalai smoked all the money in opium. They received some money from the government as blood money when her son died in the war. If only he had paid off his debts with that money, now they had the little grocery store to pay for her expenses, as well as her daughters and granddaughters. Instead, they all have to depend on Ahmad for support now.

Goli took the cup of tea from Azadeh and continued with her stories.

"Dear, it's not right to talk about dead people, but that goddamn son of a bitch hurt me deeply. No matter what I told him, it was landing on deaf ears. He said, it's a godly act to marry widows. It's what God and his prophet have ordered. I said, you fucking liar, why do you make it a holy act? Just say you want a young woman to funk up your penis! He made me so mad! I was feeling sorry for Sedigheh too. I told him, stop sending her messages and leave her alone! Let her find herself a young guy."

"So you were thinking of her too?"

"Of course. If her pappy could afford to feed her and people would stop talking about her, she didn't have to live with us. I said the same thing to Karbalai. I said, 'Listen Karbalai, if she had money and food on her table, she wouldn't marry you old fart! You are as old as her pappy!'" Goli looked around the room and lowered her voice as if she was going to tell Azadeh the secret of her life. "God knows, Azadeh, when Karbalai died, I didn't even blink. I put my veil on and on his grave just cursed him quietly. My only concern was Ahmad, who had to support his two needy women. Poor thing. He was only twenty, just out of military service. When he was sixteen we sent him to Mashad to his uncle's. There, he helped his uncle wire houses. His brother was a war hero and he was privileged that way. They told him, if he studied well, he could go to university. Sadly, he had only finished eighth grade. When Masoumeh was three, Karbalai died. You know, Masoumeh is Sedigheh's daughter. Karbalai left this little gift by his coffin. She's now seventeen, a good kid, problem free, studies hard, nothing like her slutty mom."

Goli was warmed up and was telling stories one after another. She was so used to talking about her sad life that words were just pouring out. Her tone was soft and mingled with a sigh.

Azadeh got up and put the dishes in the sink, filled up the teapot, and brought two cups and sat in front of Goli. The story was getting closer to Ahmad and Azadeh was curious to hear it. She felt that the dark spot on her mind that was Ahmad, was now growing paler. Until now, Ahmad had been this homeless, family less bum, who had no connections or attachments to anyone and anything. She could never imagine him as a responsible man with a mother like Goli. Goli poured tea for Azadeh and herself, and started again, "May God give you more, I couldn't live with the second wife in the same house. Sedigheh is a cunning person. She talks about me all over the place. I'm not stupid. I see how people deal with me in the mosque. It's not possible to argue all the time too. God bless Ahmad, a few years ago, he leased an apartment for me near the holy Imam mosque. It has a kitchen too. I am comfortable. Ahmad has good intentions and God helps him too. Ever since he came here to work for the electric company, he is financially better off."

Azadeh looked down so Goli wouldn't see the sorrow in her eyes. She never felt so sorry for anyone else in her life. She asked how long it had been since Ahmad began to work for the electric company.

"For five years, before that he was with a narcotics patrol on the Afghanistan border. He suddenly decided to become a guard and fight the drug dealers. He used to say, 'Mother, they're smuggling loads of drugs here. In all the houses you can smell opium.' My days were dark, I couldn't sleep or eat. When I saw him after two years, he wasn't the same. It was like they had taken the life out of his veins. He was like a skeleton, very quiet, chain smoking, moody, yelling at everyone." After a long sigh, she continued,

"Well, he had a right to be moody, he had seen blood. A lot of his friends had been killed in the mountains. Drug dealers are ruthless. If they caught them, they would decapitate them. I begged him not to go to the borders again. He accepted but instead, he went into Afghanistan and worked there. He said he was working in a store, which made me worry less."

Goli closed her eyes. Azadeh could tell from her lips and movements that she was saying prayers silently. She peeled an apple and put it in a plate in front of her and lit a cigarette for herself. Goli opened her eyes, put a piece of apple in her mouth, and as she was chewing it with her toothless mouth, she said, "I pray to God for this one son." She swallowed the apple and continued, "Dear, do you work? Who supports you?"

Now it was Azadeh's turn to run through a few pages of her life story and then take this story to Ahmad and prison. Although, Azadeh put the story very simply and didn't bring up the possibility of execution, her story didn't lessen the degree of Goli's anxiety. With every sentence that came out of Azadeh's mouth, Goli was agitated and cried hysterically. It was as if the flood of tears was coming out of her soul and covered her face. Her cries turned into moaning and then she was quiet. Exhausted, she laid her head on the sofa. Now she was thinking the worst. With teary eyes, she looked at Azadeh who was sitting in front of her; his stupidity has ruined her life. Goddamn you son, goddamn you! She sat straight and started banging her fists against her chest

"The dumb idiot! He stained our name. Why son, why? Why did you put that shit in this innocent girl's house?" It seemed like this was the only way that Goli could calm herself enough to look into Azadeh's eyes. She was thinking of Judgment Day and how she had to go through all that without anything good in her life to show for. All her life was stained now. Her prayers were made on the ground paid for by sinful money and the same was with the bread on her table. Everything she owned now was dirty and sinful. His face came to her mind and she loved him too much to wipe him out of her life. He was her only son and part of her being. He was her only support, her pride, and she woud defend him like a lioness in front of the entire world. As if Goli had forgiven him in her heart, she turned her puffed up eyes to Azadeh and said,

"God damn them, they must have deceived him. One must be aware of bad friends. No matter how good you are, they can turn you around. God knows my son was not into this kind of stuff, he hated even to touch this poison, let alone to sell it. He hated his dad for smoking opium, and wouldn't stay in the same room with him. My boy was clean. I know those jealous people couldn't see it, but he was so innocent and clean. They didn't want me to have this one son. This small rented house was like a thorn in their eyes. You know, dear, people are jealous. They couldn't rest until they put my house on fire." Goli put her chin on her hands and looked into the darkness outside the window. Sadness gave her pale face a state of holiness.

This made Azadeh's heart ache and she looked at Goli through teary eyes. She had never seen a face this sad and this innocent in her life. At that moment she wished from the bottom of her heart that Ahmad was alive. She wanted to say something soothing to Goli but couldn't think of anything. She was trying to help her with all her might. She had told her that she would do anything to help her and that she could stay at her house as long as she needed to so that she could visit her son. But she knew well that she couldn't support her through the dark thoughts that were going through her mind. Azadeh got up, and asked Goli if she wanted to call her daughter. Maybe talking to her would calm her down.

"No honey, what can I tell her, that I'm going tomorrow to find your brother in prison? Oh God, Fati, how can you show your face in front of your husband and his family anymore? Her mother-in-law can melt a rock with her blaming eyes. She's a witch. This is all her spell on us. Azadeh, my pain is endless. My son-in-law has given her an ultimatum that he will leave my daughter if she is not pregnant by next year. Fati loves him. Otherwise I would have made her divorce him sooner. When I talked to his mom about this, she raised hell. None of them are on good terms with me now. If they found out about Ahmad, it makes them so happy. Oh Ahmad, why did you do this to us?"

Azadeh took her to the bathroom and encouraged her to take a bath, hoping that warm water would calm her nerves. Goli bit her lip so hard that her face tensed up from pain. She looked up to heavens and with a repenting voice said, "God forgive me, I'm happy with whatever you give me." Goli didn't take a bath, but washed her face, fixed her scarf, and laid on the bed that Azadeh had made her in the family room. She was exhausted from the trip and all the crying.

She had no more energy to think of her bad fortune and fell asleep. Azadeh was lying on her bed and the misfortunes of this poor woman were hurting her soul. To her, Goli was such a simple woman and incapable of recognizing the reasons for her misfortunes. All she knew was pain, distress, good and evil, and two words that she wouldn't stop repeating: "sinful" and "kosher." Azadeh knew that Goli was accustomed to distress, she would be able to pass this one as well.

The next morning, Goli woke up with the alarm clock. She said to Azadeh about a holy guy in her dream who was carrying Ahmad's scarf in his hand, the one that she had knitted him. She had told his holiness that that was Ahmad's scarf and he had said, 'Ahmad gave this to me to give to you. Then he had given the scarf to Goli and disappeared. Goli took this as a good omen and said,

"I know it, my son will be saved by His Holiness."

Azadeh thought, the old woman found a cure for her broken heart, good for her. The doorbell rang and there was Sepideh behind the door. Azadeh was pleasantly surprised,

"I knew it! I knew you would come!"

"Of course, I told you I would come! Okay where is this lady? I can take her to the bus station." Sepideh found Goli standing by her bed, fixing it. She said hello.

"Hello pretty lady. Azadeh, I didn't know you had a guest."

Sepideh said, "Oh no, I'm her sister. I'm here to take you to the bus treminal."

Azadeh looked at her with annoyance and said, "I asked my sister to help you today. I have to go to work, I hope you two can find Ahmad today."

Sepideh furrowed her eyebrows. Goli kissed Sepideh on the cheeks with gratitude and said, "May God give you everything. I'm in debt to you all. As soon as I learn my way around here, I will go myself next time. Hopefully, his prison is not too far from here and you can go about your work too."

As Sepideh was going to say, no lady I'm not going to do this, she heard Azadeh saying, "It's better if you guys go check with the Comeeteh (the local police establishment after the revolution to monitor each neighborhood independent of the regular police force, it was made up primarily from the religious guards) first. They might know where he is."

Sepideh looked at her with obvious disagreement, and took her hand and pulled her into the bedroom.

"You know very well that I won't set foot in Comeeteh. So don't say such things again. Secondly, why can't she get help from her family? Quom is pretty close to here."

"If she had any family, she would have thought of it already. She is so embarrassed by the fact that she needs us, now don't be rude and try to talk nicely to her."

"Why? Whatever she has told you is already enough for

both of us. I have no patience to hear her cry and moan. Do you have any idea how mother was feeling since last night? She was the one who sent me here. She wanted to make sure that she leaves. Let me take her to the bus station."

"Well, why don't you stop by Comeeteh first and then take her to the terminal?" Sepideh started laughing, "Why do you play dumb? You know how I feel about Comeeteh, you let her into your home and now you take care of her too. I have to go, I'm late."

Sepideh left the room. By the door she saw Goli with her veil and shoes on, ready to go. Azadeh turned and pleadingly looked at Sepideh, her eyes were saying, can you really let her go on her own? Sepideh looked out the window and thought, what am I supposed to do? This helpless woman makes the devil feel sorry for her too. I guess I have to ignore my gut feelings and take her.

Azadeh was setting the breakfast table in the kitchen.

As soon as Sepideh saw Goli, she understood why her sister felt sorry for her and wanted to help her. But she could not see it in herself to help her. Angrily she passed Goli. Goli said goodbye to Azadeh and was waiting by the elevator.

"Dear, as a mother I was not that lucky. There was always something going on regarding my kids to make me cry and be worried. Good for your mom who has such good kids as yourselves," Goli said.

Sepideh was going to say that she was not really there to help her but couldn't say it. Instead she said:

"Is breakfast ready? We don't have time."

Azadeh smiled. Sepideh was mad because she thought Azadeh was forcing her to do this in spite of logic. Goli took her shoes off. Azadeh kissed Sepideh warmly and said,

"If I didn't know your heart, I would have never asked you for this favor." Sepideh wiped her face with her hand. "Stop it."

The day was coming to an end and still there was no news from Sepideh. Azadeh lost hope and was planning for tomorrow while struggling with her doubts. Is Ahmad still alive? She was on her way home when her cell phone rang. It was Sepideh. Her voice was tired and weak. She was saying how hard it was and they had been tossed to too many places, but finally had found him, it was so astonishing, just astonishing.

"Well, visiting hours were over, but Goli started crying, took out her martyred son's picture with his rifle on his shoulder, that picture was her key to many doors. We saw him. He is fine and healthy."

Azadeh took a sigh of relief. So Ahmad was alive. She was happy for Goli and in some ways for herself too. As long as Ahmad is alive she has to act quickly to make everything right again. He was responsible for wasting her mom's money. He was responsible for allowing the government to get all they had. He should give it back. He can get it from the same drug dealer friends. She wasn't thinking much about Hamed and the car he contributed. She knew it wasn't a big deal to him. That car was like a drop in a bucket. Hamed had more, but her mother's savings were accumulated penny by penny and were only meant for tough times. Especially with her sick heart, there was a big possibility for open-heart surgery and that was definitely going to be costly. Azadeh went straight from the hospital to her mother's house. She found Goli next to her mom, the kitchen was filled with cigarette smoke. Goli was sitting sadly with her knees tucked in to her chest. Her mother's eyes were all red from crying. Goli pressed her knees harder to her chest as soon as she saw Azadeh. Before Azadeh could say anything Goli said,

"I'm so embarrassed. Just now your mom told me how much my stupid son's troubles had cost you. If you had told me last night about it, I would have spit in his face today."

Azadeh thought, spit wouldn't replace the money. Maybe it's better to talk to his lawyer about the money. Azadeh sat next to Goli, put a kiss on her head and asked,

"How is he? He must have been surprised to see you there."

"Yeah, when he saw me he started crying. I felt so sorry for him. I told him I had spent the night at your place. He couldn't believe it. He thought I was joking with him. I told him, son, this is not the time to joke. I'm telling you the truth. Only when he saw Sepideh did he believe me. May God give you everything you desired. If it wasn't for you guys, I don't know how I could have found my son."

"Well, don't you worry I'm sure they will let him go very soon."

"He thought so too."

"He didn't tell you how long he was going to be there?"

"No, he just asked for prayers."

"He didn't tell you about his lawyer or where you should go to?"

"No dearie, there was no time for this. He only asked if I still had money. I was going to tell him not to worry about us but all of a sudden his voice was cut off. When they were taking him back to his cell I looked through the bars as far as I could." She got up and said, "I have to go. It's getting cold, I really don't want to go, but what can I do? I'll go back and we'll pray for him. I'll stay by the Holy Saint's shrine until She listens to me. I'll ask his sister to write to the officials and tell them that he's our only source of income. Azadeh, can you please take me to your home? My bag is still there. I'll go to the station from there."

Simin said, "It's too late now, I don't want you to leave. It's better if you stay here for a few days. Taxi is too expensive for you, whenever you want to leave, Sepideh will give you a ride, right Sepideh?"

Sepideh looked at her mom in disbelief, asking her, "Are you really serious?"

Simin replied to her daughter with a smile and went to the kitchen to make some rice. Sepideh followed her there and said,

"You go from one extreme to another. Do you know

how far the bus terminal is from here?"

"Well, she's our guest. Let's give her a helping hand so she won't feel all alone and helpless in the city."

That night, Goli didn't sleep and didn't let Simin sleep either. She had tea after tea and talked. She told her about all the harshness and ugliness around her, how people were hateful towards her and she was the same with them. That night she put her hideous and spinster sister-in-law through eternal damnation, and cursed her witch of a mother-in-law into the deepest and hottest place in hell to burn forever. She also talked about the times that she was naughty and mean too, like the time she poured the urine from her brother-in-law's urine bucket on his head to pay for all the times he had hit her sister and on the day of Omar Festivals (a relious festival where the shiits set the effigy of the damned Omar on fire to retaliate for the death of Ali),pretending to curse Omar, she was cursing all the neighboring women. She had also slapped a few of the neighborhood teenagers who had gathered under her window and sang

"Roghieh is like Omar, she's a son of a bitch.

Roghieh is naughty, she's the pissing bull"

For a while, every two weeks, she was visiting her son and she would spend the night at Simin's. Every morning she would wake Sepideh up and with a prayer asked her to take her to the prison. Once she went by herself but didn't get to see Ahmad. Later they told her that he has been transferred to another prison. Then she came home and begged Sepideh to take her there. Once Azadeh told her that each time, between her and Sepideh, if they're free, one of them would take her to the prison. But since she was spending the weekends with her sons, practically, it was Sepideh who had to take her all the time.

CHAPTER FOUR

It had snowed the night before and broke the freeze. The bright sun was shining on the snow-covered grounds; drivers were driving very cautiously and were honking constantly for no apparent reason. Maybe it was a habit they couldn't shake. Azadeh, alone in her car, was looking at the illegal, Afghan immigrant kids. The kids were not allowed to go to school so instead, with their snotty noses and depressed looks, would solicitate money among the cars. Azadeh stressed out, was looking in the hole in her car that used to hold her stereo. This was the third time in the past year that her car stereo had been stolen. Although, staring at the empty hole was irritating her, she wasn't actually going to replace it with another stereo. It was a waste of money. It would only last for a short time before it would be stolen again.

Azadeh was late to the hospital by about an hour. She parked her car and with uncertain steps, started to slowly walk toward the main building. All of a sudden, she stopped.

Someone was calling her name. She turned around, and saw a man with a black knit hat who was warming his hands with his steamy breath. Did you call me? Can I help you? Ahmad, who saw Azadeh didn't recognize him, took a step forward and pulled the hat higher.

"Hello miss, I see you didn't recognize me. It's been about two hours that I've been waiting for you. I was almost about to leave."

Azadeh looked at him in disbelief. It really was Ahmad standing in front of her. She had just dreamt that Ahmad was executed last night and had lost all hope. A smile came to her lips.

"I never thought they would let you go so early. Did you escape?"

Ahmad made a noise from deep down his throat that resembled a laugh.

"Thank you very much, did you expect me to rot in there forever?"

"No, but I thought they wouldn't let go of drug traffickers of your caliber so easily. It's really hard to believe. Maybe since you were in the narcotics division before, they were easy on you."

"No miss, it's not like that. If you have enough money, you can even dance with the kings. You know, the government has expenses too. I paid off and repented. They said, 'God bless you.' I wanted to ask for your forgiveness.

That day I was rushed, all of a sudden I got a brain freeze and didn't think about it. I swear on my dead father's grave, I'm so sorry. I can't understand why the sons of bitches took you. That very first day I told them, 'This lady is innocent.' Apparently they didn't believe me. Did they hurt you in the prison?"

Azadeh looked at her watch and impatiently said, "You have cost us all that we had. Mullahs have all our life savings now. Instead of mumbling this nonsense show me the money. I don't buy whatever you said to your mother. I won't let you forget my mother's money."

"Who the hell am I to ignore it?"

"Well, then you want to repeat the same things you told your mom, huh? I don't buy that you're broke. Show me the money and we'll call it even."

"You don't believe it, huh? I swear on my father's soul, I am telling you the truth. But it won't stay this way. I'll make it. A few million is nothing."

Azadeh, irritated said, "That's just the cash we paid. Go ahead, ask about the price of a brand new Mercedes, that's how much we paid the mullahs."

"Really, my mother did not mention the Mercedes. Then, those sons of bitches really cleaned you out. I'll be on it. But you have to be patient. You know I don't want to deal anymore. I want to make my money kosher and clean."

Azadeh looked at his sickly face and his cautious eyes that were darting around and thought, dirty scoundrel! He thinks I'm stupid! He couldn't make enough money with drug dealing. Now he wants to work hard and pay his debt with clean money. She bitterly said,

"I don't give a damn how, but don't forget your word. I'll wait, just tell me how long."

"I can't give you a date now, it's only been two days since I've been out, but you can count on my words. You can count on me."

Azadeh laughed sarcastically, "Okay, we'll count on you. How about if we sweared on your honor too?"

"Damn this luck which didn't leave me with any dignity!"

"Oh you know about dignity too?"

"Point taken. I deserve it. Anybody else in your place would have hit me hard in the head," Ahmad said. As he was stepping backwards to leave, he said, "Tell your mother I'm in debt to her, your younger sister has done so much it's so embarrassing, it makes me blush. My mother says we owe your family a lot. She's right; you guys are something else. I will bust my chops off to make it even with you. Give my regards to the family and tell Ms. Sepideh that I'm at her service. Bye."

When Ahmad said, 'Tell your sister I'm at her service' Azadeh knew what he really meant. Ahmad had fallen in love with Sepideh and she knew it too. Sepideh had said that she thinks he is in love with her and it is just her bad luck. Both she and Azadeh had laughed at that notion. Ahmad left, his lips began shaking, his whole body was shivering, he couldn't even take one more step. He leaned against a tree, there was a commotion going on in his heart, he could feel his love for Sepideh in his heart. His love for her was woven into all his nerves and veins. He was a desperate lover without the possibility of any future with his love. When he was in prison, as his mother was talking to him in tears, his eyes were fixated on Sepideh and he was telling his true feelings for her with his eyes. When there was a smile on Sepideh's lips he knew what she was thinking, that this guy is hallucinating. That very thought would double his feelings of sadness and helplessness. When Sepideh wasn't by his mother's side, he would ask about her. When his mother would mention that Sepideh was sitting in the other room his heart would fill with sadness. Although he kept reminding himself that he was a poor prisoner serving time for drug trafficking, he couldn't keep his eyes from searching for her. Ahmad got to the other side of the street with difficulty. Azadeh was following him with her eyes. She couldn't help thinking that the flimsy guy could be nice too, who knew?

Suddenly she saw him collapse on the ground. She started laughing as if his fall made her feel better, but it seemed like he wasn't moving and something really bad was happening. Now, it was the nurse in her that was hurrying to help a patient. Cautiously, she reached him. His eyes were closed and his body was stiff from a mild seizure however, his limbs were jerking. She leaned over, "Ahmad, What's happening?

Do you hear me?" Ahmad didn't answer. Azadeh took her cell phone and dialed the hospital. She opened his jacket buttons and felt for his heartbeat. She felt a very faint beat. She wished she hadn't laughed at him. She saw two men with a gurney rushing towards her. Ahmad opened his eyes and made a slight movement. Azadeh smiled." It must have been a hard fall. But I don't think anything is broken otherwise you would be screaming in pain right now." A pale smile crept onto his face and he muttered out something Azadeh couldn't understand. When they were putting him on the gurney he said, "You shouldn't have called them." Azadeh followed them. Azadeh met Maryam in the hospital and told her about Ahmad and what had happened to him. She told her to go and visit the monster in ER.

The next morning Azadeh heard from Maryam that Ahmad was admitted to the hospital, Azadeh was under the impression that doctor's would have given him some OTC pain meds with vitamins and sent him home, which was why she hadn't followed up on him yesterday. Now she thought the guy must be really out of luck. He was just getting ready to go home and now this. Hopefully, he's not seriously injured. After a few hours, at her break time, she went downstairs to visit him. But he was out to get some lab work done. She went to get some information from the treating doctor. The young doctor was happy to see her; "I was going to call after you. Your cousin should stay a few days here, but he won't listen, he wanted to leave yesterday, but in his state it's too risky."

-"Oh, then my cousin had a really bad fall, ha?"

The young doctor laughed bitterly. "I thought you knew about his illness. He doesn't have much time. He informed us yesterday about the brain tumor. From what he told me, taking the tumor out would lead to his death. His doctors have told him taking some precautions might postpone his inevitable death. We told him he must quit smoking and stop stressing. He didn't say anything about his job, but it must be a stressful one."

As Azadeh was walking towards his room, she was wondering why Goli hadn't mentioned his illness, considering how grave the situation was. Maybe she doesn't know about it either. Maybe Ahmad didn't want to tell her anything and upset her. Ahmad was under the covers. His boney face was colorless as if life had left his face. Upon hearing her footsteps he opened his eyes. He turned his sickly eyes towards her; "I hope you haven't informed my mother."

-"No, I wasn't even aware that you were admitted. I would have visited you earlier. I'm sorry, the doctor told me everything. I wish there was something to do for you. If you want I can call your mom now, does she know you were released from the prison?"

-"No, not yet. I was going to Quom when this fucking thing nailed me again."

_"Obviously you haven't told her about your condition," Azadeh said.

-"No she doesn't know anything. The poor old woman already has enough on her plate. If I knew there was hope I would have told her."

-"Well, she should be informed. This way she will be prepared, it's better than hearing about her son's death from a stranger."

-"No miss, she doesn't deal with this kind of stuff like others, as soon as she hears a news such as this she will have a heart attack right then and there. You know my brother was killed in the war. When she heard the news she passed out and then after that she was constantly crying for months. She was so upset that we had to take her to the hospital."

Azadeh noticed that Ahmad was talking with a lump in his throat. She said, "I'll come back tomorrow. Take care of yourself." Ahmad didn't reply, he just covered his head with the blanket. It seemed like he was crying.

Azadeh wanted to say something consoling, but she couldn't think of anything. She closed the door slowly and left. Now Azadeh could understand why he was released so early. His short time left in this world had bought him his freedom. She called her mom and told her about Ahmad and his situation as soon as she got home. It made her really sad, especially when she thought about his poor mother. Although she thought they had to inform Goli, she realized it was best to wait. Goli was now her friend and Azadeh didn't want to see her sad. Goli was waiting for the day that her Ahmad would be released and everything would be fine again and her family's name would be cleared. This was the promise Ahmad had made to his mother and that was what could sustain his mother through her long wait. Simin didn't want to make the old woman more distressed than she already was. "We have to give her the chance to celebrate his freedom first."

That night Azadeh couldn't sleep. She made herself some tea and went to the balcony to look at starry sky while sipping on her tea. She had to make herself accept that he really was broke. While it was difficult, she knew she had to forget about her mother's money. Azadeh thought about Goli and the other two women whom Ahmad had to support. She left her thoughts on the balcony and went inside to busy herself with a book, a life story of someone else.

Very early morning the phone woke her. Unexpected calls always made her nervous about her mother and sons. When she heard Sepideh's voice on the other end, she became even more worried. "Has something happened to mother?"

-"She's fine, Goli's here. She just arrived and wants to go to the hospital."

_"Have you told her everything?"

_"No, she doesn't know anything about his illness, mom told her that he's released and because he was too weak they had to hospitalize him."

_"How did she get here so fast?"

-"Can you believe that when I opened the door to her I saw her thanking a truck driver? Apparently she hitched a ride with a salt carrying truck."

_"I didn't see it in her to be so versatile!"

Ahmad opened his eyes with the touch of a hand on his face and saw his mother and Azadeh standing by his bed. His eyes got fixated on Azadeh and his face tensed up.

Goli leaned on him and put a kiss on his forehead. Her eyes got wet. She wiped her eyes with her veil and said, "I wish it was me on this bed, not you. What has happened to you in that prison?"

Azadeh interrupted her, "Goli, don't make a big deal out of it. It could happen to anyone, he had passed out, you know how bad prison food is."

She wanted to let Ahmad know that his secret was safe with her and he shouldn't be upset with her. Ahmad smiled the faintest smile that no one noticed. He took his mom's hand into his own and said, "Mother, you heard her, as soon as I eat your home cooked meals I'll be fine. Then I'll be strong enough to do everything for you." Goli laughed, "I'll cook whatever you desire, I have a very good girl on mind for you. She's Fati's friend, she's a teacher like your sister, an intellectual!"

-"Okay mother, I'll come and you can find a good girl for me."

_"Yes, you know it's time for you. Single life has made you like this. If only you had a wife and a few kids around you, you would have never gotten involved with this stuff and this would never have happened. This month we will go looking. You have to get a descent job too. I'll throw the reception party for you. Sedigheh has promised God to feed twenty hungry people if you get well. Masoumeh is already sewing you a new shirt and she'll be done by the time you come home. Yes dear, God willing we'll sew your wedding suit soon." Goli was distracting herself with her dreams and was doing the same for Ahmad by listing the good characteristics of the bride to be. From her beautiful face, full lips, and long eyebrows to her tall slim body. Ahmad was pretending to enjoy all this and was smiling at her mother's thoughts, but Azadeh could see the sadness in his eyes. Azadeh left the mother and son alone and went back to work but, all day long she couldn't stop thinking about Ahmad.

After a few days Ahmad was released from the hospital. But no one knew about his whereabouts. He had told his mom that with his record now, he couldn't get a job, so he would go somewhere else to find a good job and stop people from talking. But he didn't say where.

Goli was disappointed in him. What was the rush? Why didn't he want to spend some time with his family, not even for one day?

The day that he got out of the hospital he went to a friend's house named Mohammad. He had met him in prison. He was a translator for Afghan inmates who spoke Pashtu. He had taught theology in Kabul's Islamic school for a while, but all of a sudden he had decided to leave that life and took arms to fight against the invaders of his country. He had joined a group he had thought were legitimate, but their actions disappointed him. However, one of the leaders of the group was his cousin Sadegh Jamal. Mohammed felt that the noble cause of patriotism had been diluted by money hungry people with different agendas. He quit arms. He concluded that until people are educated about their rights in life, fighting itself won't solve any problems. Therefore, Mohammed had opened a school, but his cousin accused Mohammad of diverting kids from religion, and had closed down the school and forced the kids to work on the opium farms.

Mohammad decided to take revenge and turned a few people against his cousin and set a few hundred kilos of his cousin's opium on fire and then fled to Iran. He then sent his wife and three sons to Kandahar to hide. His brother, Hassan, joined the drug controlling forces on the border with Iran, but his cousin and his goons killed him in Mashad in revenge. After his death, Mohammad took his pregnant sister-in-law and fled to Tehran. But he wasn't living his life by solely translating in prisons. He had other projects on hand. It was Mohammad who lured Ahmad to join him. Mohammad was an experienced man. He would patiently sit in the courts and translate whatever the prisoners said for the judge. He would use his own judgment and and tell their stories such that would influence the judge to send them to hell by execution or set them free. Talking to Ahmad, he saw the good in him and also found out about his illness. Mohammed would kindly remind Ahmad about the life after death in heaven, and about all the crimes of bad people like Sadegh Jamal. Since Mohammed knew about the depth of love Ahmad had for his mom, he even made up the story that Sadegh Jamal had killed the mother of one of his enemies. He was planting the seeds of hatred in Ahmad's thoughts in different ways. Ahmad had never met Sadegh Jamal. Although once he had delivered opium to his house, but Sadegh Jamal was out and he had only dealt with his goon Ali. Ahmad had heard about sadegh Jamal's sworn enemy Molla Mohammad. What he didn't know though, was that Molla Mohammad was in fact the same guy who was advising him, Mohammad. Mohammad had shaped his thoughts without making him aware of it. His advices and the love he had for Sepideh were the only positive forces in Ahmad's life. Mohammad was telling him to use whatever time he had left on this earth to learn and open his eyes to what was happening around him. Drug dealers had ruined his life and he was having the same effect on hundreds of other lives by dealing drugs. Ahmad was analyzing the roots of hatred in himself and connected everything to the hateful act of drug dealing. He put some of the blame on the people who dragged him into it too. Mohammad's job was done. He made Ahmad conscientious enough to cooperate with the authorities and Ahmad named all of his accomplices, including Sadegh Jamal. He even volunteered to take them to his factory in a city called Meimaneh. He had done the electrical work on that building and was thoroughly familiar with all the ways and alleys. The factory was found and burned. That put Ahmad's life in prison in danger. Sadegh Jamal knew he was the snitch and would definitely send someone to kill Ahmad. Mohammad knew he had to act fast in order to save Ahmad's life. He was the one who gave the release papers to Ahmad. Ahmad couldn't believe it.

Mohammad said if it wasn't for the fact that he was sick and his brother had died in the war, Ahmad would have died in the prison. Ahmad spent a few days at Mohammad's house and then left for Pakistan to work with his friend in his rug store.

CHAPTER FIVE

The cold season was ending and the aroma of spring flowers filled the air. The sun was no longer in a hurry to leave early. The first day of spring was around the corner (Persian New Year) and the streets were filled with people who insisted on spending their last dime on Norouz (Persian New Year) and sweep up all the goods from the stores.

Azadeh had given herself up to the flow of people and was wandering around looking for Sepideh in the stores she thought Sepideh might be shopping in. She had left her work for shopping at 11 a.m. and it was now evening and still no signs of Sepideh. Azadeh checked the time and it was 10 p.m. She was starting to become worried. Yesterday a gypsy woman had appeared at her door and insisted on reading Sepideh's palm. She had told her that she has a long life, but that there are people with evil intentions in her path. The gypsy told her, "Go, leave this place. Don't let them pour poison in your cup of life." Simin, worried sick, was looking out the kitchen window, praying to God to bring her daughter home safe and sound. Her heart was palpitating, as her mind was filled with thoughts of Sepideh being involved in a car accident. She was smoking cigarettes one after the other, the front gate opened, and she recognized Azadeh's figure. She prayed, 'Oh God, oh Lord have mercy on us.'

Azadeh came to the kitchen, "Mother, don't worry, she will show up sooner or later. There's so much traffic, you know, last minute shopping. I'll prepare the fish, you make the rice."

Simin said, "I can't. All I'm thinking of is Sepideh." The sound of the clock was filling the room. The cigarette in Azadeh's fingers had a long ash hanging from it, it fell down and the cigarette burned her fingers.

Her mother said, "My heart is jumping out, where can she be?" Azadeh made no effort to calm her down. A minute ago when she did that, her mom screamed back, "Stop this nonsense! A broken car, traffic, and lots of shopping people won't keep her from calling home so we won't be worried."

"Mom, I'm worried too."

"I've called whoever I can think of. I couldn't help it, I even called your uncle."

"Why? He can't do anything from the long distance."

"What can I do? I don't have anybody else to rely on." The phone rang, Azadeh heard her uncle's voice, calling from his vacation. He was saying, if they don't hear from Sepideh for another hour, he would leave his family in the hotel and fly to Tehran.

An hour passed, Azadeh called all the hospitals, but they hadn't registered anybody with Sepideh's information. Azadeh knew she couldn't rely on their information. Now, she was thinking of car accidents too. Simin looked away from the door. "We should call the police." It was eleven o'clock, Azadeh took the phone, Simin with a broken voice said, "Let me talk to them," hoping that the police would be more willing to help if they heard a worried mother's voice. The voice on the phone put her on hold to transfer her to someone else. The hold took about ten minutes and finally another voice said,

"What can I do for you?" Simin started crying and with a sobbing voice she begged the officer to look for her daughter and not postpone it. The officer promised to dispatch the license plate number+ of Sepideh's car to all the units and if there is any report of an accident, he would let them know. At the end he said,

"If she doesn't come home tonight, you have to come down to the station tomorrow to file a report for a missing person." Simin put the phone down and with red eyes, looked at Azadeh, wondering how to wait until tomorrow. At this point Azadeh's cell phone started ringing. Azadeh rushed to get it.

"Hi, is this Azadeh?"

"Yes, yes, speaking."

"Your sister is at my house. I'm calling you from a pay

phone, I'll give you my address, you can come and get her. Don't forget to bring her scarf."

She looked at her mom whose chin was shivering and her eyes were fixated on her. She took a pen and happily said, "Thank God, mom, she's alright. I'm going to get her."

"Where from?"

She pulled her shoulders up and asked, "Pardon me, ma'am, who are you?"

"My name is Arezou, but you don't know me."

"Okay, give me your address." She put the phone down. The address was far from Simin's home. What was Sepideh doing there? She looked at her mom with a question in her eyes. Her mom's eyes were closed and she was breathing with difficulty. She put the address in her purse.

"Who was she?"

"She said her name was Arezou and she had Sepideh."

"Arezou? Do you know her?"

"No."

"Why didn't Sepideh talk to you herself?"

Azadeh had to lie and there was no avoiding it. She didn't want her mother to get more worried than she already was. "Well, her car broke down, she had called the mechanic and waited until now. So she had gone to this woman's house to use her phone. Since this woman has no phone either, she was calling from her neighbor's house. She took her purse to leave.

"Wait a minute, I'll come with you! It's not like Sepideh to go to a stranger's house at this hour of night."

"Well, maybe she had to."

"Why? She could get a taxi and come home."

"Mom, please stop making horror stories. There must be a reason that she wanted me to go get her. Maybe someone has snatched her purse."

"Impossible."

Azadeh didn't stay any longer to try to make sense out of the situation. She went to Sepideh's room and took a scarf out of her dresser, put it in her purse, and with many unanswered questions in her mind, she left the house. What are you doing there girl?

It was raining and Sepideh was driving towards her home with the windows down. She was breathing the fresh air and the raindrops were falling on her cheeks. She was thinking of a cute boy whom she had met that morning at her workplace. She was stopped at the red light. Suddenly she heard someone talking to her. It was a driver of a grey car next to her. First, she thought the young guy was hitting on her. She was ignoring him when she heard him saying, "Miss, didn't you hear me? There's smoke coming out of your exhaust." Sepideh tried to check her exhaust from the window. The driver pointed to the guy sitting next to him.

"We're both mechanics. If you park the car, we could take a look at it for you." The light turned green, Sepideh turned into the next street and parked in front of a house. The grey car stopped behind her and two guys who looked alike came out. They were dressed well and both had thick, dark hair, which had carefully been combed back. They were good looking and one looked like he was Afghan. They pulled the hood up and checked the engine. The Iranian man said, "Miss, you're lucky. If you kept on driving, your car engine would have blown up. It's too late and we're going to a party. If you call us tomorrow we can fix it for you."

Sepideh thanked him and got his phone number and was heading toward the main street to get a cab when she heard him saying, "Where do you live, miss?"

"Vanak."

"Well, it's not exactly on our way but we could give you a ride home."

Sepideh accepted the generous offer and got in their car, but after a while she realized they were going the opposite way of her house. She got worried. "I think you didn't get my address."

The driver looking dirtily at her from the rear-view mirror and with a smile, winked at her. She realized she was kidnapped when the passenger jumped into the seat next to her and pressed a revolver to her side, saying if she made any noise, he would kill her. Sepideh could not comprehend what was happening to her. She was numb and shocked. It was as if she could not see the man.

Her heart was thumping from fear. She had to run away. She had to reach the streets. She had to make herself heard by the people passing by. She looked for the door handle and started screaming at the top of her lungs. Her screams were coming from the depth of her gut.

The man like a hungry wolf put his claws in her hair and pushed her head down to his knees. He put the revolver to her neck and murmured into her ears, "Relax, relax. You don't wanna die, do you? Do you?

The magnitude of the events shook her tremendously. Now she could see herself like many of the other unfortunate girls who were taken away in the same barbaric way. If she was lucky they might leave her alive, but it was a far shot with these men.

Sepideh could not see where they had taken her. She heard a door opening and they pulled her out of the car. She was like a lamb in the wolves' mouths and she accepted her faith. They took her through a huge yard into a room where there were two other men. Their faces were covered with thick beards, but their inhumane violent nature was still apparent. One of them was sitting on a hand-woven cushion and when Sepideh walked up, he got up, took her hand, sat her beside him and said, "Listen girl, we don't want to hurt you." A teenage boy not older than fourteen came into the room with teacups. He put the tray down in the middle of the room and looked at Sepideh with horror and pity, and then left the room. The driver pulled himself closer and poured tea in the cups. The man next to Sepideh gave the cup to her, but her trembling hands couldn't hold it. She let go of the cup and the tea poured on the red carpet. The man put his cup in front of her with a smile, gave her a piece of crystallized sugar candy and with the same tone said,

"Okay girl, have you heard from your fiancée? How is he?"

Sepideh looked at his mouth in disbelief and with immense difficulty muttered, "I have no fiancée." The four men in the room started laughing. The same man said

"Girl, if you tell us where Ahmad is hiding, we'll let you go."

Hearing his name made Sepideh's eyes go wide. "Do you mean the same Ahmad who was in prison?"

They all said, "Yes."

Sepideh with the same surprised tone said, "How should I know? Maybe in Quom with his mother." A big blow to her face changed her surprised expression and made her face hot.

The struggle between her and the men was brutal. She was trying to avoid those hungry, savage eyes while the legs were beating her body. She had no other weapon except for her teeth. She was biting the feet beating her. She fought hard. Everything went dark. She felt the coldness of a blade on her throat and then nothing.

When she came to, she found herself in a dump with a few stray dogs licking her. Sepideh looked down into her lap and saw that the men had cut her braid off. She was leaning against a wall in Arezou's room.

Arezou patted her head and said, "Okay, put that braid away. Drink this. Tell me, how many fuckers were there? I have never seen such a thing. This is a mess. Good old' times, no one would hurt no one. If they didn't want to pay, they wouldn't hurt you. They would kick you out of the car and leave. Drink it girl. Your sister will be here soon." She gave a wet towel to Sepideh. "Come on honey, clean up your face."

Sepideh started to rub the towel on her face, but it hurt too much. Arezou gave her a mirror. "Look in here, you don't want to hurt yourself more."

Sepideh looked in the mirror with her swollen eyes, then she put the mirror down and looked at Arezou. All of a sudden she recognized the gypsy woman. "Was it you that was telling my fortune the other day?"

"No honey, if I could see the future, I would see my own so my life wouldn't be like this. Tell me, did the fortune teller tell you that this would happen to you?"

"Yes."

Arezou started laughing. "Well, what did you want her to tell you? Who is safe in this country? She was telling you her own fate."

Sepideh looked at the bloodstains on her dress. She felt her neck and then stared at her own hands.

"Stop this, stop this nonsense. Get over it. You're lucky

I saw you in the dark in the middle of all that garbage. At first I thought you were a dog or something. You know, you were walking bent over, looked like a dog. But it was if a voice told me to wait. It was all fate. Freaky. God must like you, honey, otherwise God knows where you would be now. This is a gypsy neighborhood. Men drink like a horse; there are all sorts of people here. You're lucky they didn't find you first. Honey, why don't you find a man, a pimp? You know streets are dangerous. No woman is safe, whore or lady. Honey, go find a man and leave the streets. If they're married then it is even better. That means they have money. Nowadays it's not like old times that if the wife found out, she would raise hell on you and then take the husband to court for everything he had, making him sorry he was ever born. Now there are no rules. There are no secrets. If the wife wants to stay, fine. If not, tough."

Sepideh's body was slowly getting colder and the pain was wrapping itself around it. She put her hands on her stomach and bent over.

"It's burning, huh?"

Sepideh started sobbing. Her tears were pouring down and she was twisted in pain. Arezou saw the blood trickling down Sepideh's legs.

"You must have gotten your period out of fright. Do you want to go to a clinic or something?"

Sepideh pulled her legs into her stomach and shook her head. Arezou gave her a rag. "Here, put this there. I hope your sister shows up. It's been two hours since I called her, hopefully she's not lost.

Azadeh had a very bad feeling. The more she thought about it, the more confused she was. Her feelings were telling her, there must be something wrong. What was Sepideh doing down there in a ghetto area? Why did she need her scarf? Her thoughts were scattered, but she knew she had to focus on the address. It was not the time to get lost. She had been driving for two hours. She passed a few brick factories and some half built houses. She passed several narrow alleyways and turned into one that was only lit by some of the houses. Some of the houses didn't have a number. Arezou's house was one of them and she was looking for an unpainted iron door. She found the house. It was a very narrow house, like a matchbox with a tiny backyard. It had a tall wall with iron rods sticking out of it to keep the thieves away. Confused Azadeh rang the doorbell, she heard the window above open. She took a few steps away and looked up. In the dim light she saw a woman's face looking down.

"Finally! I'll be down to open the door." Arezou opened the door and with a smile said, "Come in honey. Please go up the stairs quietly, the landlord is sleeping and I don't want to hear his whining." Arezou was in front and Azadeh followed her like a strange ghost. She noticed Arezou was limping and her right leg was dragging on the floor, giving her waist a pronounced curve. They reached a tiny entrance. Arezou opened her room's door. "Go in, go in honey." Azadeh saw her sister and couldn't move. She was paralyzed. She thought she might be dreaming, but her sister was real and sitting on the floor on a cushion.

It took her a moment to realize that. She wanted to say something, but nothing came out. She turned to Arezou, asking her with her eyes to tell her what had happened to her sister. Arezou took her hand, "Go in, sit down." She started putting a pillow behind her and said, "She will tell you what had happened to her, sons of bitches. This is like the ultimate savagery. I've seen violence in my time, but this is the ultimate. She must have lost a lot of blood. I wanted to get a cab and take her to the clinic but she said no."

Sepideh took the mirror and touched her tangled up and dirty hair. With her hands she wiped the blood that was streaming down her torn lip and sighed a long, deep sigh. She could not look at Azadeh, she hated her. She wanted to die, and it was all Azadeh's fault. With a bitter smile she rested her blaming eyes on Azadeh's bewildered face. Azadeh slid her eyes from Sepideh to the braid next to her. At that moment she had no thoughts, her brain was numb, the sound of Sepideh's laugh echoed in her ears and her braid was touching her face. Sepideh was screaming, "I hate you, I wish I was dead and could not see your face anymore. Look! Look what they've done to me! Now go and find Ahmad for them. Next time you'll see my cut off head! Do you understand? You dumb Azadeh! Or do you want me to look for him? Or maybe it's better to call his mother so we can both look for him! I hate you Azadeh, go die."

Sepideh flinched in pain, her torn lip hurt and blood was gushing from it onto her neck. She took the towel and put it on her lips, leaned her head on the wall, and closed her eyes.

Azadeh was caught off-guard. It was like a wild animal was pulling her heart out with its claws. A million bees were stinging her. Her skin was hot like a melted iron. She was looking at Arezou with a self-loathing look. Arezou came to her and put her hands on her shoulder with sympathy. She kissed her on her forehead. This gesture of kindness broke Azadeh into tears. Her sobbing filled the room. Sepideh started crying with her sister. Arezou was standing next to them and the scene was making her cry too. With shameful tone Arezou said,

"What have I told this poor girl? She's not a whore. Well, how should I have known? Poor girl heard it all and didn't say anything." Arezou had a new respect for Sepideh. She put her hand on her shoulder and said, "Come on now, you guys are making me cry too. Stop this. See missy, I couldn't even guess that you were, you know, okay. Well, in your shape I had no doubt that you are, you know, not so okay. You didn't say anything either to stop my blabbering mouth. All I'm saying is, forget it!"

Azadeh, who was hugging Sepideh, let go of her. There was a gnawing feeling in her stomach about the injustice of it all. She wanted to get away from that place and take her sister's revenge from those bastards. She jumped up and rushed down the stairs, her heels were echoing in the stairwell, and the landlord who had woken up was cursing at her. Sepideh, behind her, dragged her painful body into the alley and threw herself into the backseat of the car.

Arezou shouted after them, "But you're not in a shape to travel! At least drive slowly! You're going to kill yourselves!"

Azadeh's cell phone started ringing. It was her mother. She gave it to Sepideh and whispered, "Your car was broken down."

Azadeh pressed on the gas pedal and sped off. On the way, she was grinding her teeth and in her mind was lashing Ahmad and with every curse word, she pressed harder on the gas. Finally she was out of breath. All of a sudden, a strange fear took over her. She was driving, but it was as if she was driving into a storm. Her hands were shaking on the wheel. She felt like everything around her was shaking with a huge force and it seemed like everything was moving with her. She was talking to herself to hide her fear, nonsense sentences that didn't make any sense and Sepideh couldn't hear them either. Sepideh had pulled her head down her dress and was moaning from the pain that had now completely taken over her body. The night was almost over when Azadeh pulled in front of the hospital where she worked. As soon as Sepideh saw the hospital, she said in protest, "Azadeh go home, just go home!" She wanted to go home, wash up, and in the security of her room cry over her bad fortune. Azadeh turned around and inquiringly looked at her. She had a question on her mind and was hoping that the answer would be negative.

"Sepideh, what do you mean?"

"I wish I had died when I was unconscious." She said these words with a heartbreaking cry. Azadeh felt as if

Sepideh's tears were cutting away and piercing her soul. She held on to the wheel with all her might and screamed a scream which unraveled all the threads of her being and then an excruciting pain took over her body, a pain so unbearable. She saw herself all in red, screaming to let everyone know what has happened to her sister. She was about to call her uncle to tell him about the rape, but she couldn't. For a second she saw him dead in a car crash. She came out and opened the door.

"Can you walk? Or should I call for a wheelchair?"

Sepideh, submitting to Azadeh's will, hung on to her and they walked into the hospital. In the hallway, Azadeh saw her friend Maryam who looked at Sepideh. "What happened, was she in an accident?" Azadeh couldn't hold back her tears.

"Maryam, help, call the doctor."

"What happened?"

"You'll find out."

Maryam ran to the end of the hallway and came back with a wheelchair. They took her in, examined her, stitched her cuts, took x-rays, and gave her strong pain medications. Sepideh lost control and was constantly crying. Maryam, who now knew the story, took Sepideh's hands in hers and was trying to calm her down. Later, a few guards came to take a report. Doctors had to report the incident to them. They were all around her in a circle, shouting and talking all at once, asking questions, or blaming Sepideh for what had happened to her.

"Why did you get into the car of a total stranger? If you were covered properly, no man would ever dream of doing this to you. We are telling you this for your own protection. What did they look like? Please give us all the details."

Sepideh looked like an innocent lamb encircled by wolves and was staring at them with fearful eyes. Azadeh broke their circle and shouted, "Enough! Can't you see what a miserable state she is in? This is not the time for nonsense! Leave her alone! We'll be back tomorrow to make the report."

Maryam took Azadeh out. "Don't say anything, you'll make trouble for yourself. They have no idea what's going on. Let them follow their own procedures."

"What are you talking about? What procedures? You know very well, everyday so many girls, all raped and beaten up are brought here. Is it their fault now for getting into strangers cars or not being covered properly? How much coverage is enough? Scarf, pants, and long dress are not enough? How stupid could they be?"

"Azadeh dear, calm down. Go home, I'll stay with Sepideh all night. Don't worry."

Finally the guards left and Sepideh, under the influence of drugs, was able to sleep. When she finally fell asleep, Azadeh went back home. The night was gone and the sky had the blue tint of early morning when Azadeh finally got home. She found her mother asleep on the sofa. She threw a blanket on her and went to her room. It was her old room and her mother had kept it the same way, so that whenever she spent the night there she wouldn't feel like a stranger. She threw herself on the bed and started crying with her pillow in her arms. Her mom woke up with the sound of her crying and rushed to her room, worried.

"Why are you crying? When did you come back? Where is Sepideh?"

Azadeh looked at her and didn't say anything. Simin looked out into the hallway and asked again. "What's going on?" But she didn't wait for an answer and ran to Sepideh's room. Azadeh went after her. Simin was looking around the room, searching for her.

"Where's Sepideh?" Azadeh took her hand and sat her down on the bed. Her brain was numb and she couldn't say anything. She sat next to her mom with a bent head. Her mom took her chin and pulled her head up and asked, "Has something happened to her?"

Azadeh looked at her mom's face, which was starting to turn blue and with trembling lips, said, "Mom, calm down. She's okay. You heard her on the phone." "Yes, I did, but where is she now?"

"Mom, please calm down. She's fine."

Simin shouted, "Why do you lie to me? Tell me where she is! What has happened to her?"

Azadeh fixed her eyes on the Chinese wisteria tree,

which was showing off its blooms in the dim light of dawn. She was afraid to look at her mom. Her tears were rolling down and she started telling her mom about the horrible things that had happened to Sepideh. Simin was quiet. She didn't utter a word, nor did she shed any tears. She took Sepideh's picture, which was framed on the nightstand and stared at it. She was crying on the inside and the sounds of her heavy breaths were unlike anything Azadeh had ever heard her mother do. Her silence was the calm before the storm. Azadeh was praying for her mom to cry, to scream, to fight. She took the picture frame out of her hands.

"Mom, for God's sake, say something! I promise you I will get revenge." To make her mom calm, she was willing to do anything, find Ahmad, make justice, anything and everything. She was talking with the heat of rage, hoping to release the rage in her mom. But Simin seemingly removed, wasn't listening to her nor was she crying. Azadeh saw how her efforts were wasted and her mom was deeply wrapped in her own pain. Her stomach from all the stress was in pain. She got up, went to the kitchen, and came back with two cups of hot tea, gave one to her mom. A bitter smile came to Simin's mouth. She put the cup on the nightstand and with her body bent, she went to her room. There was a lot going on in Azadeh's mind. She was blaming herself for everything. Who the hell do you think you are? A complete idiot who couldn't see the obvious! Why didn't you see Ahmad as the criminal he is? Instead you felt sorry for Goli and this is the price you paid for that. She was feeling the ultimate guilt. The guilty feeling and shame were torturing her to death. Why didn't she see the real danger? Why had she ignored the fright in her mom's voice the night that Goli landed at her door? Why did she insist on sending Sepideh to the prison? Why didn't she see the danger in sending her sister to visit Ahmad in prison? Maybe Ahmad had introduced her to his inmates as his fiancée. In her mind she was hitting Ahmad with a blame stick. You bastard! You knew damn well in what type of shit you were involved in! Why didn't you have the sense not to mention Sepideh anywhere? You will pay for all this. I will hunt you down and will give you to the animals who are after your worthless life.

She heard her mom talking to her uncle in the kitchen. He had just arrived in town.

"Your uncle will be here in a few minutes to take me to the hospital. I talked to Sepideh's doctor too. She will be released. You had better go home and check on your kids."

There was an emotionless emptiness in her voice that scared Azadeh. She didn't blame her for it. It was all her fault, she couldn't even blame her if her mother disowned her. She said with an embarrassed tone, "I'll come with you guys. I have to talk to Sepideh too. Although, I think it's better for her to stay in the hospital for a few days, I know she wants to come home."

Simin didn't say anything. She was looking for her shoes.

Uncle was driving in the direction that Sepideh had given him, but there was no sign of her red car. As he was driving towards his sister's house, he was thinking of those men who had assaulted Sepideh and knew that it was almost impossible to catch them. They were not some random dirty, old men that he would be able to find by searching the ghettos and crack houses. These were professional drug dealers about whom he had heard horrible stories. He looked at Sepideh's face in his rear-view mirror. She had leaned her head against the window and her face was filled with sadness. Trying to say something encouraging he said,

"Dear Sepideh, we will find them. Hadji Mehdi is our ally. We shouldn't lose hope." He was talking about Hadji Mehdi because he really had no other connection in law enforcement.

Azadeh replied angrily, "But, uncle don't you think that Haji is only useful for your business? Our only way is to find Ahmad."

-"Find him to do what?"

-"Maybe he will pity us and show his face."

By pitying she meant Ahmad's love for Sepideh, which was the only hope Azadeh had in finding Ahmad. The uncle turned around and gave her a knowing look, like she should have known better to say such things. Azadeh ignored the look, her mind was now focused on Ahmad. Uncle parked by his sister's house and asked his niece, "Sepideh, do you think you can handle the police now?"

Sepideh didn't reply and followed her mother inside, limping.

Azadeh said, "Uncle, I think it's best if she rests for a few days. You know that the police was informed. Maybe it's better if we went to the same station."

-"Okay, but do not procrastinate."

-"But, she is so scared I don't think she can even talk."

_"Okay, let her rest now, I'll come back this evening to take her. You should cut all connection with Ahmad's mother. I'll send someone right away to put an alarm in the house. You take care of yourself, even when you are in your car. Lock yourself in. Don't forget, we have to take that woman with us to the police station. Her testimony is very important for us."

Azadeh thought her uncle was too naïve. With or without Arezou the police won't be able to do anything for them.

"You know, Uncle, her house is too far. What if we go all the way and she is not home?"

"Take Sepideh with you there. If she's there, call me and I'll meet you there. Call me."

Azadeh went to Sepideh's room. She was up to her neck under the covers and was sleeping almost unconsciously from the drugs they had given her at the hospital. Azadeh couldn't get herself to pull Sepideh out of that relaxing state. She closed the door behind her and left. She was only focused on Ahmad and wouldn't listen to anyone else either. She didn't take her uncle's advice and decided to call Goli right away to see if she had heard from Ahmad. She couldn't stay at her mom's either. She felt like she wasn't welcomed there. At that moment she was willing to surrender to that feeling.

When she said goodbye to her mom, her mom didn't even look at her. Azadeh, with a heavy heart, went to spend some time with her sons, but first she stopped at her house to call Goli. When she was talking to Goli on the phone, she couldn't get herself to tell Goli about all the horrible events. Azadeh felt that if she told Goli about it then, the old woman would start wailing and bring the heavens down, and more over will get the next bus to Tehran and slow her down in her search for Ahmad. She should make Ahmad aware by some other means. She heard from Goli that Ahmad is in Pakistan now and has no phone number. Goli also told Azadeh that she hasn't heard from him for a while now.

"Well, if he calls you, ask him to call me. There are some papers from prison that he must sign."

As a precaution she refused to give her home phone number and only gave her the cell phone number. Azadeh, with teary eyes, called Hamed to tell him how she can't look into her mother's and Sepideh's eyes. She felt guilty and afraid, and could see the fear in their eyes. She was telling him that she has to find Ahmad by any means possible. He was the only person who could stop the next tragic event from happening. Azadeh was trying to change Hamed's opinion of Ahmad. She was saying that Ahmad is not as bad as he seems to be, plus he is sick and dying. Most certainly he won't stay impartial if he hears about the tragedy that has happened to Sepideh. She told him that she can't trust the police and that they won't do anything to help. It was only Ahmad that could save them all. Hamed, with half closed eyes, was listening and then he smiled and said, "As easy as that, Ahmad will come and put himself in danger for you guys! Well, life is precious, he's not a piece of wood. He's human. Believe me, dying people cling to life harder than you and I. Think straight and don't waste your time."

"But he's my only hope. It's impossible to live in fear, waiting for Ahmad to die, hoping that everything will be done then."

Hamed nodded in disagreement and said, "Believing in him is like believing in a frog to turn into prince charming. This fucking bum is involved in this mess up to his eyeballs. You should pray for his death instead of these hallucinations that he will try to do something real for Sepideh. It's better for her and your mom to be away from here for a while, until everything is alright again. How about Europe to your cousin Farhad? Maybe Sepideh will fall in love with him and will stay there."

"What are you talking about? They have threatened Sepideh to find Ahmad. Otherwise they will hurt us again."

"Well, good luck. Go ahead, find him. Let me know how it goes."

This time he started laughing out loud. Azadeh got up and said, "That's exactly what I want to do. I won't let go of Ahmad. I wish you knew me better."

A few diffcult days passed. Simin had to greet friends and relatives who came for New Year's ceremonies with a smiling face and wish them a happy New Year. She postponed visiting them until Sepideh felt better. One day,

Azadeh got up really early and went to Sepideh's room, asking her to get ready so they could go to the police station. Sepideh turned her back, "What for?"

"Don't you want them to be caught by police?"

"So what? What difference does it make to me?"

"Sepideh, don't talk like this. We have to go to Arezou's house too before she leaves her house."

Azadeh put her veil and dress on the bed and went to tell her mom.

Simin said, "Okay, you do your best. It's at least some action. Maybe they'll calm you down, but don't you dare call Goli. We have to keep this as quiet as possible."

Azadeh felt a softening in her voice. She felt a trace of feelings for herself in her mother's words too. It made her heart warm. She kissed her mom with loving eyes and left.

As she was driving, she was talking like she was standing in front of the police. "You shouldn't leave them alone and ignore this tragedy. You should take their threats seriously and assign a guard for my mother's house for her safety." She wanted to transfer her thoughts to Sepideh. Sepideh's eyes were closed and her head was on the headrest.

"I wish you could control yourself and tell them everything instead of crying. You know, if you only cry, they won't take you seriously. They might feel sorry for you and that won't help us. You have to ask them to follow up on your case and catch whoever did this to you and take care of our safety too." She was constantly talking, encouraging Sepideh to be brave, but Sepideh was only hearing her voice without comprehending what Azadeh meant. She was so engulfed in sorrow and fear that her brain wouldn't take in any advice.

Arezou looked down at them from her window with astonishment and said, "Come on up. The door is open."

"No, we're here to pick you up on our way to the police station. It's getting late."

"Honey, come up, what's the rush? Come up, the police station is open twenty-four hours a day. I haven't had breakfast yet."

Azadeh entered a small and very modest room that she hadn't notice the last time she was there. The walls were covered with a faded blue paper and there were few pictures of Shah, the queen and Ali the Shii Imam (prophet's son- in-law and his fourth successor) with his famous sword in his hand. There were also a few pictures of the young Arezou in a puffy skirt and her long curly hair on her naked shoulders too. Azadeh looked at Arezou. In the daylight she could see her more clearly. A heavy thick layer of makeup couldn't cover the dips of chicken pox on her fat face. There was a tattood circle in between her eyebrows and that made her brows unnaturally wide and long. Her body was on the fat side. Azadeh sat down next to the New Year's ceremonial setting. (It is customary to set a table for the New year with tulips, mirror, red fish, sweets, coins, apples, vinegar, garlic, and Quran on it) A tall, blue carafe got her attention. She took the lid off and smelled it, then she put it back, laughing.

"I thought there was rose water in it." Arezou laughed heartily and showed off her yellow teeth.

"No sweatie, every year on the New Year's I drink my wine first to give me a good buzz and then I summon my mom's spirit and talk to her, after that I pray to Imam Ali." Then, when I'm really buzzed and half asleep, I can feel my mom stroking my hair as if I'm a child again and I rub myself against her like a kitty cat." Arezou poured tea in the cups, gave one cup to Sepideh and said, "I see you're getting better. Now, where are you guys headed?"

"To the police station. It doesn't make a difference which one, they're all the same." Arezou laughed and nodded.

"I don't want to discourage you and don't want you think I don't want to come with you guys. No, I swear to all holy, but you should know you are wasting your time."

Sepideh looked at Azadeh and said, "I say the same thing, let's go home."

"No, we won't go back. That's the reason this country is full of criminals."

Arezou said, "Okay, we'll go. We'll make an event of it. At least we won't get bored. There are always a lot of people at the police station yelling and screaming. It's like a movie. Sometimes they get into a fight and there are fistfights, kicking, scratching. Finish your tea." She put some feta cheese on a piece of bread and swallowed it with a sip of tea. She got up, took a lipstick out of her purse and put it on her fat dark lips. Azadeh looked at her rouged lips and said,

"Maybe they'll give you a hard time in there."

Arezou laughed, rubbed her lips together, and put the lipstick back in her purse. "I'm too old for them to give me a hard time. Okay I'm ready." She put on her veil, "Let's go." Azadeh saw Arezou's landlady in the yard, said a hasty hello, and left the house.

Sepideh said, "Azadeh, I'm scared. For God's sake, let's go back." Azadeh ignored her and through the half closed door, looked at Arezou who was getting into a long discussion with the landlady.

"Come on Arezou, you can tell her everything when you come back." After a few minutes, Arezou came, and breathing heavily, threw herself in the back seat.

"She's so nosy, wants to know everything. She's a crackhead, she made me smoke a few times too. She says booze will take life out of your body, but drugs give you life." Then she laughed heartily, "Have you seen her? She's like a sick stoner and she says drugs give you life."

Azadeh laughed and looked at her in her rearview mirror. Before Sepideh said anything to her she knew that Arezou must have spent her life in prostitution. Although she was a middle-aged woman, the stamp of her profession was obvious in her demeanor. Arezou was careless and talked fearlessly. She was very easy to get along with and laughed easily. She believed she was worthless and there was no place for her in this society so she didn't try to cover it up. Shamelessly, she told them her life story on the way to the police station.

When her stepmom kicked her out of the house, she was only thirteen. Her sister, Souri could not keep her at her house more than a few months since her husband's dirty looks and evil intentions frightened her. Souri gave her to Akbar Chassis and after two shots of vodka she was not shy anymore and slept with him. One day when she was very happy, she was dancing for him and Akbar sold her to Jalal, the owner of one of the taverns in the red zone. Her name was Sakineh, but Jalal said Arezou is sexier. She was a good dancer and all the losers in the ghetto were her clients and would spend a lot of money on her. But Jalal wouldn't give her a dime and when she was asking for her share of the money she had earned, Jalal beat her up. Once, Jalal threw a shot glass at her and split her head open. From then on, she stopped dancing for him and he then sold her to Heshmat Chicken. Heshmat then took her to a whorehouse since she was funny and slightly fat. She had a lot of clients. There were a lot of guys who fought over her. There was a temple in that neighborhood and whenever she was sad and lonely she would go there and lit a candle for her mom's soul. Her mom had died in an accident when she was ten. When Shah left and Imam came, the Islamic guards raided the whorehouse and kicked everyone into a bus, but she was stupid enough to stand up to them. When she regained consciousness she found herself up to her neck in splints with broken arms, legs, and hip. They wanted to kill her, but she got lucky when one of the Islamic guards turned out to be one of her old clients and stopped them. She spent six months in the hospital and ten years in prison. When she came out, she went straight to one of the houses that had been made after the revolution as the supposed new legal Islamic houses for prostitution called House of Piety. She was told that she could work legally there but the madam of the house, who put the pictures of all women in a book, had told her that since she was too old, plus the fact that she was limping, she couldn't put her picture in that book. But when she saw Arezou crying helplessly, she took pity on her and let her clean the house once a week. Now she has several houses.

"God bless the madam." With the money earned from cleaning houses, she could barely make ends meet, but she was thankful that she could at least have food and pay for her rent. The homemade booze has damaged her stomach and lately it was making her dizzy too, but she was happy with it. That night when she found Sepideh in the dumpsters, she was coming back from cleaning up the madam's house. Azadeh was looking at her in the mirror. She felt sorry for her and said, "You're a good woman."

Arezou sarcastically said, "Really? What has made you see me as a good woman?" The praise was like medicine on an old wound and she said with a smile, "Lovely. You're too nice, I'm not worth it."

Azadeh said, "Arezou, what difference do you see between yourself and that madam?"

"Well, we're both ladies. But between me and her, the

difference is the sky."

"That's true, but in my opinion you are much better than some of them."

"Are you kidding me? There is a big distance between us."

"Have you ever hurt anyone or made anyone cry?"

"No, no honey. Am I sick to do that?"

"Lied? Backstabbed anyone?"

"Who am I to backstab people? I was always minding my own business. But honestly, I have lied a lot. Well, if I didn't lie, I couldn't take care of my business and I wouldn't even have this little income. Madam, when she gave me money, she said 'First, go and repent. Cleanse yourself, then come into my house and touch my stuff.' I said cleanse myself? Why? And she said 'because you have slept with men without being married to them.' I took the money and bought a pair of shoes and a backpack for the neighbor's kid. With the rest I bought a few bottles of vodka and some rosary beads which I took to Madam and told her, 'I just got back and cleansed my soul, as clean as it could get." Arezou laughed and put her hand on Sepideh's shoulder. "I did the right thing, huh? Say something, you're making me depressed."

Azadeh said, "I think you did the right thing. That kid must have been very happy. Do you remember Mavash (a dancer in the Shah's regime for the cabarets and was famous for helping poor and unfortunate people) the dancer? My mom liked her dancing."

"I'll never forget her. I used to dance just like her, but I wasn't rich like her to support families. Do you know what the mullahs did to her grave?"

"No, but why do you want to know?"

"Well, I heard when mullahs saw people going in throngs to her grave and praying for her soul, they spread the rumor that they have heard the dead complaining that the dirty dancer is burning their souls and asked for help. So the mullahs took out her remains out of the grave and only God knows what they did with them. I don't know how true this story is but, it's not farfetched."

To Azadeh, Arezou with all the dirty and ugly stories of her life, seemed more beautiful than the most pious woman, who were now in charge of destinies of thousands of women like Arezou.

"What do you wish from God, Arezou?"

"I wish mullahs would go and Shah would come back."

Despite her will, Sepideh had to think hard and tell her story in broken sentences to the Hadji with thick eyebrows who was looking at her indirectly. She had to make an effort to bring out each word. Her voice was exhausted and satiated with fear. She would be quiet for a moment and look at her hands, then with a deep sigh she would continue. Hadji's secretary, who was a young woman, was staring at

Sepideh while her fingers were typing her words. All of a sudden, the door burst open and a goat jumped in, followed by two bloodied men. Arezou burst into laughter and said,

"Is the goat here to bear witness?" Hadji looked at her angrily and told the man,

"Do you think this is the barn? Take the goat out and tell me what is going on."

One of the men replied, "Hadji, the missus is coming back from her pilgrimage tomorrow morning. I gave money to this one guy to buy a sheep for sacrifice in her honor, but he gave me this bony goat in the backyard. Now he won't take it back claiming that I asked for a goat."

The goat dealer started swearing on all that is holy that the guy is lying and that he really had asked for a goat.

"Well, take the goat back and bring the sheep."

"Okay, that's what I'm saying too. Pay the difference and I'll bring in the sheep. But he is refusing to pay." In the meantime, the goat started staring at Hadji and peeing in his office. Hadji got up, kicked the goat with all his might and shouted,

"Take him out right now!" The goat baa'ed and fled with the man after him. Arezou's laughter filled the room. Hadji sat down angrily.

"God is great. These people have no brain. Okay sister, you were saying..."

Azadeh couldn't help but think, you are no better than them, if mullahs had not filled your head with shit you would have had some logic too.

Again Arezou started laughing. This time, an angry couple entered the room. Sepideh stared at the couple, like a turtle staring at her eggs, waiting to hear their story about their domestic violence dispute. The man was loud and abusive. The woman was defensively fighting with him. Hadji, after hearing the story, started blaming the woman.

"Well, you went to a friend's house without your husband's permission and then hit him in the head with a ladle, and now you don't expect him to fist you in the mouth?"

Now Azadeh and Sepideh were laughing too. Arezou, laughingly said, "Good for you honey. This time, hit him with a brick. A ladle is too old fashioned."

Haji, as if repulsed with Arezou's rouged lips, said, "Damn the devil, you shut your mouth woman and cover it with your veil." Then he turned to the woman and said, "You be quiet and go home. You should obey your husband. You know what consequences disobedience has, don't you?" The woman said, "No I won't obey. I will divorce." She left the room, but her voice could still be heard, "I won't obey

Finally, Sepideh completed her story and the secretary put the typed up paper on Hadji's desk before leaving. Hadji said a few meaningless sentences. Arezou got up and said,

"Let's go, my legs are burning." Uncle, who had just

arrived, said,

"Ma'am, please sit down. Hadji, who will take care of this family's safety?

"Well, first this sister's file should be sent to the appropriate sections. When they approve the paperwork then God willing we will act on it."

Uncle said, "What are you talking about Hadji, are you saying my niece is lying?"

"No, brother. All I'm saying is that there is a process."

"Nothing will be done by just a few prayers. Please do something, it seems like you didn't grasp the enormity of this crime."

"My men are at work, my brother. God willing we will catch them."

Arezou said, "Did you hear that uncle? Now, let's go." She started limping towards the door and said out loud, "This is all bullshit! They're only forceful when it comes to us. As much as they act concerned about covering women, they are not concerned about the real criminals putting women's lives in danger. If this veil would make anyone respectable, I should have been called 'The Honorable Arezou.' Let's go, what are you waiting for?"

That day, Azadeh took Arezou to her mother's house and gave her a few bottles of wine to repay her for her troubles. Arezou spent a few hours with them, and told Simin about Jalal, Akbar, and Souri.

CHAPTER SIX

Azadeh knew that Goli would give Ahmad her message, but in spite of what she expected, a few weeks had passed with no sign of Ahmad. One day, she decided to go to Quom and show the real Ahmad to his mother. She planned to ask Goli to inform Ahmad about the disaster and ask him to come and take away the evil shadow of fear that hung over her family. She could not have more sympathy for Goli than she could have for her own family and Sepideh. On that Friday, she made up an excuse for Zohreh that she had a cold from walking in the rain and couldn't make it to visit her sons. However, Zohreh didn't believe her. Zohreh had seen Azadeh still take her sons to the movies despite having a real cold or fever. Now why was she afraid of making her sons sick this time? But she couldn't find any logical reason for her lying either. She dialed Azadeh's home number, but she had already left. Zohreh, annoyed, thought that she had to find out what was going on. Azadeh didn't like lying to people about her actions but she knew well, if she said the truth, there would be havoc. Even mentioning Ahmad's and

Goli's names was forbidden. Her mother had gone as far as changing their telephone number so that Goli wouldn't be able to call her. She was terrified of having any connections with them.

It was an hour before noon when Azadeh arrived in Quom. She took a cab to Goli's house, which was the ground level of a two-story building. She dialed her house from the cab to make sure she was at home. If Goli knew she was going to her house, she would call everyone to go there. Azadeh had been told that all the people who's pictures Goli had shown her were looking forward to meeting her. But Azadeh had no time for a social visit. She only had two hours to say whatever she wanted to say to Goli and go back. Goli opened the door. At first she was surprised to see Azadeh in a black veil. But then she became very worried. She thought that Azadeh must be the bearer of bad news to pay a surprise visit to the house. She thought of Ahmad, her face showed her concerns and grew dim. Azadeh felt Goli's concern, but kept quiet. She said a very formal hello.

"I was hoping Ahmad would call me, but he hasn't. Is he still in Pakistan?" All of a sudden the worrisome clouds went away from Goli's face and with a sigh of relief she said, "My dear, you almost gave me a heart attack. I thought maybe you have some bad news from him. Yes dear, he called me a while ago. He's busy with work, maybe he didn't get a chance to call you. Why didn't you call ahead about your visit?"

"Well, I wanted to call you, but this was better. No one should know about my visit here, especially my mother and

Sepideh."

"Goli, we should leave this place," Azadeh continued.

"Leave, to where dear? Pilgrimage can wait (there is the shrine of Prophet Mohammad's great grand daughter in Qom and people go there for pilgrimage), but in a few hours it will get better and you can actually touch the shrine. I'll make tea, you must be exhausted."

"I'm not here for pilgrimage. I'm here to tell you about something and it's better if you don't stay here."

Goli, astonishingly said, "What do you want to say? Why can't you say it in here?"

"I can't." Azadeh put her shoes on. Goli put her veil on.

"Dear, you're killing me. What's going on? Why not here?"

"I told you, no one can know about me here. Maybe Sedigheh or one of your other friends will show up."

"Sedigheh won't dare to show her face here. As you wish, I won't tell anyone." Goli said that and started walking with fast, but small steps. There was already a big crowd gathered around the shrine. A melting pot of men, women, young and old as well as monks were gathered and there was the loud, muffled noise of crying, praying, and reciting Quran. Azadeh started to think that Goli was taking her inside the shrine.

"But Goli, we can't talk in here." Goli didn't answer,

she passed the shrine and further up, she sat under a familiar tree that had just begun blooming. The voice of the pilgrims could be heard weakly and sounded almost like a whining. There was nobody around. Every now and then a few people would come, but since there was nothing to do there except walk, the wanderers would go back to the shrine.

Azadeh sat on the ground next to Goli. She felt the coldness of the ground and said, "This is too cold for your bones, let's go somewhere else."

Goli said, "Dearie, let's get a cab. We can go to Hamid's gravesite. There are benches in there too."

"No, it will get late then. If it doesn't bother you, let's stay here."

"Okay dear I'm okay. Tell me what's on your mind."

Azadeh looked down. It was too hard to give bad news and make a mother cry. As she was telling the story, Goli started crying. Her heart shivered for Ahmad and she cried for Sepideh. Goli was overcome with fear and couldn't understand why they were looking for Ahmad or what he could have done. All she could think of was to find him and warn him to stay wherever he was to keep him alive. She was thinking of Sepideh too. She was feeling deeply sorry for her. She was whispering to herself. Sepideh was always sympathizing with her, would willingly deal with the crazy traffic in Tehran to take her to see her son, and would wait for her in the sad prison yard so that she could talk to her son and cry for him. She was never showing an impatient face to her to make her uncomfortable. She was like an innocent angel.

Azadeh said, "But Goli, why did those goons think Sepideh was Ahmad's fiancée? Do you know something?"

"How should I know dear?" She was cursing herself now. Goli was wishing she would have stayed quiet when the prison guard asked her about Sepideh's relation to the prisoner and she had answered that she was his fiancée. That night, Goli embarrassed and frightened went to Sedigheh's house to warn them to be careful and asked Masoumeh not to talk to strangers in the streets and do not stay out at dark. It was the last days of spring and the dream of Ahmad's cooperation was out of Azadeh's head and was instead replaced by hatred for him. She couldn't believe that even after he was informed about this mess, he was still so careless as not to even call her out of curiosity. She had heard from Goli that Ahmad was still in Pakistan and didn't want to show up in Iran at least for a while. But on the contrary, to what Azadeh was thinking when Ahmad heard what had happened to his beloved, he fell like paralyzed with sickness. He could only blame himself for this disaster. I'm as stupid as a cow, a shithead, a dumbass. Why the hell didn't I think straight and put her in danger? He, like his mother, had a wish in his heart and he had spoken of his wish to his cellmates. He told them Sepideh was his fiancée and now he was burning with guilt. The only thought on his mind was revenge. He was planning to go after Sadegh Jamal and put a dagger into his heart. His days were like his nights, hatred had taken over his entire being. He couldn't stay in Soltan Abad any longer. The revengeful thoughts took him back to Tehran.

CHAPTER SEVEN

Sepideh had terrible migraines and spent much of her time in her room in the dark. Her doctor recommended that the curtains be pulled down. The routine social gatherings, her sessions with her psychiatrist and even the traditional remedies were not helping. She was living in a constant state of fear. She would wake up in darkness and stay there in her bed until the pills would force her back to sleep. Her life was at a stand still of nothingness. All her friends came to visit and they all had something nice to tell her. Some would insist on standing by her and helping her pull herself out of this abyss in an effort to try to let their friend breathe again. But the faces and bloodshot eyes of those men, the flash of their daggers had all in all captured her into this nightmare and Sepideh had no way out. Simin was intermingled with her daughter's pain and would cry rivers of tears. With a cup of fruit juice, she would go to her daughter's room, sit next to her and try to calm her with soothing words. Simin would beg her to come out of that room and watch a video or something. But all of of her efforts were in vain and after a few minutes of waiting helplessly, she would go back into the kitchen and light a cigarette. She was smoking up to two packs a day now and her breathing was toiled. She had nothing else to do except staring at the small circles in the air. She had lost her desire to clean up around the house. It was months since she had worked on the backyard. There were weeds all over the place and they had even grown to cover the rosebushes. There were no more fish in the pond since there were no sounds of footsteps in the backyard to scare the cats away. There were signs of death and destruction surrounding the house and the occupants of that house were slowly surrendering to despair. There was a deep difference in living and staying alive. Watching this had destroyed Azadeh too. She was forced to work and that was the only way to keep her mind from going crazy. But she was sloppy at her job and her supervisors had given her several warnings. The next misstep would lead to her termination.

Summer arrived and the hot days spread into the city. With these hot days Sepideh's condition got worse. Her headaches were so bad that her energy was constantly drained. The painkillers didn't help anymore. Her thin face was pale and there was no sign of life in her. It seemed as if her blue eyes had turned gray from the constant fear. Azadeh, exhausted and stressed from work, was always going straight to her mother's now. Her mother was always anxiously waiting for her so she could tell her about Sepideh.

"Azadeh, what do you think I should do? I make her everything she likes, but she still doesn't eat anything. I could only force her to have a glass of milk. I think she has increased the dose of her pills, the whole day she was sleeping like she was unconscious."

Azadeh couldn't even stand listening to her anymore. She didn't even want to convince her sister to pursue her old lifestyle. It was inevitable that the day would come since she had been sleeping calmer. With the time passing, it seemed like that horrible event had started and ended in the same day and there were no consequences to it. Though, it was too late for Sepideh to think like that.

It was the last day of summer and the heat was receding slowly, but Sepideh was still burning with the fire of fear. She had surrendered to it and was waiting for her death. Azadeh wasn't expecting anything anymore. All she ever thought about was to bring her sister out of this abyss to another world filled with the delicate bloom of happiness. Azadeh had actually been thinking about Hamed's suggestion and was planning on sending her mother and Sepideh off on a long trip, a trip that might have no return for Sepideh. Her only concern was how to convince her mom to stay away from her beloved home and live in London. But on the other hand, she knew that her mom could not leave Sepideh alone in London and return to Iran. Their mental attachment to each other was undeniable. For her mother, it was as if she had poured all her love into Sepideh's wellbeing and she couldn't imagine living a life without her. Azadeh was debating if her mother could leave her homeland and spend the rest of her life with Sepideh in a foreign land. Finally, she made up her mind and decided to gather up the courage to tell her mom that she could be in love with this land as much as she wanted, but she had no right to pull Sepideh with herself along into this fire. It was Sepideh's right to feel safe. It really doesn't matter where on the face of this earth she finds that secure place. In her mind, she could see herself winning over her mother. She was so sure of it that she was even thinking about the practical planning of the trip. The main obstacle though, was that even in spite of her dad's execution, the whole family was still banned from leaving the country. But to Azadeh, this was not a big enough obstacle to make her change her mind. She had to make the arrangements for Sepideh and her mother to leave the country at any price. It wasn't an easy task and required a lot of arrangements. The huge country with all the long borderlines was now heavily watched with a human wall of patrols. The prisons along the borders were full of people attempting to cross the borders illegally, but she was hopeful to find the right people, who for the right amount of money, would find any hole along this human wall and smuggle the unfortunate to the other side and show them the ways to get asylum from their destination countries. But how was she supposed to come up with the money? That was the only discouragement she had. The only way she could provide the money was by selling her mother's home. She was weighing all the outcomes of the plan and could imagine her mother yelling at her. She knew her mother would tell her about their beloved country, the sympathy for her people and the fallen soldiers who defended their motherland. Her mother would tell her about her little garden, the little crows on the weeping willow, the smell of roses, and the freshly rained soil in the back alleys. And Azadeh knew she would be against leaving her husband's grave.

She was driving to her mom's with a hopeful tune in her heart. The day was lingering and it was a very pleasant fall day with a slightly cool breeze. When she got to her mother's, she went straight to the garden and hosed it a few times. She washed the brick walkways and covered the wooden table with a tablecloth, put the food and dessert that she had brought on the table. Simin, pale faced, was standing in the doorway, watching her. Azadeh smiled. A faint smile came on her mother's face.

"What's up? Are you celebrating something?"

"Yes, a big celebration. Please come and have a seat. Food will turn cold. I'll call Sepideh. I have to pull her out of this dark house. Sepideh was asleep. Azadeh pulled the curtains to the sides. "Get up! I have good news for you." Sepideh was blinking in the bright light.

"First, pull the curtains down, then tell your news." Azadeh cursed the psychiatrist.

"Enough with sleeping, get up, and go to the backyard. Mom is waiting. I got kabob and it will get cold."

Sepideh turned in her bed. "I'm not hungry, leave me alone." Azadeh threw the covers away angrily.

"Have you looked at yourself in the mirror lately? Do you see what you are doing to yourself?"

"Okay, you go. I'll come later."

"No, get up now." Sepideh got up and Azadeh helped her to the backyard. Azadeh was nervous and was swallowing her food without chewing while constantly complimenting the food. Why she ate so much was beyond her. She even put a lot of food on her mom's and Sepideh's plate and was insisting that they finish all that too. Simin was looking at her in amazement and finally asked, "What's going on? Something happened?"

"No, nothing, I'm just happy." "Happy? Maybe you heard something from the police department?"

"No mom, I'm not thinking of police, Ahmad, and all those losers anymore. Now I'm thinking of a solution."

Simin pushed her plate away, lit a cigarette, and said bitterly, "Okay, if you see a solution, talk about it." Azadeh felt it was time to start talking, but the words that she had carefully thought of in her mind to start off with were now fleeing her mind and she was drawing a blank. She started worrying that she might lose her courage and end up postponing her talk to an unknown future. She went straight to the heart of the matter.

"Mother, don't you think there's a land somewhere beyond the borders that could embrace you?" Simin's fingers, with the cigarette still in between them, stayed still in the air.

"I don't understand. Who's going to embrace me?"

"What I'm saying is, to leave this place. Go to a place that will give Sepideh peace and she will feel safe and secure."

"Where is the safety that Sepideh is going to feel? What do you have in mind for us now?"

"Mom, don't you want a good life for Sepideh? Well, get her out of here, to a place that she can live without fear. Go to Europe, go to our cousin Farhad, or wherever you want. If you say yes, I'll take care of the rest." Simin pressed her cigarette onto a piece of kabob and said,

"Did you have a lot of food last night too? You're talking nonsense, stop it now, I have no patience for this nonsense."

Azadeh answered bitterly, "No I won't. My sister is perishing before my eyes."

"What are you talking about? You know how we manage to live. Say we stay with Farhad for a while, how? With what money? Plus, no country will give us visas." Azadeh looked around the house.

"If you can part with this house, I'll take care of the rest."

Simin looked at her in astonishment and said angrily, "You mean, we sell our house and become homeless, is that right? Huh? You're crazy. I never thought you would have such expectations from me."

"Well, I was expecting you to suggest it," Azadeh responded.

"Suggest to leave my house and go after a dream in God knows where, I can't believe I'm hearing this from you. Let me remind you about our roots in this country. Good or bad, it's ours."

"But mom, it seems we are only getting the bad and that's ruining us."

"Well, we should endure. Forgetting is a blessing that God has given us. Sepideh won't stay like this forever. Finally this nightmare will end and she will resume a normal life."

"You're right, but for how long? Don't you see that Sepideh is perishing more and more everyday?" Azadeh turned to Sepideh and said, "Why don't you say something? Do you think mom is right? Will you overcome this nightmare eventually or do you want to stay with it forever and take us with yourself too?" Azadeh was furious. She didn't expect for her mom to be so naïve and take her daughter's illness so lightly.

Sepideh heard what Azadeh was telling her but she couldn't comprehend these moving words. Hurt, she replied, "Do you think I want to live like this? Don't you think I know you are suffering with me? It's my only wish to get out of this slump."

"If it's your wish, you aren't doing anything to fulfill it."

"Azadeh, you're crazy. Sleep or awake, they won't let me go. Only I am aware of the hell I'm living in."

"But you're pushing away the hands who want to pull you out of it. From all your doctors' instructions, you only take the pills. You don't do anything to busy yourself. You left your job, left all of your friends. When was the last time you had a visitor? Even your friends are giving up on you? Believe me, the worst is over. They are not coming after you, but you don't want to accept it. You are isolating yourself in your room and the thought of those men has crippled your brain." It didn't go as well as Azadeh expected. She cleaned the dinner table and said, "Mom, I'm leaving but you think about it before it's too late and we lose Sepideh forever."

Simin looked at Sepideh who was walking towards her room, to sit there and cry in her loneliness. Her twenty-four-year old daughter seemed like a hunched-back old woman, who was leaning against the wall to pull herself forward. Her eyes filled with tears "We have to endure." After a glass of wine, Azadeh was hiding herself and her sadness behind the smoke of her cigarette when her cell phone rang. She answered reluctantly and immediately recognized Ahmad's voice. All of a sudden all the numbness was gone from her body and mind. She shouted, "Where the hell are you, you worthless punk? You dying shit! Why don't you die and leave all of us alone?"

"If I was a bastard it would have been done by now. I wanted to call, but you know, it didn't happen. You shouldn't be scared anymore. Nobody is going to hurt you. They're gone. They knew your sister didn't know anything, otherwise they would have finished her off."

"Where the hell are you?"

"Right here, in this hell. If you want, I'll give you my address and you can spit in my face. I well deserve it."

Azadeh screamed, "Spit on you? I'll chop you off and send your pants to your friends."

Ahmad laughingly said, "Okay, whatever, but don't tell my mom about me. Don't say anything to anybody. It's better this way, it's only between you and me."

Azadeh didn't know what to say, she was about to hang up when Ahmad said, 'Listen lady, I have something for you. I have to see you."

"Okay, I will come along with a few policemen."

"Relax, why police? I didn't do anything. I'm one of the good guys now. If you knew me well, you wouldn't say this."

"Oh yes, I know you. I know what a bastard you are. Tell me what plans you have in your brainless head. Why do you want to see me?"

"I swear on my dad's grave, there's no plotting. I want to tell you everything that has been getting piled up in me before it's too late. You know what I'm saying? I'm worried for my mom. I swear I'm worried for you too."

"For us? What do you take me for? You are such a fucking bastard, you don't think about anything else! You have no idea what you've done to us, do you?"

"I know, I swear on my dad's soul, I know. You want to see me or not?"

"Now, yes. Now that I know you have money and aren't broke anymore. They say you took a lot of their money and disappeared. Now that you have kept alive, which I wish you weren't, the least you can do is to share some of that money. I'm coming to cash out your debt."

"Okay, I'm at your service. Whenever the money is ready, I'll call you up. Now if you have a pen, write down the address."

Azadeh thought, the bastard is playing me. But, she said, "Go ahead, in what hole are you hiding?" She took down his address and phone number, and then crumbled the paper while talking out loud, "He thinks he's dealing with a dummy?!" She was confused, why did Ahmad give her his address and what did he have to tell her? Why was he so at ease with her, like a long lost cousin who was just found?

An hour passed. She decided to check the number, found the crumbled paper, and called him. When she heard his voice on the other end of the line, she asked, "Are you really at Evin Village?"

Ahmad, who had just suffered a seizure, answered weakly, "I'm almost dead, why would I lie? I was just playing black jack with death." When she hung up for no apparent reason, she decided to keep their conversation a secret.

Weeks passed. The passage of time didn't bring the blessing of forgetting to Sepideh. Now, Simin began thinking about the trip too. She couldn't be apathetic to her daughter's condition anymore. One day, Simin decided to make a painful call to Azadeh.

"Maybe you're right. Sepideh is getting worse. We must

do something."

Azadeh, had been waiting for this day impatiently and said, "I know it's too painful for you and giving up this house with all these memories is difficult. But you will get Sepideh back in return."

Simin sighed, "I hope so. That's the only hope that keeps me going."

Azadeh could feel the anxiety in her mother's words and knew instantly what Simin was thinking.

"How do I leave you alone here? I wish you had found your soul mate by now."

The next day, the human-trafficker, whose name was Darius, came to Simin's house to tell her about his plans to put Simin's mind at ease. But to the contrary, he made Simin more worried, sad, and disappointed. She was wondering how she was supposed to hide in a roadhouse in Tabriz. If they were lucky, they would be transferred to the other side of the border by car or on mule's back amongst the sacks of potatoes, and then tear up their passports, surrender themselves to the police in Turkey and ask for asylum. Sepideh was a little bit better now and was spending a little less time in her room. This move and leaving the country illegally would determine her future life. She thought that maybe Azadeh was right and she should try her luck somewhere else. Simin, relying on a little bit of English that she knew, was more willing to go to England, plus Farhad's residence would be a support for them. But Darius didn't promise London. He was thinking more of Scandinavian countries since he had more experience with them. Simin didn't have a pleasant picture of those countries in her mind and was sadly thinking about the long, cold winters there.

Everything happened quickly. The house was put up for sale. The very first day the same Hadji who was the head of the revolutionary guards, magically appeared and surprised Simin. She was thinking after all they had been through with him before, he must have given up on the house. But Hadji had brought his checkbook with him thinking that he could break the spell with offering a small deposit in cash and get the house for a fraction its worth. But Simin was harsh. "Okay Hadji, just say I'm here to rip you off and quit the drama. What do you take us for?" For one more time, Hadji was rejected. He left in dismay. But in spite of the very promising market for the house, two months passed without any prospective buyers.

That was too strange. Azadeh got to the bottom of it. It was found out that Hadji really didn't lose hope and was bullying away any serious buyers. One stressful day, Azadeh called Zohreh. She couldn't keep Ahmad's phone call a secret anymore. She had decided to pay him a visit and wanted to tell Zohreh about it. Zohreh picked up the phone herself.

"Listen Zohreh, I found Ahmad a while ago. I want you to come over. I have to tell you something, but you have to keep it a secret."

"Good for you. Have you struck gold?"

"I have a good feeling about it. I have a hunch and I

think I should see Ahmad," Azadeh responded.

"Say no more, I'll be right there." Azadeh didn't think Zohreh would get there so fast. When she opened the door, Zohreh jumped in. "You crazy. First tell me how did you find him?"

"He called me and gave me his address."

"Are you kidding me? It's impossible!

"Look, this is the address. I hope he hasn't changed it, I want to go see him."

Zohreh took her eyes away from the address, "Why?"

"I knew you would ask that. Maybe I can get some money from him and send mom and Sepideh on their trip."

"Dream on, you can try a million times, but nothing will ever come out of it."

"Well, I have to put pressure on him and do my best. I thought it would be better to see him face to face rather than just calling."

"You are willing to risk your life based on a maybe? Forget about him and don't cause any more troubles for yourself and us."

"Who said I'm going there?"

Zohreh smiled and said, "Oh I see, you want him to come over here. Are you going to offer him some wine and then ask him politely to write you a check too? Don't be crazy, leave him alone."

Azadeh said bitterly, "What do you suggest? To leave him alone now that I have found him?"

"Are you that naïve? Have you forgotten who you are dealing with?"

"No I haven't. But I can't just let him be either."

"Yes you can."

Azadeh saw that there was no convincing her and she didn't want to continue the argument.

"Well, you're right. I had a hope for mom's sake but, I should forget it."

After Zohreh left, she called Ahmad immediately. He was expecting her phone call.

"Finally!"

"Don't be cute, I want to see you."

"Well, I want that too. Please come over, you have a car and I'm sure you haven't forgotten my ugly face either."

"No, I won't come over there."

"I can't show my face outside yet. Swear to my dad's soul.

Are you telling me the truh?Because if I find out you aren't..."

"If I wasn't, I wouldn't give you my address. I know you don't want my mother to see my death yet."

Azadeh thought, bastard! He knows me better. She hung up without telling him anything.

A week passed and Azadeh still hadn't made up her mind. She was confused and that made her focus all her attention on Ahmad. Finally one day she paid Zohreh a visit.

"I can't take it anymore! And don't you try to change my mind either! Tomorrow I'm going to his house. I thought that you should at least be aware of it."

Zohreh, stunned, ironically said, "Well, you're right. At least one person should know where to go to collect your dead body. Have you completely lost your mind? Do you have any idea what you're after? A useless dream! I can't believe that your only motive is money. Maybe you're in love and don't want to admit it."

Azadeh said bitterly, "I wish you knew how much I hate this man! He could have prevented a disaster, but he didn't. Now accept that I have the right to go after him. This is the least he can do. There is no other way, I have to do my best."

The next day, Azadeh drove to Ahmad's address. Her increasing anxiety was apparent. Her foot on the accelerator was shaking. She pictured his house as a remote place. It was a humid, but pleasant fall day. The sun was slowly starting to set as she turned into his neighborhood. Her heart was pounding and anxiety was taking over her entire body. She started feeling the pain of anxiety in the pit of her stomach. She sat there motionless for a moment. She knew very well that she couldn't go back. She had to overcome her fears so she got out of the car. The alley was so narrow that no car could fit into it. There was a water canal in the middle of the alley filled with filthy water. She passed a few houses with peeling paint and bellied out walls as if any minute they would crumble. As she was looking for the house numbers, she found herself in front of his house. Then his hiding place is this hellhole? She had been expecting a better house. Hesitantly, she pounded on the wooden door. In a minute, a young woman with olive skin opened the door. She was wearing a black dress that covered her whole body down to her ankles. Her braids were showing from under her gray scarf. She looked at Azadeh with a recognizable sadness in her eyes and asked, "What can I do for you?"

Azadeh was surprised and for a second she thought that maybe Ahmad had brought her all this way for nothing. She replied, "Doesn't a guy named Ahmad live here?"

"What is your name?"

"Azadeh."

"Wait a minute please." She closed the door. Azadeh sighed in relief. He was telling the truth after all. The woman came back and in a welcoming tone said, "Please come in." Azadeh followed her through the backyard, which looked more like a chicken pen. The woman opened the door. "You wait here, Ahmad will be here in a minute." Azadeh entered the room and was filled with smells of incense, dampness, and sadness all at once. The floor was covered with a new gelim rug and the bedding was rolled against the wall. The dirty walls had once been painted green, but were now covered with pictures of Afghan men in arms. There was a gas top stove in one corner with a boiling pot on top of it. Azadeh saw a four or five year old girl who looked exactly like her mom, they looked like they were molded from the same material. Her long hair was pinned with a gold pin, and with a smile she was playing with an old doll. Then she saw Ahmad coming in, dragging his skeleton of a body with the same old black leather jacket that she saw the last time.

"Hello there. I was tidying up the other room. This little girl's name is Malihe. Did you say hi, Malihe?"

Malihe nodded several times and then said, "Hello." Azadeh smiled at her and followed Ahmad to the other room. That room wasn't much different than the first room. Ahmad offered the cushion for Azadeh to sit on.

"Welcome."

Azadeh looked at him in annoyance and said, "No, I'm not welcome. This is not a social visit. I have risked a lot to come here. Nothing other than terrible things have happened to us because of you."

A smile came to Ahmad's black and lifeless eyes. "But don't worry. No matter how keen those dogs are, they can't track me down here. This place is safe."

"Exactly. That's why you're hiding like a mole in here

and we had to suffer because you. I wish you had a little bit of conscience to prevent this disaster."

"You're right, but how could I have known they would come after you? Suppose I give myself up to them. What good would I be to you guys then? I told myself as long as I'm alive and in this world, maybe I can do something for you to make up for everything."

"Like what? What good have you brought us alive that your dead body wouldn't have? You know, maybe you dead would have been more useful to us. It seems like you don't grasp what you have done to us."

"I swear to God I know. I'm not stupid, I know."

"I don't care what you have done to them. But I have to find out why they came after Sepideh. On the other hand, you're saying they're gone now. Well, then why don't you show your face around if they're really gone?"

"Listen lady, I wasn't bullshitting you. You should know that." At this time the same woman, who seemed to be the lady of the house, Shirin, entered the room. She put a tray with two cups of tea on the floor and left the room with a smile on her face.

Azadeh said, "When did you get hooked up with this poor woman? Does your mom know about this?"

Ahmad laughed, "Wife? That's all I need in this mess. You see how I look. I can hardly manage to stay alive, let alone think of messing around with women. This is my friend's house, Mohammad. This woman is his wife. They have nobody here. All their family and relatives live in Mashad." He passed the tea to Azadeh and asked, "How are your mom and sister? I swear on my father's soul I always think about them."

Azadeh answered bitterly, "How do you think they are feeling? I'm trying to tell you that physically and mentally Sepideh is not doing well. The life you have caused for her is so frightening that she is even scared of her own shadow. They have decided to leave the country, do you understand? They have to leave everything behind and run away. I don't care what you want to do and how you can come up with the money. I only care about my mom's house, which now she has to sell for a fraction of its worth to get rid of this nightmare. I know you took the drug money and split. Return some of that money and we can call it even. This is the least that we expect from you."

Ahmad bent his head. "What the hell? Sure. I'll think about it. You have every right to that money. Your mom shouldn't sell her house, I've got to do something about it." He looked up towards the ceiling. "Don't you think the same? Maybe, whoever the hell, is sitting up there forgot about us. Please God, Give me a break and let me help a lady!"

Azadeh said angrily, "Stop the nonsense, and show me the money. Quit the drama."

All of a sudden they heard a door closing and Ahmad looked out the window and said, "That's Mohammad. He's a good guy, I met him in prison."

"And you say he's a good guy, to you all the criminals must be good guys."

"No, lady this poor guy is Afghan, in prison he was a translator for Pashtu. He is a Shiite like us. He used to be a clergy but early on, he quit."

"I'm not here to hear stories. Tell me about the money."

"I told you, I'll think about it."

"Think about what? What are you waiting for?" Ahmad didn't know what to say. In reality, there was no money. But at the same time, he was thinking of Sepideh and wanted to help out. He rolled his hand up and down his face, thinking about a good answer. With a long sigh he said, "It takes time. You have to wait. God willing, within the next two weeks I'll come up with something. About Mohammad, his luck is the same as mine. He was stupid enough like me to join the party. He says he wanted to fight the evildoers, but not with guns and bullets. In his dreams he thought they'd give him the medal of courage. He had taken all the little boys out of the ruins of war to supposedly save them from the warlords. Did you know that they hunt down the little orphan boys and before training them to be killers, they rape them. They pass them around until they break and become their slaves. Everybody knows this. There's no hiding it. It's so routine for them that they think it's like a part of everyday life, like going to restroom. That's how they make their army. Anyway, Mohammad spent his own money to buy books and pens, and gave it all to them. The poor guy wanted to educate them, but the party didn't like it. They took everything away. Instead they gave the boys some razors to shave the opium plant to extract the juice."

"What about you? You were one of them, one of the drug dealers. Now overnight you have seen the light and want to change the world? How about from now on we call you the 'holy dealer?'"

Ahmad laughed, "Well, how about that? I have a heart too. You know Azadeh, I can't get wise on my own. Someone has to shake me up. I swear on my father's grave, when I heard about you guys from my mom, my heart was broken. I never imagined these fuckers would come after you." Ahmad put a cigarette between his lips and stared at the lighter's flame. Azadeh saw the tears in his eyes that would fall and disappear inside his black unshaven beard. She really looked at his face for the first time and asked herself if he's really sorry for what he has done to them.

Ahmad coughed a few times and pressed his cigarette butt in the ashtray and said, "It was really hard in the prison. Not that they tortured me, no. It's not about that. They left me alone. The prison doctor had told them that I was dying, but my life was bitter as poison. When I looked at the cellmates, I hated myself. Though many were young, they didn't have teeth. No teeth or no meat on that bones, they had nothing. When I talk about this, my head wants to blow up. I'm a human being too. I wanted to do something for them and their families."

At this point the door opened and the same lady came

in with a tray and took the empty cups. She asked Ahmad, "Brother? Does this lady stay over for dinner?"

Azadeh replied, "No, I have to leave, thank you."

Ahmad said, "She's a nice woman. Mohammad is nice too, he knows a lot. He makes good money too. But there are a lot of demanding, needy Afghans around him. There's nothing left for him. Taliban torched his house in Afghanistan. He wasn't home, but his poor wife and kids were asleep and burned to death. But, those bastards still wouldn't leave him alone. So he fled and came here." Ahmad told Mohammad's life story as he had heard it from him.

Azadeh said, "I can't understand why this man is your friend and has let you in his house."

Ahmad laughed, "Well it's a God loving act. I'm changed too."

Azadeh replied with a bitter smile, "You can't exonerate yourself without giving us our lives back."

"I know, that's why sometimes I just want to be buried under the ground. When I think of it, I can almost smell my skin burning. I swear on my dad's soul, I am burned in this life. This is a time that no matter what, your conscience overcomes you and you question your actions to God. It's so unrealistic that even now when I talk about my life, it seems like a dream. I can't believe it. What happens when one loses his dream?" Ahmad smiled and shook his head. "Well, I looked at the people who crossed the borders to join the party and I asked myself how can I ge like these guys who spall money than they can count? I realized then that I didn't want to stay at the border any longer to inspect people's underwear. Then, I no longer laughed at the guy hiding behind the burka before throwing the burka away and beating him to death. You know what? I was a black sheep between the revolutionary guards. I didn't look like them and I wasn't pretending to be pious like them either. I was like a puppet; I did everything they told me to and that's how I was mixed up with them. There was always something on my mind and that was my mom and sister's lives. I wanted to help them out. Give money to Sedigheh so she could sleep at night and give my sister a good dowry when the time came."

"So you went to fight with the oppressors, but became a dealer yourself."

"You know what? I'm too chicken to do any of this. I'm too weak and skinny to be fit for fighting and martyrdom. I told them the same thing. I begged them not to send me to fight Taliban. Just play me around on the borders, something simple. They all looked at me and laughed. The Hadji said, 'Do you think that we use our rifles to fuck each other with it? This is a war.' Excuse my language. This life has taken away my manners too."

"Yeah, I can see that."

Ahmad stroked his forehead as if looking for his thoughts. "What was I saying? Yeah, Hadji said, 'This is war and we will train you. If it works then great, if not then we'll put a scarf on your head and give you something simple to do. But there are conditions for that too. We have to be able to trust you.' Well, I said, 'What the hell? Why do you make it so hard? I have a certificate from the government. My brother was a war hero. All I want is to be around you guys.' Hadji said, 'You will when the time is right. We have to turn your brains around to empty it from everything from before.' Everything was different over there, even God. At night you dreamed that you were put on fire alive and when you woke up, you realized you had pissed on yourself." Ahmad covered his mouth and laughingly said, "No, I can't stay polite. Sorry lady."

Azadeh thought, so up till now you were polite?

Ahmad continued on, "When you are with them, you don't think about the consequences. It's like you are sleepwalking and following orders. They make you so busy and brainwashed with their religious stories that you forget you're human. You even doubt yourself. They wanted you to think only about the afterlife, but I realized I was there to fix this world. Their words didn't fall too deep into my brain. My heart wasn't following them. I was telling myself to fill up my pockets and run away. It was all lies and stupid me, I thought all I had to do was to blow some bullets on the border, then I would be done and they would pay me a lot of dough for that. Well, that was what I had heard and when I asked Hadji if they were involved in drug dealing, he said it was just rumors spread by our enemies to make the party look bad. But they were smart. They knew I'd find out so they started giving me a hard time and at nights they put me on watch so I wouldn't leave. You know, they were so good at keeping everything a secret. Wow, it seems like it was yesterday when Hadji put a package in my bag. This was when my tumor started to grow. I remember the terrible pain in my head. I was very scared. I asked him what could happen on the other side. He said, 'Don't you worry. The border guards are with us.' I lost control and told him, 'Hadji, there's something bugging me.'

'What?'

'What do you guys do with the money?'

'We buy arms.'

'What about those poor people? The addicts, the lives that get destroyed?'

'Are you blind? Don't you see all the people we lose in the war? What if a few hundred who don't believe enough, die this way? Fuck all of them for Imam's sake. We are fighting the oppressors and that needs money.'

'Hadji don't you find me worthy?'

'Why?'

'Well, now that I'm crossing the border, why don't you give me more?

'You're the newcomer, a little chicken, can't expect to bear the weight like a camel. You have to prove yourself first.' In short, for the past few years, he gave me small loads, money was small too. But he was sleeping on loads of money, an American bed, and his kids were enjoying the money too, all the dollars which were meant to buy arms."

Azadeh was all ears. Although it was a sad story, she was fascinated by it.

"Well, I kept thinking the Taliban had made up the rumors about the party to make them look bad. So it's all true after all, huh?"

"Yeah, there's a lot going on over there. You know, lady, the point is that we have no time to waste. I want to pay my dues to you, all I'm thinking about are these three poor women, who's going to take care of them after me? Yeah, sister as long as there's life left in my body, I have to do something for them. The only way is to somehow get into their system, get money for you guys, and save your mom's house."

The truth was that up to a few minutes ago, it didn't occur to Ahmad that there was another way to get revenge from Sadegh Jamal. Now he was thinking of kidnapping him and taking all his money. He was so excited and the cigarette was burning in between his shaky fingers.

Azadeh laughed, "Promises, promises. Leave these imaginations for later. For now, show me the money. I don't know what you've done, but they're not after you."
"No, all of a sudden my conscience has found the courage. I know I did some damage to them." Ahmad was yawning nonstop. He scratched his wet eyes and lit another cigarette.

Azadeh looked at him and said, "Are you hooked on

drugs too?"

"Why? No, getting high is not my thing. It never was. When my dad was smoking opium I didn't like it. I think I was fifteen, sixteen years old then. One day I saw him sitting by the pipe, snoring. My mom was in one corner crying. I couldn't take it any longer. I took the pipe and threw it in the pond in the backyard. The pipe went under the water; my dad beat me to death. When I could get myself out of his hands I hit him in the chest and ran away. That day my mom packed me a few clothes and sent me to Mashad to live with my uncle. I didn't see my dad from that day on, but to tell you the truth, I cried a lot on his grave."

Azadeh got up.

"Where to? Not that I want to make myself worthy of your presence, I'm worthless as coal, but I wish you could stay longer. God knows I'm not that bad. I've done some good too."

"Well, good for you. If you really have done good things, let your mom know so that she can be pleased with you at least a bit. You don't want her to know after you're gone, do you?"

"Bingo. That's all I want too. I want her to be happy with me. Now, whenever I talk to her she curses the day I was born. She said that if I go after drugs again she will wipe me out of her memory. She is right to do so. She always thought her son was working hard, wiring electricity into houses. See lady, aside from my mom, I want to have some respect from you too. Maybe you can forgive me."

Azadeh said with a sour tone, "No, we have passed the limit for forgiveness. You know what deep sadness you have brought into our lives. There's no use for us to know what you've done or what you want to do. We have no interest in hearing it either. If we have tolerated you so far, it was all for your mother. Otherwise, we could have treated you completely differently." As she was opening the door, she said, "Don't forget your words. Hurry up, they don't have much time." Azadeh closed the door behind her. Her cell phone rang. It was Zohreh, who had been worrying about her. In the backyard she saw the mother and daughter washing dishes. She bent down and kissed the girl's round face, and said goodbye to the little Afghan woman.

The next day, after finishing her work at the hospital, she drove straight to her mother's house. She found her in the kitchen washing vegetables. Simin gave her some to clean too and with a long sigh said, "Azadeh, what do you suggest we should do? I don't feel right selling my house to this guy at such a low price. At the same time, it seems like we have no other choice." There was such sadness in her voice that it ached Azadeh's heart. At that moment, her only wish was that Ahmad wouldn't disappoint her. As she was cleaning the parsley leaves, she said, "Mom, wait for a few more weeks. Maybe there won't be a need to sell the house and that man can take his dream of having this house to his grave."

"What are you talking about? If you think we can mortgage the house, you're wrong. I asked around yesterday. Banks won't give much of a loan and if we don't pay them on time, the house will be reposed. You know very well we can't pay the banks."

"I know, that wasn't what I meant."

"Then, what? What other way is there?"

"We just have to wait."

"Wait, wait? For what? Are you waiting for magical checks to fall from the heavens?"

Azadeh smiled and said, "That's exactly what I'm waiting for. Trust me mom, there will be another way."

"What way? What are you talking about?"

"You just have to wait," Azadeh responded. Simin shook her head as her fingers worked faster at the parsley. Azadeh knew what was going on in her mind. Her mother was thinking that she was crazy and talking nonsense. Although Simin was very worried, Azadeh, ignoring her anxiety, was trying to keep her hopeful by pretending to look for prospective buyers.

A few weeks passed. Simin called Azadeh after receiving a phone call from Darius, the human smuggler.

"I'm going to call that evil of a man right now and give him the deed to the house. Enough is enough. I don't even know why I have waited so long. As long as there is such a snake blocking the way to this house, no one will ever buy it. You should lose hope too. Accept that you won't be able to find a buyer for this house. Darius just called and is pressuring me. He said in a few weeks he wants to move us along with a few others."

Azadeh had nothing to say. She was losing her faith in Ahmad too. She had called him a few times, but heard the same worthless promises. She could not keep her mother waiting for her imaginary buyers any longer. But at the same time, she didn't want to lose hope. She decided to go to Ahmad's house the next day and hear what he had to say. She asked her mom to give her until the following night.

"No, I won't wait any longer. I can't understand what you're waiting for either."

"Just one more day mom!" Then, she immediately asked for a day off from her supervisor. On her way back, her cell phone rang. She couldn't believe what Ahmad was telling her on the phone. She was besides herself and tears of happiness were rolling down her eyes. Ahmad had the money and was asking her to come and get it. It felt like God was playing games with her. This wouldn't be the first time that Ahmad would find a light in her bleakest moments, and then start a new game that would take her in a different direction. But for now, Azadeh didn't care if the whole world knew she had met with Ahmad the drug dealer. She was intensely happy with herself. Stubbornness had paid off and now the house with all their memories was her mother's to keep. She said aloud, "Ahmad, I believe you." She kept repeating it as she was walking towards the break room. She saw Maryam in there and excitedly told her everything that Ahmad just told her. But Maryam did not show any enthusiasm as she expected her to.

"Why don't you believe me? There's a whole bunch of money waiting for me."

"Yeah, I believe your naivety. But I don't believe that son of a bitch. He wants to lure you into his house and find a companion for himself in that hellhole of a house. If he had the money, he wouldn't stay in that place. Don't believe this bum. Don't even say a word to your mom about this either."

"There must be a reason that he is still in that house. He could have told me there was no money and left me alone. What would I have done if he had said that?"

"Nothing. But this son of a bitch has found a listening ear. He doesn't want you to leave him alone like everybody else did." Maryam killed all the enthusiasm in her. Azadeh left Maryam to refrain from losing her hope.

That evening, as soon as she got home, she dialed Zohreh's house, but Zohreh said the same things as Maryam. She was saddened that her two friends thought of her as naïve and even stupid. She didn't want to go to her mother and hear the same things from her too. She thought, I will go to her when I have the money to show her. At the same time, she thought Zohreh and Maryam could be right too. Their heads were filled with stories of cruelty and violence from drug dealers and they couldn't see them in any other way.

The next day, it was around noon when she got to Ahmad's house. In the room, she saw a man that she guessed must be Mohammad. He was a man about fifty, with quiet manners. He was short with high cheekbones, and wore the Afghan costume of white linen pants and long white shirt. Mohammad got up, put his hand onto his chest, and bowed. "Come on in. You are welcome in my house." Azadeh sat down on a cushion on the other side of the room. Ahmad seemed too sickly, so much that Azadeh was hesitant to ask him about his health. He was very pale and was only skin and bones. Azadeh had brought a box of sweets with a few bottles of vitamins. She gave them to him and said, "These are vitamins, they're good for you. I can see you're not doing so well. If you want, I can arrange for you to be admitted to the hospital."

"No lady, I'm not feeling very well, but hospitals won't do me any good either. Anyway, in the end, I will die. This is my mom's bad luck. Everyday that passes, it seems like I'm getting closer to the grave. It's pulling me in." Ahmad blew his cigarette into the ceiling and with a short breath said, "I'm too stubborn though, I have to wrestle with death first, finish my business in this world, and then I'll go to the next world. I know it is the stress that is making me worse. I was feeling better a few weeks ago." Azadeh looked at him through the smoke. She saw the fear of death in his eyes. Ahmad, all of a sudden remembered why Azadeh was there, got up, took his jacket off the wall, and pulled an envelope out of the inside pocket. Azadeh saw a pair of handcuffs hanging from the hook.

"Did you kill a police or a revolutionary guard? "

Ahmad, understanding why she said that, pointing to the handcuffs, said, "These are Mohammad's. They're ancient. I can't figure out where he got them from. Here you go sister. It's not all the money, but it will take care of your business for now. I think now my big toe is out of hell." He started laughing, which made Mohammad laugh too.

"Don't worry my brother, we won't let you burn in hell. All these people who have made this world a hell for others will burn with eternal fire in the real Hell. I'll find them over there and with a small bribe I'll get us out of there."

Ahmad laughed. "No worries, yours truly is used to burning. I have shed my skin so many times that now it is as thick as leather."

"That's what you think, I can still see you can cry when you're sad," Mohammed said.

"Believe me, I wish I didn't care, but I do. It's the sadness, it comes out of nowhere and makes me cry." Part of him thought it was from love. "Well, I have a right to happiness too, everybody is telling me I'm going to hell. That's fine, but I want to die with a clear conscience. You know, it doesn't let me be. Day and night, my conscience is begging me to do something before I die. That's right, it wants to die in peace. I'm not like those Hadjis who calm their conscience with sacrificing sheep and goats. Poor sheep who are used to soften disturbed consciences. As soon as life gets rough and makes people feel guilty, they sacrifice the poor animals to pay for their sins."

Mohammad said, "You know brother, you're looking at this world through the wrong eyes. Sacrificing is good. It helps the poor."

Azadeh said, "No, Ahmad is right. They take people's hard earned money, then, give it back to them as charity."

Ahmad shook his head and smiled. "Sons of bitches. They take everything and then give us promises of the afterworld."

Mohammad laughed out loud. "Promises for the poor in the afterlife, but a bounty in this word for Mullahs!"

Ahmad said, "No matter what, you're a clergy to the bone."

Azadeh was very curious to find out why Mohammad gave up his life as a clergy and was able to make himself content with his current lifestyle.

"Mohammad, as I hear it from Ahmad, you had a change of heart and left Feisieh (the theological school). It sounds strange to me. You must have had a strong reason for it."

Mohammad stroked his beard and said, "The lazy hands that don't do the laborious work will work the rosaries. When you see yourself and the poor laborer, who is bearing the weight of your life, your conscience won't sit right with you. I sat in on too many lectures and heard too many things. The more I heard, the more I hated the perspective of that life. A few righteous clergies are enough for country. The rest are lazy butts who only work the rosaries.

Ahmad said, "They're not that lazy either. I saw them in town putting chains on a monkey's neck. The monkey was screaming and showing the place for friends and enemies by pointing to his eyes and his butt (in Persian culture, to show the value of a good friend, they say he/she is as precious as eyes and enemies are as worthless as excrements coming out of the body. Ahmad hints to that here. It is also an old trick where people would train the chained monkeys to point to their eyes and butts as if they were pointing out the place for friends and enemies)."

Azadeh said, "That's right, it's the story of the monkey and the chain of life…"

Mohammad said, "People shouldn't be blamed my sister. Have you ever been to Afghanistan?"

"No, I haven't. But I am aware of their problems." "In there, everything stinks of backwardness. People are sick, but they don't know how they got poisoned. They are used to their own stink. There's the death veil of dark ages over our country. In that veil, sadness, tears, hunger, and death are a normal way of living. Those who say they are fighting the evil Satan are darker than Satan himself."

Ahmad looked at Azadeh and said, "All of these slogans are empty talks. All lies. Fighting with the Great Satan! They're all sharing the same bank account as Satan. Mohammad, leave these things alone. The good old Satan in Heavens is no longer evil compared to these ones on Earth."

Mohammad laughed and looked out the window. It was time for his prayers. He got up and left the room.

Azadeh said, "I can see that both of you are regretful

of your actions, but what's the use? There's no benefit for anyone in regretting. What good comes out of hiding here for his people?"

"You're right, he likes to work here."

"Why? Maybe he can do a lot for his people."

"He wants to, but he can't. If he sets foot on the other side of the border they will kill him right away."

"Why? What has he done? Who wants to kill him?"

"The drug dealers. The Party people. He's not as innocent as he looks. He's always on the go. Here, with his clergy way of talking, he makes the prisoners talk and then he gives the information to the police. So far he has caused a lot of drug busts, but he's naïve because he think the police burn the drugs. I won't insist on telling him the truth either. This place is like K'aaba to him (the holiest place for Muslims). Let him walk here and pay his pilgrimage every Friday through his prayers, ask for death to America. Let him be happy with his words."

"He doesn't look like a hero."

"How about yours truly? Do I look like a hero?"

"I've heard so many strange stories from you guys that I think you are capable of anything."

"Oh boy, even when I did right you called it wrong. When dealing with criminals, you have to do the same. But Mohammad used his brain and he's right. When you have hatred in your heart it makes everything tainted. If I had used good judgment, then I wouldn't have caused so much trouble for you and myself. But this time I know what to do."

At this moment Mohammad walked in the room and heard his last sentence.

"There's no next time. Listen boy, quit it and leave it alone. Why do you want to cause trouble? Don't you know who you are dealing with?" Then he turned to Azadeh and said, "I'm aware of what you've been through, you have been in my thoughts, but we shouldn't do anything to risk our necks. Ahmad simply doesn't understand this. You should just be happy with the little damage you have caused them."

Ahmad said, "What's the use? That son of a bitch didn't miss a heartbeat. I've heard they are running the same opium houses again."

Azadeh, confused, was looking at Ahmad and then Mohammad. "What are you guys talking about?"

Mohammad said, "You know sister, when Ahmad was in prison, he revealed a lot of names."

Ahmad said, "Yeah. I started a fire into their business, but what's the use."

Azadeh was looking at him in amazement.

"I can't calm down. If they'd left Sepideh alone, I would be done with them. But what can I say? Sepideh is on my mind constantly. What kind of a man would I be if I don't do anything to get revenge?"

Azadeh, as if hit by lightening, stood up and yelled at him, "If you wanted to do this, why didn't you use your brains to see if it would us?"

Ahmad dropped his head, "I told you before, I didn't think straight?"

"Well, it's quite possible, since there's no brain in your head."

Mohammad said, "Sister, calm down, he knows what he has done."

"I don't understand you."

Ahmad looked up, "See lady, you must have guessed it by now. When I was in prison, they traced everyone who had contacted me in there. They knew something was going on and I was about to mess with their business. So they must have thought Sepideh knew about my whereabouts.

Mohammad looked at him with blame. "Don't beat around the bush, tell this sister the truth."

Ahmad dropped his head again. "Okay, I'll tell her. Well, it was so stupid of me, it felt as if I had been bewitched by Sepideh, I couldn't think straight. Maybe I wanted to show off too. I wish I didn't. Anyways, I told everyone, the girl who comes with my mom was my fiancée, not knowing that my mom had said the same thing to the guards."

Azadeh couldn't believe it. "Is that what your mom had told you?"

"Yes, poor thing has spoken out her wishes. How could she know? She's never been to prison to know how it works. In there, you cover your head under the blanket so that if you sleep talk, your cellmate won't here it. I knew this and I still talked."

Azadeh had a dual feeling about all this. She knew he was the cause of all the disasters, but at the same time, somewhere in her soul she was admiring him and believed he deserved a better destiny. She sat down and said, "Did you really mess with them?"

"Well I had to do something. I couldn't just sit around and cry over my broken heart like a little girl. When I was in prison, I wasn't such a hot shot. But I have changed a lot in the past few months."

"So you know them personally, huh?"

"Yeah."

"Well, what are you waiting for? Why don't you give their names to the police?"

Ahmad started to laugh and Azadeh didn't like it. "See lady, if it was that easy, I would have taken care of it by now. But they're more careful than to leave any links or evidence. For smaller charges, they will send someone to take the blame and go to prison. But I'm after the big boss. He's from the other side of the border, but his operations are on this side and he's doing very well. A few times I delivered him the best kind of opium, the royal opium, but son of a bitch doesn't show his face to anyone. Well, I guess since he has a lot of enemies, he can't show his face to anyone. He's killed a lot of people, so he must be scared." "What I don't understand is if you knew about his hiding place, why didn't you take the police to him? If you're scared to do it, let me know, I'll be happy to do it." She was frustrated by his calmness. She took out her notebook to write down the address.

Ahmad, with the same calmness, replied, "He's mine. I have plans for him."

"No, you're lying. Why have you let him be free for so long?"

"It's impossible. He's a turban-head. At most, he'll be held for one hour. They'll send a bag of money to the judge and buy the whole court. Then when he finds you, he will have you skinned like a sheep with your body hanging. I'm not the killing type. The only way for me is to snatch him and hand him over to someone who can finish him up quietly. Then I will give the news to the papers that Hadji is missing and there's a cash reward for whoever finds him."

"It's not as bad as you say. Even in this system, there are people who are not afraid of turban-heads and want to take this snake and have him prosecuted."

Ahmad said, laughingly, "They're not hiding lady, everybody knows them. The big ones are invincible. The ones you hear about in the news are the foot soldiers, worthless to their operations. Still, busting these worthless people is better than nothing. It will make a mother of an addict feel better when a she hears about a drug bust on the radio. Secondly, I'm after money. I told you, I need to provide for a lot of people. This son of a bitch is like a bank. I must be a total idiot to let all his money go to waste."

Mohammad turned to Azadeh and with an ironic smile said, "He's dreaming. He has this idea and knows very well that it's impossible."

"Yes, it's easy to dream, but still everything is possible. I swear on my pappy's grave, I'm thinking about it a lot."

Azadeh said, "What's the use of dreaming when there's nothing to do about it?"

"I didn't say there's nothing to do about it. There are some preparations to do first. When those are taken care of, I won't waste any time."

Mohammad gave him a knowing look and shook his head. "Brother, don't you dare bring these people to my house. You know I'm minding my own business and living with my family worry free."

"I know, you've got to look after your family. Rest assured, I won't do anything to risk your house and family. You're right, I shouldn't be playing with the lion's tail. Who do I think I am to do such things? I have to do as much as I can handle. I'll think of something else."

Azadeh got up. Her head was full of all the things

she had heard and they worried her. It was late at night when she got home. The next morning she got up with a headache and a bad feeling in her stomach. She felt like she was sick of everything. When she saw the money on the table, she didn't feel like she wanted the money anymore. All the excitement that she had yesterday was gone. Now she could only see the lifeless eyes and shaky bodies of the thousands of young addicts who were sitting on the streets. With great effort, she tried to wipe those images out of her mind and she tried to just concentrate on her mom. She thought to herself, her mother's problem is not just losing a house, it's the only thing remaining from her hard life. She had to preserve the house.

She went to her mom's house and found her in the kitchen cooking. She hugged and kissed her mother. "Mom, don't worry. When you're not here, I'll plant the pansies and geraniums in the garden in the summertime. I'll take care of the cherry tree and make cherry jam. I'll feed the little sparrows, they're used to the taste of your bread. And I'll make sure that cat won't fish in your pond. So when you come back your pond will be full of red fish."

Simin put the fried cutlets in a plate and said, "Sweet dreams."

Azadeh took the money bag out of her purse and put it in front of her eyes. "My dreams came true."

Simin's jaw dropped, worriedly looked at her and said, "All this money, where did you get all this money? Where from?"

Azadeh laughed and replied, "Obviously, from the same person who took it from you." "What do you mean? Who took my money?"

"The government turban-heads. I took it back."

Simin, confused, shook her head. "Stop playing with me. Tell me, how did you get this money?"

Azadeh, eating the delicious cutlets, told the whole story to her mom. Simin, in silence, stared at her. She was happy to see the money, but was disappointed at what Azadeh had done. Bitterly she said, "What have you done? Didn't you think about the risk and the possibility that I might not see you ever again?"

"Well, I should have, but you know me."

"That's right, I shouldn't be surprised if they bring me your head one day. Tell me, how am I supposed to leave you here alone and live in a foreign land, worrying about you day and night." Then she sighed in silence. She could never get used to her daughter's reckless behavior. She had always let Azadeh do whatever she wanted to, but at the same time, she always worried about Azadeh.

Azadeh laughingly said, "Mom, don't worry, be happy. This is a dream come true. I'm done with Ahmad. This is the end. I couldn't rest until now. Now I want to spend time with my kids, it's been so long. Maybe after you guys leave, I'll take a mini vacation and visit Auntie in Mashad. Then I'll move here, I have to break my lease as soon as possible."

Simin, with a worried and concerned tone said, "Azadeh, you have to find someone for yourself. You can't live alone forever."

"Well, you're right. I have to choose amongst all the eligible lovers that I have." "Stop joking. You have had very good suitors. I wish I knew who you were waiting for."

Azadeh playfully teased her, "A prince on a black donkey."

Simin laughed too. "Why don't you take my words seriously? I guess you forgot that you're a woman and your hard days of old age are awaiting you. Find yourself a companion and give me some peace of mind too."

"You're right, I will think of something especially since I will be very lonely soon."

Simin knew Azadeh said that just to make her happy. She knew Azadeh was hardheaded and didn't want to fall in love and end up connecting her life to someone else's. Regardless, she said, "I hope you do this and let us know too."

"And I hope Sepideh will get better and we will see the better side of life again. Maybe we will hear her music again."

Simin, after a long sigh said, "I miss her music." At that moment, they both heard the music being played. Azadeh turned her head and saw Sepideh in the door. She got up and lovingly kissed her sister and after a long time, saw happiness in her mom's eyes.

CHAPTER EIGHT

Winter came and Sepideh and Simin's trip was going to start in a week. Now Azadeh, with the passage of every day, was finding herself closer to losing them and couldn't stop thinking of the lonely days awaiting her. She was imagining them in a foreign land, a land that they were still unsure of where it would be. She saw it almost impossible for her mom to get used to Europe, but she was hoping that the positive effects of this move would allow her the strength to get used to the unknown faces and would ultimately let her suffer less.

Sepideh was still in a trancelike state, caused by the medications she was taking. Traces of her pain were still apparent in her face. Deep down, Sepideh blamed herself for not being able to cope with her problems and returning to a normal life. She could see her mother's sadness. She had heard her sobbing many times. It was impossible for her to live without her mom. At the same time, she hated being this dependent on her. To some extent, she blamed her mom for her own inability to climb up the mountains of her destiny. She couldn't help thinking, 'Mom I wish you would let me find myself without you. Why don't you ever leave me alone for a minute to taste independence? Why did you make me so accustomed to your love and care that now I can't be without hearing your lovely voice. Your daughter has grown up now. Stop calling me at work and don't ask your brother to give me fewer responsibilities at work.'

But Azadeh was convinced that her mother would leave Sepideh in another country one day and return home. Although she had no idea about life in the western world, she knew enough that they would have to try twice as hard to make a living. Life is faster there and one cannot fall behind. Sepideh would be able to prove her abilities to her mother with all the work she would have to accomplish to survive.

On the first day of winter, Simin, her eyes filled with sadness, looked at her suitcases next to the door. Some friends and relatives had come to say farewell and wish them a good trip. She cried when she kissed her grandchildren's faces for the last time. She didn't know if she would ever see them again. Sepideh, paler than ever, sank into the couch and couldn't stop thinking about her unclear future. The future that everybody thought was best suited for her and continued to push her toward it with best wishes. She was encouraging herself with calming thoughts of sleeping without seeing the horrible faces of those men in her dreams again. She didn't want anything else from life. She didn't expect happiness since being away from her beloved sister and dear friends wasn't going to be easy for her. She was leaving in an effort to find herself again and make her family happy.

Neither of them slept that night because they were trying to prolong the time they had together. Darius was on his way. He was coming to take them on the path to an unclear future. Their first destination after passing the mountains was Ankara in Turkey. They were supposed to spend a few days there in a cheap hotel. The hotel was home to many Iranians waiting for their visas to a dreamland and Darius was their hero. It was six in the morning when the doorbell rang. Simin felt anxious as if the reality of leaving was just occurring to her. She closed her eyes to hide the fear behind her eyelids. Azadeh looked at her. The guilty feeling filled her heart and burned her whole body. She wanted to say something, but what could she say at that moment? She had interfered with the story of her mom's destiny. Now she could do nothing but watch the story unravel in silence. They kissed each other one last time. Simin stopped at the backyard door and with wet eyes looked at her garden for the last time. She felt like she was losing whatever was left of her life with this move. Azadeh hugged her tightly and cried. Then, sobbing, she bent and kissed Sepideh in the car. She didn't know how long she waited there. The car had disappeared a long time ago but she was still looking into the far distance. It was the sound of the garbage truck that brought her back to reality and she went inside. She felt an indescribable feeling. The feeling of loneliness engulfed the house. She looked at her mother's slippers, she would never hear her footsteps again. There wouldn't be any traces of the life that she knew anymore. In the absence of her mother and sister, who would she seek to soothe her in the hard life? She picked up Sepideh's Tar and ran her fingers through its chords. When she heard the sound, her heart filled with hatred for all men. Ahmad appeared in front of her like a bad omen. Anger took over her entire body. She screamed with all her might and threw whatever she could grab. Her legs took her to the kitchen. She sat on her mother's usual seat by the window, lit a cigarette, and at that moment something came over her. She was tempted to call Ahmad and relieve her anger by shouting at him. She wanted to tell him, "I will give you a place, bring that devil here, and you will see how I will take his life." She couldn't stand her mother's home any longer. She wanted to calm herself by holding her children.

Zohreh opened the door to her. "So good of you to stop by. I didn't sleep at all last night, you were on my mind and no matter what I couldn't get rid of my thoughts."

Azadeh smiled, "Where are the boys?"

"Hamed took them for a haircut. I know you're missing your mother and sister."

"Oh, you have no idea how much I'm missing them."

"I know, it's so hard for you to be away from each other."

"It's so hard, I don't think I'll ever get used to it. Do you think I should accept that it will be like this forever? What have we done to deserve such hardships? It looks like our destiny is set up in a way that we are always against the stream in the river of life. I feel like everything is against me."

"Dear, you know this was the only way for Sepideh. Don't worry about your mom. She'll get used to it. When they settle down you can visit them. Don't take it so hard on yourself."

Azadeh spent the whole day at Zohreh's house. They talked and she spent some time with her boys. It was dark and there were few stars in the cold, vast sky when she went back home. She sat again in the same place in the kitchen and stared at the moon, while slowly sipping on wine. The half moon looked like a bad omen causing her all the bad luck she could imagine. She slowly got drunk, and put her head on the kitchen table and fell asleep.

When she woke up, she didn't know if she was asleep or not, because she woke up thinking of Ahmad and all those men. A week after her mother's departure, she broke the lease on her apartment and moved into her mom's house. She wasn't completely done with moving when in her surprise she heard Goli's voice on her cell phone. She was very friendly to her on the phone. Goli's voice sounded so sad that immediately Azadeh thought something had happened to Ahmad.

"Goli have you heard from Ahmad?"

By hearing his name it was like something broke in Goli's heart and all Azadeh could hear was her sobbing. In between her sobs, Goli said Ahmad is still in Pakistan and he had broken the lease on her house. Ahmad had called Goli and told her to move in with Sedigheh. It had been awhile since she was living in Sedigheh's house. Goli said she had gone to the shrine everyday and had asked the Saint to help her. She wanted to talk to someone and when Simin didn't answer the phone, she had called Azadeh to talk. Azadeh didn't want to tell her about her mother's immigration over the phone. Although, she herself wasn't in a situation to sympathize with anyone, she still tried to calm the old woman down. After she hung up, she kept on thinking about her. All of a sudden it dawned on her. She felt like all the bricks from her house were falling over her head. A deep sigh came from her heart to her mouth. It was clear, the money that Ahmad gave her was the cause of more hardship in another woman's life in an effort to soothe their tragic lives. She felt the ultimate sorrow for Goli. Tears came to her eyes, what a messed up life! The poor woman's only happiness in life was having her own space and now she had to be a guest at her husband's wife's house. Azadeh's conscience was bothering her. Goli was like a heavy weight on it. She decided to go see Ahmad and confirm her thoughts and ask him what will happen to those three poor women after he is gone.

It was a late afternoon on a Friday when she started out toward Ahmad's house. Ahmad himself opened the door to her. He told her that Mohammad and Shirin had gone to Mashad but in reality, only Shirin was sent there and Mohammad had gone to Pakistan to plan with the help of his friends to set the opium farms belonging to Sadegh Jamal on fire. Ahmad had guessed the reason for Azadeh's visit.

With a sad smile he asked, "When did you talk to her? You didn't tell her, her bastard son is in Tehran, did you?

How was she? Was she well?

"No, what's left for her to feel good about? If you had told me, I wouldn't have let you do it."

Ahmad ran his fingers through his short beard and said, "Did she curse me a lot? You shouldn't think about it too much. It will change. I told her she has to be patient. Sedigheh is not as bad as she says. She doesn't do anything to her, it's our mom who's the trouble maker. If my mom puts on a good face she won't have such a hard time over here."

Azadeh said bitterly, "Good face! What do you expect? As far as I know your mom is a very proud woman. It must have been very hard for her to share her husband."

"Well, it's not Sedigheh's fault! She had to marry my dad out of desperation. My mom won't let go, she is still cursing my father. I know she's sad and hurt. She's not the only one. There are women in her situation all over the world. Nowadays women themselves find the second wife for their husbands! It's not the end of the world that she's still getting upset over this. I understand her hurt, but what can I do? I had to get the money from somewhere."

"At least tell her about your schemes."

Ahmad shook his head, "If it were that easy I would have told her already."

"What did you tell her then? Of course lies, as usual."

"I swear on my pappy's grave, I don't want to lie to her,

but she starts crying and hits her head." With a deep sigh coming out of his bony chest he said, "Poor woman has cried all her life. There's no end to her sorrows. It's like sadness is attached to her like a little bell. Ok, let's talk about something else. It will get better. I'm not dead yet. I will take care of her."

Azadeh staring at the ground quietly said, "You must still be thinking about becoming invisible and fixing everything, huh?"

"God bless you...yes. I'm thinking of it day and night. I don't want my mom to become homeless before they put me in the grave. My sister and Sedigheh will find a man to take care of them. But that poor old woman!" He couldn't continue. He lit a cigarette.

"So you haven't found a house for your plans."

"There are a few houses, but they're not safe. They'll catch me before I can do anything."

"Why not here? It seems okay."

"No. First of all I have promised Mohammad not to do it here, secondly the street is too narrow. You saw that even a donkey can't pass by the narrow walls. The guy is supposed to come here unconscious and leave unconscious. For that a car has to come all the way to the door."

"How long are you going to keep him?"

"Only for a day, enough time to go to the bank and come back."

For a short moment Azadeh hesitated. Half of her felt numb to everything and the other half madly wanted to do something. Finally she said, "Ahmad, I'm not saying I'm very brave, but in this situation something must be done for that woman."

Ahmad sharply looked at her, "Meaning?"

"I'm saying, if you can't find a place for one day I can let you use my house. It seems like your plans are simple and risk free, but I don't want to be involved."

Ahmad started laughing until his bony body was shaking. Finally, calmly and seriously he said, "No sister, stop dreaming, it's not as easy as you've heard. If it's not done right then we'll have to go somewhere no one can ever hear from us. Everything has to be done correctly and precisely, very very carefully. No loopholes, of course I'm not scared of anything. I've been in the hole too; it's no big deal. So the only thing left is fear for your life. Well death is coming my way regardless. A few years sooner or later doesn't make a difference."

"Are you going to be doing it all by yourself?"

"No way, how many eyes and hands do you think I have? There are a few of us. The guy is too big so we have to act big too."

Azadeh got up. "Well I wish you success. I hope you get my sister's revenge too. It's not fair to return that bastard without harming him. Also I'm going to Mashad to visit my relatives for a few days. You can use my house in my absence. As soon as I'm back I'll call you to see what you have done!"

"It seems like you don't want to let go of this?"

"That's right. I have a bad feeling. Let me be frank with you, I want to help you, but I also don't want to get involved."

Ahmad didn't say anything. He looked into Azadeh's eyes and in them he saw that she really wanted to be a part of this. A look of satisfaction came across Ahmad's face and Azadeh saw that. She closed the door behind her and left.

All week her thoughts overpowered her and she decided to go to Zohreh with them. Zohreh had become her only companion and confidant. There was no one else that would watch over her and that Azadeh could trust more. Zohreh was anxiously sitting in front of her to hear what Azadeh wanted to tell her.

Azadeh, was excitedly trying to piece her sentences together. She was puffing on her cigarette repeatedly and her sentences made no sense.

Zohreh was looking at her in disbelief. "Azadeh, what are you saying! Is it bad news?" Zohreh was thinking of Simin.

Azadeh looked down and fearing that she might change her mind, started talking slowly and cautiously told Zohreh whatever was on her mind.

Zohreh was looking at her with a dropped jaw. She

couldn't help but look down at her. 'She never thinks of her responsibilities, how can she think this way and gamble with her life in spite of her responsibility as a mom?' Zohreh thought. Her face turned unfriendly and with a dry tone she said, "I'm disappointed in you, how can you be so careless about your children? No matter how kind I am with them I cannot replace you in their hearts. Stop this nonsense and find a harmless hobby for yourself."

Azadeh realized that Zohreh was right. In all her scheming, she had though of herself as someone without responsibilities. This was the first time she wanted to do something just for herself and thinking about it had satisfed her. She didn't want to argue with Zohreh anymore. So she just said, "You're right, I have to calm down and forget about all this."

Zohreh said, "I want to believe you, but something in your eyes tells me not to."

Azadeh laughed, "Don't believe them, you're right. I was only thinking about myself. Now I have to think about my sons, Kaveh and Kayvan."

Zohreh felt proud, she was feeling superior to Azadeh. Thanks to her, she had reminded a selfish mother of her responsibilities. Zohreh felt proud to have Hamed's heart all to herself. Azadeh could see Zohreh's feelings on her face and couldn't help thinking, she doesn't know I have never felt any jealousy toward her.

It had been a month since Simin and Sepideh were in Ankara, Turkey. Living in a hotel had exhausted Simin. Her days were spent with travelers such as herself. They would gather up in the lobby and tell each other their life stories, exaggerated stories and they were all aware of the exaggerated melancholy without actually mentioning it. They would talk about prison and the torture they endured. They spoke of what a bad fortune it was to be related to the royal family because now they were haunted by the revolutionary guards. The "rich" people couldn't show their faces in public and had become bored with the religious government so they gave away all their wealth just so they could leave the country. Though some of them were "wise" enough to keep their villa by the sea for hard days!

But Sepideh's story wasn't one that she could just share with the others. She would show a pale smile and answer questions by responding, "Nightmares, I left to get away from my nightmares."

Sepideh had actually begun to sleep better and her appetite had also improved. She had grown accustomed to using words like smuggler, foreign currencies, phony passports, and guards. Unlike her mother, she wasn't getting bored just waiting. She had found a few friends in that hotel too, a few ditzy girls who were just happy to be able to wear whatever they wanted to.

Simin, seeing the improvements in Sepideh, was hopeful to her complete recovery. Simin thought, maybe if Sepideh recovers fully, she won't need her medication anymore. She had told Azadeh that Darius the smuggler is making arrangements to send them to London.

Their words were comforting to Azadeh. But she had become bored with her own life. She was in such controversy within herself that it was taking up her energy. A strong feeling, even stronger than her bond with her children, was pulling her. She wasn't even thinking of her mother and sister anymore. Her only comforting thought was revenge. A vague suspicious feeling was telling her that Ahmad hadn't told her the entire truth. This Hadji must be one of those motherfuckers who had Sepideh under their fist. She was certain of this suspicion.

CHAPTER NINE

The changes in Azadeh's behavior were obvious to Zohreh and she knew she couldn't ignore them any longer. She became worried about her and knew Azadeh was lying to her about cutting ties with Ahmad. She knew by experience that a woman like Azadeh is not afraid of anything. That was why one night she called on Azadeh unannounced and made her tell the truth.

Azadeh opened the door to her. Zohreh was so preoccupied with her questions that without the usual greetings, she threw herself on the couch and said, "I'm here to find out what's going on. You have changed tremendously, like there's nothing left of you. Can you even see the people around you? I don't think so. You are so preoccupied with yourself that even your sons are mad at you. Your visits are shorter every week. It's like seeing them for you is a task that you want to finish as soon as possible. Tell me what's going on! It can't be your mother and sister. As far as I know, they're fine. There must be something else. If you're still thinking of that addict bum, tell me. I hope he dies pretty soon and his power over you will cease."

Azadeh was quiet. She understood what she was hearing and knew she couldn't find any excuse for her behavior. She didn't even have an explanation. On the other hand, if she said anything about what was going on in her mind to Zohreh she would raise havoc and get everyone on her case. Although, she wasn't afraid of anyone, she knew if Hamed knew he would call her mother and worry her. For a second, she thought of confessing everything to Zohreh and trying to get Zohreh on her side. She thought she might have a chance at her kindheartedness.

She told her, "This was what I have caused for my family. Although I did my best to make everything okay, these guilty feelings won't leave me. Now, I feel I have to get revenge on these criminals and that is the only thing that will calm my soul." She told her about Goli's homelessness and how Ahamad was like the modern Robin Hood who is risking his life to defend the poor. Azadeh really believed in what she was saying and felt so excited that it brought tears to her eyes.

Zohreh was looking at her with a deep piercing look. It was hard for her to understand what she was hearing, Azadeh a hijacker! Now she was convinced that Azadeh had gone mad and had made up that story. She began doubting that Azadeh had gotten the money from Ahmad. Maybe that was a delusion and the money had really come from another source.

Her face slowly calmed down. Her dry voice was blaming and with a sympathetic tone she said, "Dear Azadeh, I understand you. I know it's not easy for you. No matter how much you busy yourself you're still lonely. But you can help yourself get rid of these delusions. Why don't you make yourself happy with what you already have? Why don't you take a vacation with the boys? They'll be happy. They have missed you too."

Azadeh sighed from the bottoms of her chest. She looked at her kind eyes and thought, 'why can't these eyes see me? Are my thoughts like a children's story that she can't take them seriously?' Then sadly, she said, "Dear Zohreh, please for God's sake try to understand what I'm telling you. Maybe my judgment about myself is not a fair one, but I have always felt that I have never been a good wife to Hamed and a good mother to my kids. I have never been satisfied with myself. My years with Hamed were so dark that I couldn't watch my children grow. Even now, I can't see clearly through the darkness. I'm not saying you can't have expectations from me, but please have some understanding too. If I seem so desperate it's because I am the only one left for myself. That's why I don't want to sit and cry anymore. I'm tired of empty talks. Now, these thoughts are the only things that satisfy me. I want to feel my own soul. See Zohreh, I want to become a memory. Then when my boy's think about me, it's a different memory than what they might have now. They won't talk about the grandma's old house with its big pond and huge windows in the backyard. The hawk is not a carving on the stone for them anymore. The hawk has flown away and has made a mark, even a small one on their memory. My sons and I will pass these days. When they say goodbye to their childhood and transform into grown men, they will forgive me."

Zohreh, amazed and helpless, was staring at her as if she was seeing an alien. With a nervous tone she said, "Azadeh, you are lying to yourself. I know you have a loving heart. I know other people's sufferings hurt you. But that doesn't mean that you should risk your life. You are looking for excitement. Life is too boring for you. You want entertainment."

Azadeh replied bitterly, "What are you talking about? What entertainment? I'm not asking you to understand, but I wasn't expecting your hurtful words either." Now Zohreh looked at her suspiciously. She didn't want to be considered as a conspirator in a situation like this.

"Well, you know better. I won't say anything anymore. But, you should know I never expected you to involve yourself in these sorts of schemes. This is not in your character. From now on I don't want to know about your affairs either. Go ahead and find some other ally for yourself."

She got up and left without saying goodbye. Azadeh knew what Zohreh was going to do next, which would inevitably ruin her plans. She had to deny everything the best she could. Before her phone would start ringing, she went out into the streets. The color of the sky reflected how she felt, dark and gloomy. She started walking on the sidewalk. She was engulfed in her thoughts. She was picturing capturing those evil men, the lives of those three poor women, Masoumeh's future, and other lives. The more she thought the more she was convinced that this is "the place" to find herself.

After walking for hours, she returned exhausted, but hopeful. As she expected, her uncle and Hamed had left more than ten messages. She unplugged the phone and went to bed. Without expecting to fall asleep, she picked up a book, but her thoughts were too scattered to be able to follow the book. She missed her father. She picked up the photo albums and started going through them. On the first page she saw a picture of herself at about eight years old with her school uniform on sitting on her dad's lap. She looked at her dad with teary eyes. He looked worried because he knew what his destiny had in store for him. She pictured her mom in the kitchen by the window and started talking to her, listened to Sepideh playing Tar, it sounded like a lullaby to her ears. Her eyes filled with sleep and she closed them.

She woke up with the doorbell ringing. It was morning and there was a pale sunshine lighting up the room. She got up, annoyed and opened the door to her uncle. At the same time, the elevator's doors opened and Hamed walked out. He said hello and with a grim face threw his giant body inside and stared at Azadeh. Azadeh looked at him too. His look was exactly the same as when they used to live together under the same roof. He had a gray suit on, one hand in his pocket and with the other hand he was playing with his mustache. Azadeh wasn't intimidated by his anger. With a smile on her face she passed him to go to the bathroom to wash up and get ready for a fight. She could hear him telling her uncle that she had lost her mind. He was telling her uncle that he wanted to go after Ahmad and beat him up, so that he wouldn't show his face around there.

Azadeh came back to the room with the same smile on her face. Her uncle said,

"Sit down, is this true?"

"What?"

"Your stupid scheme?"

"Oh Zohreh. She makes everything so out of proportion it was just a dream I was telling her about. Rest assured, I'm scared to do such things."

Hamed looked at her with cutting eyes. "Stop lying, this bum is playing with your mind. Zohreh told me you have gone to his house several times. I'm mad at Zohreh too, she should have told us sooner. We wouldn't have let it come to this. It's not important to me what you do with your life, but I'm here to remind you of our kids. You are the stupidest mother on the face of the earth without thinking about your kids at all. You are acting like a naïve person who can be conned and used. If it weren't for the boys I wouldn't even set foot here today. To hell with you. Give me this bum's address so I can send his mother to his funeral." Hamed was so mad that he didn't care what he was saying in front of Azadeh's uncle.

Azadeh's face was hot and her eyes were burning with anger. She couldn't help thinking, 'he really is here to remind me of my sons?! The same guy who used to do the same things that now he was accusing her of! Who is he kidding?' She screamed back, "If you really wanted me to be with my kids then why did you ignore all those cries and beggings when I was begging you to give them to me? You took them from me and gave them to a stranger, now you're telling me to be a mother and stay with my children! How can you even suggest that I was the one abandoning my kids when it was you who took them away from me?" She was so mad that she forgot why Hamed was there. She even forgot about her uncle. The old wounds had opened up and anger was pouring out. Her uncle tried to calm her down by making her sit down. But Azadeh was too agitated. Her uncle gestured to Hamed to leave. Hamed slammed the door behind him and left. Her uncle took her hand and calmly said, "Dear, he's right to be angry at you. You are his kid's mom. You still have a place in his heart."

Azadeh swallowed her tears and said, "I don't want that place. When I was living with him there was no place for me in his heart, now there's no use."

"Didn't you forget how hard he worked to get you out of prison?"

"No, I haven't, but I will also never forget that he took my sons and left my house to take them to Zohreh. That day he broke my heart so badly that there's no room for forgiveness." Azadeh started crying.

Her uncle gave her tissues and continued, "Dear, it's not a good reason for you to forget your children and go after adventures."

Azadeh sniffed and said, "Don't tell me you believed her too."

"Are you telling me these were all stories?"

A smile came to her face and she said, "An action story with no definite ending yet. I will finish writing it in my mind one day. By the way, I'm planning to take a few days off and visit Auntie in Mashad. I'm exhausted. Lately there has been too much pressure on me. You know."

"I know, I know."

"I wish he knew too and wouldn't say all those things to me."

"Okay, don't let those things bother you too much. You have lost a lot of weight. Why don't you come for a visit? My wife said you haven't called her lately either. Come to dinner tomorrow. I'll ask her to make your favorite. You haven't had a good meal lately."

"Okay, it's getting late, you'll be late too."

Azadeh looked at her watch, and hurried to get ready to leave the house with her uncle. That afternoon she called Ahmad and said that next week she would meet him to talk about her offer. The whole day she worked hard to get away from her thoughts. She felt very energetic. Her job didn't require her to put much effort. After years of assisting doctors in surgeries it was like second nature to her. At the end of the day she went to her manager's office. She had a lot of vacation time saved up, she could easily get a month off.

A week had passed and Zohreh hadn't called on her. Although, she was trying not to think about Zohreh, she was missing her and expected that she would call her out of curiosity. She couldn't help thinking how lonely it was to not have anyone to talk to. She realized that although she felt close in her heart to Zohreh, she was at the same time too far away from her in her mind.

It was the end of January and the snow had turned the city completely white. Azadeh spent the whole day cleaning the house. She could not just sit and rest. When the last rays of light were diminishing, she put her coat on and started out toward Ahmad's house to hear of the unfortunte people's destiny.

At his house she was introduced to a guy named "Mr. Ali," who seemed to be the brain of the operation. He was about thirty years old with a dark face and black thick hair. Mr. Ali looked at her with his slanted eyes, it was a look that seemed to belong to someone else. It made her uncomfortable. The gravity of the situation grew two folds on her, and she felt scared. But she knew there was no turning back. She had convinced herself to be brave and had pushed herself to go forward. So she had to stay brave until the end.

She took her eyes away from Mr. Ali, lit a cigarette and stared at the lines on the carpet. Mr. Ali who seemed very serious and tough, started questioning her. Although, he knew everything about her and had no doubts about her motives, he had to do this to test her strength and bravery. Azadeh didn't understand why she needed to be brave and what use they could have for her since she wasn't supposed to do anything. She was only giving them her house for one day while she was visiting her aunt in another city far away. She couldn't take it anymore and asked him exactly what she had been wondering

Mr. Ali replied, "You're right, you're out of the operation, but what if once everything is arranged all of a sudden you decide to back out? Then all the plans are ruined and we'll all be arrested."

Azadeh said fiercely, "No, there's no backing out. Although I disagree with you about wanting to have this guy killed, I am going along with it.

"I thought if we give this guy to the authorities then all his money will end up either with another mullah or in the hands of Palestinian Hezbollah, neither of them is acceptable." Ahmad said, "Don't worry, you want him dead, he'll die. His life is dependent on his bank account. When you take that from him, he'll die on his own."

Azadeh spent the first week of her vacation with her kids and the next morning was the day that she was supposed to go to Mashad.

It had been an hour since she had returned the boys to

their father's and was pacing in the backyard impatiently. It was Friday evening. Mr. Ali was supposed to arrive any minute. He was supposed to stop by and get the house key from her. Now that it was time for real action, Azadeh was petrified. It was like the excietment of these plans had left her body and mind and now she was seriously thinking about what she was about to do. She was listening for the doorbell with anxiety and expectations. It seemed to her like the entire neighborhood knew about the plans and would call the police as soon as they saw Mr. Ali. She peeked into the street and checked several times. Finally, she heard footsteps behind the gate. Hastily she opened the door and saw Mr. Ali with a young guy behind the door. After they came in, Azadeh checked both sides of the street before closing the door. Mr. Ali checked the backyard, rubbed his short forehead and with a solemn look said, "Scared?"

Azadeh felt that if she said no they would know it was a lie and with a bold smile replied, "I hope no one saw you guys."

Mr. Ali said, "Not that everyone in your neighborhood knows me or knew what I am doing here. If it's okay, I'd like to check the house out."

Azadeh led the way and they followed her into the house to check each room. Azadeh was surprised. Mr. Ali seemed cool to Azadeh. He was walking as if he had been there before and the house was not unfamiliar to him. Mr. Ali, after inspecting the whole house, chose Sepideh's room as the most appropriate for his plans. It's window opened to a small courtyard surrounded by tall walls from three sides. He stuck his head out of the window and looked up. "I looked around, behind these walls must be another backyard."

"You're right, there's a green house on the other side."

Mr. Ali inspected the iron bars on Sepideh's bed and said, "It's not the season for gardening so there shouldn't be anyone there."

While closing the window Azadeh said, "Maybe, but you still be cautious. Everything has to be done quietly." "Don't worry, no one will notice anything. But we have to bring some stuff in the house."

"That's your business. I'm going to be gone for ten days. I hope there won't be any trouble. I want to come back to the same house with everything exactly as it is now." Azadeh closed the door behind them, took a sigh of relief, and poured herself a glass of wine to calm herself down. But it was useless. Even wine didn't have the same effect on her anymore. With a heavy head she threw herself on the bed. She lost track of time until there were only a few stars in the sky and sun was sneaking in through the gray clouds. She had to get ready. A taxi was supposed to pick her up to take her to the train station.

As soon as she was settled on the train, she tried to calm herself down. 'Don't you even think about it for a few days. Don't look back or forward. Take it easy and enjoy your trip.' As the train was moving she busied her mind by thinking of a place far away in wilderness and she imaged herself moving along the river and prairies. But it was impossible for her mind to relax. It kept going back to the events in the past..

In her car there were three other women, two of them were sisters. One of them was a young woman with an incurable disease and was going on this pilgrimage to the eighth Imam to beg him for a cure. (Shiit's believe in twelve Imams who followed the Prophet Mohammad, the Eighth one, Imam Reza is buried in Iran and is very dear to Iranians) Her face, with beauty that was fading away, was smiling. She was hopeful to survive. She believed completely in her belief that she would be cured by the Imam and was excitedly telling Azadeh about it. Azadeh prayed for her with all her soul and tried to show her sympathy in her face. At that moment, Azadeh was thankful to God that she didn't have to worry about her own health.

Her aunt's house had a delicious familiar aroma. It awakened the forgotten memories of her childhood. The past years with lovely memories of summer vacations and playful times with her cousins came rushing back to her. The memories and all the auntie's kindness helped her be hopeful about the success of whatever was going on at her house and she wished Goli back in her house again. She wished Arezou walk with no limp and stop slaving her life away for the worthless Hadji Khanoum. She could see lives, which weren't horrible anymore and mothers who could teach their kids "mother is the breadwinner of the house" (in the first grade book the first sentence kids learn is Dad is the breadwinner of the house). Unfortunately, these sweet dreams didn't resonate with her for more than a couple of days. Her soul was in turmoil. Although she was trying to calm herself down she couldn't. All the worries were part of her soul now and they would turn into nightmares at night. When she woke up, her mind was racing and she could see the faces of all the men at her house walking in front of her. Her aunt and cousins were noticing her miserable state and simply thought it was because she missed her mom and sister.

As the days passed, something started bothering her. She thought Ahmad would have contacted her and told her about the plan by now. She was very anxious to know how everything was going. If it weren't for Mr. Ali, she would have called them by now. She couldn't even guess what had happened. Maybe the plans had been compromised and they were all captured, or maybe they didn't care about her and divided the money amongst themselves before they split.

It was very early in the morning when she arrived in Tehran. She got off the taxi in front of her house. She hesitated for a while before entering. Something was wrong. Finally, she turned the key in the lock and went in. She put her suitcase in the hallway. It seemed to her that there was someone in the house breathing heavily. She looked in Sepideh's room at the end of the hallway. Her ears had led her there. It was a long breath as if someone was asleep. She got angry thinking Ahmad had crashed in her house while she wasn't in there. She knocked on the door angrily. The room seemed too dark to her. In the very dim light she could figure out a man lying on the bed with his hand cuffed to the bedpost. She was about to scream, but controlled herself. This must be the guy, but why?

She closed the door slowly and frantically ran in the living room, "What the hell were you doing the past ten days?" But there was no one there. She checked the other rooms and called for Mr. Ali and Ahmad, but there was only her own voice. She thought the only thing she could do was to go to her own room, lie on her bed, and wait for them. She thought they must have gone to get the money.

Two hours passed. She figured she had to forget about Mr. Ali's orders and call them. She dialed Ahmad's number. What was that? The ringing was coming from the kitchen. Oh well, then you're here. Are you deaf? She ran to the kitchen, but she was stopped at the door. She froze when she saw Ahmad's body on the floor. When she was able to move, she bent over him, "Please, no, oh God no, not now. Ahmad please wake up, please?" His face was horrible. His skin under his beard was blue and his head was tilted to one side. It looked like he was dead. Azadeh felt for the pulse on his neck. It was warm and there was still life in his body. She straightened his head and put a wet towel on his face. Then she pulled his body towards a wall and space skinny legs against the wall to help rush the blood into his body. She had to call for paramedics. She almost dialed the phone number of the hospital where she worked, but stopped. It wasn't a wise thing to let her coworkers know about Ahmad's presence in her house. She called another hospital almost an hour away. Then she thought of inspecting his pockets to see if he had her keys. In his pockets she found his gun, her own key, and another small key. She put them all in a drawer in the kitchen. She then lit a cigarette and looked into the front yard. All of a sudden she felt an urge to go in Sepideh's room and beat the man up before Mr. Ali came back.

She pushed her cigarette into the ashtray and put her mom's veil on and covered her whole face with a black shawl. The only thing visible on her face was her eyes. Slowly, she opened the door and in the dim light of the lamp, she saw the thick black curtain covering the window. The warm air in the room smelled like the man's stinky breath. She took a step forward. She glanced over his face and body, and his turban by the bed. It was the same man she had pictured, middle-aged, dark-faced, with a long beard starting from underneath his eyes all the way onto his chest with a few strands of hair on his bald head. She felt a mixed feeling of fear and hatred. She was possessed by temptation and excitement. She was filled with the temptation of revenge. Her excitement climaxed. She was breathing heavily. Her heart was pounding. The guy was not moving, his mouth was open and she could hear his breathing. She could hardly control her hands, her shaky fingers were reaching for his throat. But before touching his throat, she pulled her hands under her arm with a quick move. Tears rolled down her eyes. What a useless thought. She couldn't use her hatred as a weapon and take someone's life. She looked at the man's hands and the handcuff seemes familia to her. They were the same ones she saw before at Mohammad's house. At that moment, she heard something like a body dropping down to the floor. The noise was coming from the window. Shakily she went to the window and through the drapes looked outside. But her view was blocked by the planks on the windows. Why all these precautions? So they lied to me, this guy was supposed to stay here for a few days. She felt helpless. What if Mr. Ali doesn't show up and this guy wakes up and starts screaming while the paramedics are here to take Ahmad to the hospital. What am I supposed to do then? She thought it better to move Ahmad's body, but to where? The only place that the guy's scream won't be heard by anyone is the backyard. A lump came to her throat. "Ahmad, forgive me." She stood up by Ahmad's body, took him by his armpits and pulled him into the yard and laid him under the willow tree near the gate. Then she took a pillow from the house with a blanket and threw it on his body. Then she sat next to him and started crying. A teardrop fell on Ahmad's closed eye. A few crows sitting on the nearby branches started crowing and pointed their beaks towards him. Azadeh scared them away, "Get the hell away, he's still alive!"

The paramedics arrived sooner than she thought. She explained to them that he was the plumber that she knew and had called for some repairs but all of a sudden he had collapsed.The paramedics took Ahmad to the hospital. When she heard from the nurse that Ahmad was climbing death's wall, she knew she had to let his mom know about him. She was holding his cell phone, hoping that Mr. Ali would call and tell her of his whereabouts. A few hours passed and the sun started to set. Now it was the night owl sitting on her soul's wall. She was engulfed with fear. She was expecting another hard blow to her life. She went to her room and collapsed on the bed. She was thinking about how to tell Goli about Ahmad. What if Mr. Ali didn't show up that night, what was she supposed to do with this guy, how was she going to explain it to Goli? If she knew Ahmad had another day she would have waited. But she didn't want Goli to have to visit her son in the morgue. She picked up the phone and dialed the old woman's number. She didn't give too much information over the phone. She knew with the slightest news, Goli would get the next bus to Tehran.

Now the darkness had spread. Fear, sadness and restlessness all at the same time were gripping her. The sound of the man's breathing sounded like death to her. The intervals between his breaths were getting shorter, indicating he would come to in a short while. Suddenly he started coughing. Azadeh put her hand in her pocket and grabbed Ahmed's gun. Slowly, she walked towards Sepideh's room and opened the door. She stood in the doorway and looked at the half conscious body of the man.

Her whole body was overcome with fear and cold sweat was dripping from her face. She took a half step forward. The man moved and his colorless lips uttered a few incomprehensible words. Without even moving, he opened his eyes. There was surprise in his eyes. He turned them to Azadeh and with a deep voice asked, "Where am I? Who are you?"

Azadeh mumbled, "Hell, I'm the angel of death." The man pulled himself a little bit upward and turned his wide eyes around the room. It seemed like he couldn't figure out the time or the place. He leaned his head against the bedpost and closed his eyes. His breathing was regular and his bony chest was going up and down rhythmically. It seemed like he would regain his consciousness in a few minutes. Azadeh's state of mind was indescribable. Her legs were buckling under her weight. She sat down and leaned against the door. She was afraid to lose sight of the man. Although his hand was handcuffed to the bed, Azadeh still didn't feel safe. She was afraid he would leap at her.

Finally, Hadji turned his head and opened his eyes. It seemed like he just remembered everything that had happened. He managed to hold up his neck and tried to turn in bed, but the handcuffs were holding him against the bedpost. He turned back and stared at his hand. Then he pulled himself forward, sat in the bed with his legs dangling and saw his turban on the floor. With an unexpected fast movement he leaped toward it, grabbed it, and put his finger in the hole on top and with his finger started feeling for something in there. Suddenly his face turned yellow, amber yellow. Then he fell back on the bed, pulled his legs up and stayed still like that.

Azadeh got up and looked at him in disgust. What was he looking for in his turban's hole? She tried to come up with an answer, but it was useless.

The man turned and with crusty eyes looked at her. It was like in his desperation he was trying to figure out his guard. The room was hot and now it smelled like a dead dog, nauseating. Azadeh was about to leave the room when she heard him.

"What are you going to do with me?"

She replied calmly, "You know better. Did you think we brought you here to party?" Hadji grabbed his beard from his chin and stroked it down to his chest.

"You useless whore. Osman is that you? fucking fagot , are you pretending to be a woman?"

Azadeh was almost about to break his jaw but, she thought this guy must be one of the guys who raped Sepideh. So she calmed herself down. She didn't want to give the man any clue as to who she was. At the same time, the guy was her prisoner and she was in control until Mr. Ali got there. She should show him her authority. So she finally said, "Hadji, if you don't shut your mouth, I'll waste a bullet on you. Now it's up to you."

Hadji started cursing her as he was wiping the spit off his mouth. Azadeh couldn't take it any longer,She closed the door and ran to the kitchen. She took out the gun and grabbed its short muzzle with her fingers. What am I doing with this? I can't even kill a cockroach with it, let alone this bearded son of a bitch.

Helpless, she went to her room and cried. She had risked too much without evaluating her real strengths, now she was like a stuck mule in mud, didn't know what to do with the guy until Mr. Ali got there.

She jumped up with the sound of the doorbell. At that moment, hearing Mr. Ali's voice was her only wish, but at the other end of the intercom was Goli's voice. It was 9 o'clock at night. Through the window, she looked at Goli's little figure in the backyard. It seemed smaller than usual.

Azadeh hid her worries under a smile and said hello to the old woman and even put an icy kiss on her cheek. Goli took away her veil and said, "Dear, I missed you so much. Sedigheh told me you have sent Ahmad to the hospital. God bless you. How is he? The same as the as last time?"

"Yeah, like last time, he was here when it happened."

"Why? Why do these things happen to this miserable son of mine?" Then she looked at Azadeh from top to bottom. "Why do you look like this? Where is the rest of the family?"

"I'll tell you later." "Later? What happened? Is Sepideh okay?"

"They're okay. It's been a few months since they've moved from here. Out of the country."

Goli with surprised eyes asked, "Why?"

"Well, you can guess why. Sepideh was getting worse everyday. They had to leave this place."

"I'm so sorry. But what was my boy doing here? How could he show his face to you? How long has it been since he's back?"

Azadeh remembered Ahmad had told his mother he'd gone to Pakistan.

"I don't know, he didn't tell me."

"God bless you for taking care of him. Did doctors say why he passed out?"

The phone rang. Azadeh jumped to get it. It was Kayvan her older son, checking to see if she was back. Azadeh, with a heavy heart, told a whole bunch of lies to her son. She made up a story about water pumps blowing up and there's water everywhere, so they can't come for a visit for a few days. She had totally forgotten about Goli sitting there. She was looking into the backyard with sad eyes expecting Mr. Ali.

Goli asked, "Dear, which pump is broken? Is there water anywhere enough for a cup of tea?"

"Oh, I'm sorry Goli, I'll make tea for you right way." Goli followed her into the kitchen and saw the water pouring into the kettle, but she didn't ask any questiosn. Azadeh, as she was turning the stove on, said, "Goli I know it's late, but I think it's better if you went to the hospital tonight."

Saying this, without waiting for her response, she started dialing the number for the cab company. Goli looked into her eyes, "Would they let me in at this hour?"

"Yes, I'm sure they will. But before you go I have to tell you something."

"What? Is Ahmad going to die? Oh my god!"

Azadeh with a short cry said, "Please for God's sake be quiet. I was going to tell you to be careful in the hospital and don't say anything to anyone. I have told them that Ahmad was my plumber."

Goli, bewildered, looked at Azadeh "Who?"

"Ahmad passed out when he was here."

"But you're saying there was a plumber here!"

Azadeh shook her head, lit a cigarette, opened the window to get some fresh cool air. Goli asked, "Should I brew tea?"

Azadeh poured hot water over a teabag and put it in front of her. "The cab will be here soon." Goli looked at the teabag and said, "Thank you dear, teabag is okay."

As the doorbell rang, Goli drank the whole cup in one sip. Azadeh opened the door and said, "Listen Goli, Ahmad has learned plumbing. When I found out I asked him to take care of my plumbing problem. Now hurry up the cab is waiting."

"Well you should have said this in the first place, then neither of us would get confused." As she was getting to the door she put her hand to her heart and said, "Dear boy, you're too weak to do that sort of work." As she closed the door behind Goli, she heard Hadji's grinding cough in the hallway. Then the coughs got louder and Azadeh heard him spitting. She covered her face and body again, and with a glass of water went to the room. Hadji rubbed his eyes when Azadeh turned the light on. He took the cup of water from her and looked inside it.

"Don't worry I'm not poisoning you, its just water."

A smile opened his mouth revealing his big and yellow teeth. He poured the water into his mouth in one motion and as he was looking at Azadeh threw the cup at her. It was a plastic cup and rolled under the bed. Hadji wiped his mouth with the blanket and loudly said, "You fucking son of a bitch. If I get a hold of you I'll have you hung from your ass. I'll have your balls pulled out of your mouth. You think you're hiding from me you mother fucking faggot."

Azadeh closed the door, but she could still hear him cursing. As she was looking outside his last sentences were echoing in her ear. "You think you're hiding from me you mother fucker." She thought, who did he mean? Whoever it was, he must know him. Then something came to her mind. Is it Mr. Ali or the guy she saw with him or someone else? She didn't want to get worried, but she couldn't help looking at the clock and wondering when Mr. Ali would come back. All of a sudden thinking that Mr. Ali had taken off with the money, she started trembling. It was well past eleven o'clock and she was almost sure that she would never see Mr. Ali again. For a second she thought her life was over and she wasn't thinking about her dreams being taken away by bad luck anymore. Ahmad was dying and Mr. Ali was gone. The other guy was as good as gone. She was left alone with this man in her house. She started smoking cigarette after cigarette. She was so mad at herself and was blaming herself for being too emotional and acting on her emotions instead of on her logic. What was she thinking about? Letting these men take over her life like this! She wanted to live courageously and do whatever she wanted to do and let the hawk of her dreams fly freely! Bullshit, courage needs balls which you don't have, hawk!!! You are not even a sparrow! She had trusted men unconditionally and instead what she had received was deceit

Then she thought she had heard Hadji. She ran inside. Hadji was screaming, "Hey whore. Where the hell are you? I have to go pee."

Azadeh wanted to ignore him, but his screams were driving her crazy. Her eyes were burning with anger. She yelled at him from behind the door, you can shit on yourself for all that I care. But she couldn't just ignor him, so went to the bathroom and took out the razor, scissors and everything else that she thought could be used as weapons. Then she went back to Sepideh's room and opened the door. She had to figure out a way to release his hand without him attacking her. At the same time Hadji was thinking exactly the same thing, how to attack her, take the gun away, and kill her.

"Ok, get up and lean against the bedpost!"

"You Medoussa, I can't hold it, I'm gonna shit on you now"

"Against the bedpost"

Hadji was still trying to figure what happened to the two men who jumped him in the car and put a syringe to his neck. Now there was only this woman who was either crying or screaming. There was an obvious scheming along with violence evident on his face. He was checking Azadeh with his eyes behind his bushy eyebrows. Azadeh noticed this so she stood up behind him like a pillar and with a commanding voice mixed with fear, said "Bring up your hand and put it behind your head."

Hadji turned his head and brought a demeaning smile to his face, brought his hand up, and put them behind his head. Azadeh as if she was in a sauna, under the veil and shawl, was sweating like a dog. Fear of getting attacked had made her very alert and her eyes were watching Hadji like an eagle. In a split second she turned the key in the cuff and then it was released from the bedpost. She pulled his hand so hard that he screamed in pain. Her fingers were working so fast like she had no control of them. She put the other hand in cuffs too. Then she pushed his head forward and put his handcuffed hands on his belly. She leaned against the wall and sighed in relief. She held the gun and as she was pointing at him with shaking hands inched her way towards the door. "Now get up."

Hadji looked at her and laughed harshly. His yellow and thick spit started running on his beard. When he stopped laughing he said, "That son of a bitch faggot couldn't find anyone braver than you to give a gun to? You whore, go wash dishes or something. Now open my hands. How am I supposed to pull my pants down?"

Azadeh looked at his loose linen pants and said, "You can, walk."

Hadji got up and spat on the carpet in front of him then started walking. At the door he paused and checked the hallway, then he looked at Azadeh and said, "Seems like you're all by yourself."

At that moment Azadeh could envision her body hanging from the cranes. Hadji was finding out about her situation. She harshly said, "When it's time, others will come."

"Oh it's not time yet, huh? Okay, I'll wait." Hadji in the bathroom checked the feminine towels. "Okay, I see now. The faggot desired a woman." The bathroom had a little window into the backyard and from behind the trees the sky was showing. Hadji looked up at the window, pulled himself up, and pushed on the window. The frame moved a little and the window cracked open. He pulled his neck up, but couldn't reach the window. He looked around to find a stepping stool or something but he couldn't find anything. Then he started screaming.

Azadeh behind the door, was thinking about the end of her life as she knew it when she heard him screaming for help. She jumped in the bathroom as fast as lightning and pointed the gun at him. "Shut up you stupid asshole!"

Hadji left the window, pulled his pants down as he was staring into her eyes, and sat on the bowl. Azadeh stood there with pointed gun as Hadji was trying to do his business. It took him nearly ten minutes till he finally got up and washed his face. Hadji was so happy. He was thinking to himself, 'this whore is bluffing. She's not a pro, this is her first time. All she has is that gun and there is nobody else. Ali must have tricked her. If Ali the faggot can trick her, then I can trick her too. I'll talk to her and promise some money to her, maybe I can fuck her too, well, we'll see...' Azadeh's scream brought him to reality.

Azadeh handcuffed him to the bed the same way she had

un-cuffed him. Then she went to the roof and looked for a thick rice bag. She folded it several times and covered the bathroom window with it. She was lying on the bed thinking about Goli. Hadji was awake and was complaining of pain in his hands and legs. She could hear his moaning and it seemed like he really was in pain. Then Azadeh realized that she hadn't fed him. Maybe that's why he's moaning. Reluctantly she got up and went into the kitchen. She fixed him a butter and jam sandwich and went into the room. Hadji was throwing up with his eyes closed. Everything that was in his stomach was falling down his chest and his bony legs. Azadeh grabbed a red towel and came back to the room. Then she left the sandwich and the towel next to him and left. When she heard the doorbell she knew it was Goli. She had almost given up on Mr. Ali. It was twenty-four hours since she had last heard from him. Goli's facial muscles were tense and her eyes had no expression. There was no hope in them. Her old beliefs "the holy grave of the saint, the moon in the sky, the green robed man in her dreams," which would warm her heart and give her courage before were useless to her. Her Ahmad was dying, Azadeh took her hand and sat beside her on the couch. "How was he?"

"Bad, he's dying. I heard it with my own ears when the nurse was talking to his doctor." She slipped down on the floor and started hitting on her head. "Ahmad, my Ahmad, my soul, my breath, my everything. Oh Ahmad."

Azadeh was watching her, but her whole attention was to the hallway and knew that Hadji must have heard Goli and was making plans. She put her ear on the door. There was no snoring sound. Son of a bitch is awake! Oh God, what should I do? She went back to Goli with the utmost feeling of helplessness. She tried to quiet her, but it was too late. Hadji had heard everything, what bad luck.

After an hour Goli lost all her energy and exhausted, fell on the carpet thinking about her life. Azadeh, ignoring her, was looking outside, puffing on her cigarette nervously. Goli turned around and looked at her. She had felt that Azadeh was not paying attention to her, but was expecting sympathy from her. Azadeh felt her disappointment, but there was nothing she could do. All of a sudden she thought of dinner and hurried to the kitchen to make some eggs. Goli slowly followed her. Azadeh put the skillet with eggs on the table and lit a cigarette. But Goli only drank a few cups of tea and went to the room next to Sepideh's where she had spent many nights there.

Azadeh, exhausted, took a shower and let the hot water lash on her skin. Then she went to her room and dropped on the bed. She felt an unpleasant numbness taking over her body and her head started spinning. Sleep was taking over her. She got scared, got up, leaned on the wall, and pulled herself to the kitchen. She put the cold fried eggs into her mouth and swallowed without even chewing. Then she ate a few spoonful's of honey and went to the room where Goli was to talk to her. But she didn't find her in there. She found her in the backyard with a blanket around her, sitting on the steps. She sat beside her. Goli, who had heard the coughing in the next room, thought that guy must have been Azadeh's boyfriend.

"I'm waiting for morning to call my daughter. She must be worried sick by now. I wanted to call her before but it was too late. I didn't want to cause too much trouble for you and your boyfriend. Go to him. God willing, you'll marry him and won't be lonely anymore."

Azadeh looked up and sighed into the sky. "Goli, what do you see in this sky?"

"Nothing, a sad sky as myself."

"But I see two stars in that corner, there, where the sky is the darkest."

"Oh yeah, those two next to each other, yes I see them."

"I want to tell you, you and I, right now, are like those two stars. Those two, in this vast sky, only have each other." Azadeh put her hand on Goli's and kissed her on the cheek. "You know, everything has changed here. It's my fault. I made a big mess for myself and I can't even talk to anyone about it or ask for help. I'm so glad you're here, you have given me strength."

Goli sighed and said, "Okay, if I'm alive after Ahmad. Who has made the trouble for you? Is it this guy here? Are you married? Or is he having cold feet?"

A really sad smile came to Azadeh's face. "No, nothing like that. Goli, it's a secret. I want you to keep this secret forever."

"You go get some sleep, I can't concentrate on what you are telling me. I'll go to the holy shrine of the saint and cry until I die. Why should I live anymore? What is left for me except for two bloodied crying eyes."

Azadeh, sympathizing, said, "I have to talk to you tonight before you see this guy. There's a lot you have to know. The guy that you heard is a mullah that Ahmad has brought here."

Goli turned her head towards her with an inquiring look, wide eyed and eyelashes stuck together from crying. Azadeh dropped her head and told her everything.

It was dawn, sadness and fear had turned Goli's face dark. That look with her dropped jaw and knitted eyebrows was blaming Azadeh. She was thinking, everybody had done her wrong and used her. They had taken away her rights as a mother and taken away the days she could have spent with her sick son. Goli stood up like a dry bough broken under pressure. Her back was bent. She leaned on the wall and went to the room.

When the sun was lighting the room up, Azadeh opened her eyes. Goli had gone to the hospital without waking her up. Azadeh finally had a chance to concentrate and find a solution for the mess she was in. She wasn't thinking of Mr. Ali anymore, she had given up on even seeing him again. Who could help her now? She was desperate and helpless. Her brain was useless to her now.

CHAPTER TEN

Hadji had spent the whole day snoozing and now that it was evening he was wide awake and was stomping with his feet like an angry bull. Pain in his legs and arms were killing him and he was cursing Ali. The snake he had taken care of for the past seventeen years now had shown his true face. Ali's face when he was a teenage boy came to his mind. He shook his head with sorrow. He first saw Ali when he snuck his hairy head into Hadji's backyard to check out his twelve year old daughter who was washing clothes. Hadji had beaten him up badly and when he was beating him, he saw the look on Ali's face. In the midst of all that, he noticed his face was trying to protect himself from his beating. That look turned Hadji on. He pulled him into the back rooms and raped him then threatened him that if he said anything to anyone, he would have him and his mom beheaded. When Ali was scared out of his mind, he patted him, and gave him a few coins. That same day, he sent him a pair of new shoes too. Ali was an orphan and from that day on, he became like one of the household members there. Hadji was still at school in Kabul to become a mullah. When his schooling was done, he was promoted to a full mullah and gained influence. He became rich by harvesting opium and then moved to Tehran to start his own drug ring there. His right hand man was Ali. He couldn't trust anybody else. A few years ago, Ali even took a bullet to save his life. Ali was his driver and would go everywhere with him. It was a few years that Ali wouldn't let him come to his bed anymore, but still Hadji was taking care of him. What a mistake. Why did he get so careless with Ali? He should have known there was something going on when Ali came back from a visit to his mom in Afghanistan. Ali wasn't the same obedient slave as before.

As he was feeling sorry for himself, he was looking at his turban and its hole. He was sucking on his yellow thumb, hoping that the smell of opium under his nail would calm him. Since last year when the opium in his snuffbox got soft from his body heat, he wasn't carrying it on himself anymore. That day, Ali jokingly suggested to him to put the box in the hole in his own turban and he did just that. The box was always with him just in case he was away from home and his pipe. He could put a piece of opium under his tongue until he got back. Hadji didn't know what was in store for him. He was sure Ali had gone and crossed the border to Afghanistan to get his mother and disappear somewhere. But he couldn't figure out his reason for waiting and what they had planned for him. If he was to die, why hadn't they done it yet? Maybe they wanted to leave him alone so he would die on his own from withdrawal. Thinking about death scared him so much that he started screaming and yelling madly and frightfully.

Azadeh, snoozing in her room, jumped up from his screams. She was almost sure someone must have heard him through the blocked windows. She ran to the room to quiet him down, but as soon as she got to the door, she hesitated. She had to hide her fears from Hadji, she opened the door and looked into Hadji's dark eyes calmly. Hadji was staring back at her. He couldn't see her eyes from the slit that was open from her shawl. He just heard her saying "You'd better shut up. You must have figured it out by now that no one can hear you here. So calm down and don't do anything stupid."

"Listen to me woman. I want to make a deal with you. I'll double whatever they're paying you. Come to your senses woman and let me go. I swear to my four sons I'll do anything you ask me to. I'll buy you a house; I'll take care of you. I heard you crying and talking out loud. It's obvious you're not made for these sorts of things. They must have been tricked you into this. God is my witness, I'll save you. If you want, I'll marry you so you can get part of my inheritance. I can even put you in my will so you get everything. I'll take you places, I'll take you to Macca for pilgrimage, whatever you want." Sweat was running from his forehead and dripping into his beard. He had pulled his legs into his chest and was massaging them with his free hand. Azadeh laughed by looking at his old and skinny body. He reminded him of what Ahmad had told her once. Hadji was addicted to opium. 'I don't think this skinny old wretched of a man can survive without his opium. What if he dies on me?' Thinking about the possibility of his death gave her shivers.

Darkness had covered everything, when the doorbell rang there was no worries or anxieties accompanied with it. Azadeh hugged Goli and let her cry on her shoulder as long as she wanted to. At the hospital they let her be with her son as long as she wanted to and then she closed his eyes with her hands to put him to rest forever. His death was the saddest of all deaths. He didn't die among familiar and beloved faces, but on the cold hospital bed in a strange city with strangers around. This hurt Goli the most. In her mind, Ahmad wasn't the small-framed skinny guy that he was, but rather a tall handsome man that the ground would shake when he walked. His face was lit with holiness and he was a hero, who only thought of others. Now, Ahmad was a martyr to Goli. His small flaws were all forgiven and she could barely remember them. A martyr whose picture she had to put next to her other son's, Hamid.

Goli didn't stay long. The same night she returned to prepare for his funeral. When leaving, she kissed Azadeh and as her bitter tears were rolling down her face, she asked, "Now what are you going to do with this guy?"

"I don't know, I just want to find a way to keep him quiet so I can visit my sons tomorrow. I'm afraid Hamed will bring them over unexpectedly." Azadeh was doubly sad that she couldn't be with Goli at this time. She should have helped her and her family through the last night, and accompanied them to the hospital, but she had to stay and deal with this son of a bitch.

It was around noon when she pulled herself out of bed with her pounding headache. She had to get ready to leave. She went to the bathroom and her reflection in the mirror frightened her. Her face was full of anxiety from apparently hiding a secret. She looked exhausted, and the lines around her eyes and lips had become deeper. 'If Zohreh sees me in this state, she will become suspicious. Maybe she even will get tempted to stay with me.' So she decided to go straight to her son's school. She would pick them up and take them to the movies. Then she could drop them off on the way back and run away without encountering anyone. She looked in the medicine cabinet in search of a strong painkiller. But there were only a few aspirins. She took the bottle and with a cup of water, went to Hadji's room. She looked at him, who was massaging himself and moaning. She didn't even consider him to be worth hating.

"Do you want to get rid of the pain?"

Hadji looked at the bottle in her hand and said, "What are you cooking for me?"

"Nothing, I just want you to shut up for a few hours."

"Don't be crazy woman, let me go. Give me the phone. I'll have them give you one hundred million dollars."

"Okay, whenever I make up my mind I'll give you the phone." She threw the aspirin bottle on his lap. Hadji took four pills and put his tongue in his mouth. Azadeh took his thumb and put it in the turban hole. She took pity on him and wanted to calm him. She couldn't figure out why. Although, she was missing Goli during these tortuous days and nights, now she had time to sit down in her loneliness and think about her life. Hadji was a stinking creature to her and his stench had satiated the air in the room. His moaning and begging were making her nauseous. He was a begging wretch, always asking for aspirin. She would just throw a handful of aspirins in front of him and go back to the kitchen to drink coffee and look at the papers. She was expecting to see his picture in the papers. Surely, somebody must be looking for him by now. Apparently, nobody was missing him and this seemed strange to Azadeh. Maybe this wretched shit is not much to be missed after all. Or maybe they are looking for him quietly and as soon as they find him, they will kill everyone involved without making any noise.

She was so preoccupied with these thoughts that she couldn't think about her mother and Sepideh anymore. One day, she received a letter from them, which she just threw in her room unopened, hoping to get to it later. It was a week since she was with Hadji in her house and her vacation was about to end. She had to hurry up. She was constantly thinking without coming to any conclusion. She couldn't come up with any plans to get rid of him. She didn't see it in herself to be able to deal with the situation. She even thought about telling everything to her uncle and asking for help. But every time she wanted to pick up the phone, a voice from deep down her soul warned her not to involve him, not to take the fear into his household. She had to keep it to herself and await the horrible fate she would receive when Hadji's gang came after her. Plus the fact that she knew her uncle would most probably give Hadji to the police to deal with him. She could do the same thing and buy herself a life in prison. It was a nightmare that was frequently visiting her in which Hadji's men were kidnapping her sons. Then she was thinking about her life after all those years in prison and that was unbearable too. She saw a future for herself being treated as a crazy, mad woman, who deserved whatever happened to her. People making fun of her and calling her crazy, death would be better than that fate. After the dream she had last night, she spent the entire day thinking of the desert that she would leave Hadji at. This was a dream that she wished for in reality. Something was telling her she should bring that dream into reality.

She decided to go for a drive before sunset to check things out. She drove around for a while and finally found herself in an abandoned landfill type of place with a few people digging around the trash. Two of them ran towards her. She got scared and drove back home. She spent the rest of the night thinking of that place. If only she could overcome her fear, maybe then she could abandon Hadji in there.

The next day, in hopes of becoming braver, she drove to the landfill when it became dark, but ended up returning even more afraid.

CHAPTER ELEVEN

Goli's moments were filled with sorrow for Ahmad and anxiety about Azadeh. She knew she couldn't do anything for her but this disaster rested on her shoulders. She couldn't stop thinking about Azadeh, and how frightened and lonely she must be feeling. She was feeling that too. Ahmad came to her in her sleep a few times and had frowned at her. She even heard him telling her, "Mom, you can leave me, go and help Azadeh."

As soon as the Seventh night of his passing was done (In Shiit tradition the seventh night after the death is when the dead person is crossing the realm of life to death with no return), she couldn't stay in Quom any longer. She made up a story to her daughter and started toward Tehran. Azadeh was lying on the bed and reading her mom's letter. They were fine and everything was going well, and in a couple of weeks they were going to London. Azadeh took the pen to write them that she is fine, and that life without them is too lonely and sad. But she couldn't write. She imagined her mother being happy and worry free about her, thinking that finally she was spending her time with her kids relaxed and happy. She got up to call her kids and tell them about their grandma, when the doorbell rang. She got scared; who could be coming to visit her unexpectedly? She thought that maybe it was her uncle. She wanted to open the door, but she was worried about Mr. Ali. Slowly, she went to the backyard and looked from underneath the gate. She saw a suitcase and long veil. With a smile she opened the door. Goli came in and Azadeh hugged her tightly.

"I didn't expect to see you so soon!"

Goli looked up at the sky, "Where do you think we are right now?" The sky was filled with stars.

"We must be those two."

That night, Goli went into Hadji's room to check on him when he was asleep. She was hiding behind Azadeh and saw him in the shaky light of the candle. "Dear, this skinny ass is nothing to worry about. Give him to me, I'll dump him somewhere myself."

While she was locking the door, Azadeh said, "That's what I'm thinking of, I have even found a spot. It's a landfill, we'll go and dump him there."

Goli, cautiously said, "Yeah, that's a good idea, we'll dump him. God willing, dogs will tear him apart so his family won't even get his remains." Azadeh cried in her heart, she could see how simple and childish her plan was. Despite expectations, Goli wasn't that much impressed by Hadji and wasn't scared of him at all. She could even see how little and insignificant he was. This was worrying Azadeh. She could even imagine Goli chatting with him.

"Goli, I need to talk to you about a serious matter. I need your help." Azadeh explained all her plans slowly and in detail. The desperation was apparent through her tone and in the look in her eyes. Goli's face turned white. Now, it was what Azadeh had expected. Goli was frightened by the responsibility given to her and she was trying to hide her anxiety unsuccessfully. She knew when it was time to act, her body would get weak and her tongue twisted. With fear in her eyes she looked at Azadeh.

"Dear, maybe I won't be able to pull the guy out of the car as fast as you're expecting." Then she put her hands in front of Azadeh's eyes, "See, I'm shaking even now."

Azadeh shook her head sadly, "Goli, I understand what you're telling me. Pray to God as you usually do and ask him to give you strength."

"God damn you Hadji, I wish you were dead instead of my Ahmad. Now at my age, I have to pull your dirty body to places. Maybe we can just dump him somewhere around here or even in front of a mosque so we don't have to go to a dumpster."

"If none of the houses had windows, we could. In the landfill, there are only rats and dogs."

CHAPTER TWELVE

It was four in the morning on Friday. Friday was the day Azadeh was going to dump Hadji. By experience, she knew that at dawn the nightwalkers would reside and the city rests, letting the streets relax and breathe. She usually spent the whole night waiting for the first ray of light, but now she preferred the darkness. It was a cover for her secrets. An hour ago she had given a few pain killers to Hadji and now he was deep asleep after a long painful day, so deep, that he didn't feel Azadeh's presence next to him. He only heard her saying, "Take it easy, we're taking you home." He didn't get a chance to say anything or look at Azadeh. His mouth was taped, his head covered with a cloth and his whole body covered in blankets.

Unexpectedly, Hadji was heavy. She couldn't carry him more than a few steps on her shoulders. She put him down. She pulled her gray Fiat as close to the gate as she could and opened the trunk. Goli was watching the street. She pulled Hadji to the gate with great difficulty and used all her strength to dump him into the trunk. As she was pulling and pushing she could hear Goli praying in a loud voice. She left Hadji on the ground.

"Do your praying later, come and help me."

Goli breathed heavily while rolling her eyes trying to show Azadeh, "I told you, I can't help."

Azadeh's brain was burning like a furnace and she was at the height of her stress level. Uncontrollably, she started hitting herself on her head, covered her face with her hands and started crying. Goli joined her in crying. Then Goli tied her veil behind her neck and said, "Okay, let's do it together. I hope a hundred dogs will tear your body, you evil man. With that she kicked him hard. Why did you let them bring him here, did you want disaster for yourself, girl? Oh, my god, he is so energetic all of a sudden, look he's running towards the yard, hurry Azadeh"

Saying that, Goli herself, got a hold of the man's head and pulled him down to the ground. She pulled him towards the gate and Azadeh held on to his legs.

Hadji, exhausted after fighting, was lying still on the ground. He was so motionless that for a second, Azadeh thought maybe he was dead. At that time it didn't matter to her if he was alive or dead. She didn't even check his heart. Goli was holding his head with two hands. Azadeh took his arms and legs and lifted him. Goli lost control and dropped his head on the ground. It made a sound and Hadji started moaning in pain. Azadeh, nervous, pulled him up from under his waist and with one motion dropped him in the trunk. Then she sat behind the wheel. In spite of what she expected, there was no less traffic than normal days. When she got to the stoplight, she was so nervous that she passed it without stopping. She was praying that there was no police, but that didn't happen. She saw a police car speeding up to her in her rearview mirror. She looked at Goli, whose dentures were chattering in her mouth.

"The police is following us. If they stop us, don't forget what I told you to say!"

Goli looked back and didn't say anything. Azadeh turned the radio on to cover the chattering noise. At the next stoplight the police pulled her over. Azadeh was looking straightforward. She didn't want to lose her cool. The officer knocked on the window and signaled her to roll the window down. Her heart was pounding as she tried listening to any possible noise coming from the trunk, she rolled the window down. Goli with closed eyes, had her head leaned against the window.

"Is she sick?"

"Yes officer, my mom has asthma, I'm taking her to the hospital."

The officer said, "Hurry up then."

Azadeh sighed in relief and pushed on the gas pedal. She saw in her rearview mirror that the police car was escorting her. Goddamn it, maybe they sensed something. The thought of landfill vanished from her mind. She pulled into the freeway and sped towards the hospital where she was working. When she got there, the police car just passed her. As Azadeh got out of the car, she noticed that it was early morning. She wanted to go to the landfill, but was afraid that police might be watching her from a hidden place. With trembling hands, she opened the door for Goli. Goli was looking for the landfill, but she couldn't find it. Everything was hazy to her. With difficulty she pulled her numb body out of the car and hung onto Azadeh for support. She was going to ask about the landfill, but no voice came out. As Azadeh was pulling her body she could feel how badly she was shaking underneath her long veil. She got worried. She fetched a wheelchair and rolled her inside. Her face was turning blue, her whole body was shaking, and cold sweat had stuck her dress to her body. Her jaws were loose and her mouth open. She looked so bad that they promptly admitted her and started the treatment. Her blood pressure was high and she was about to have a stroke.

After a few hours, she picked her up and with a bag full of medicine drove her home. What a disaster! She was constantly checking her in the mirror. The police turned out to be the good luck for them, a guardian angel. She was calm and didn't care about Hadji anymore. Even if he was awake and screaming in this traffic, no one could hear him. When they got home she saw her neighbor. Ignoring the neighbor, she helped Goli into the house and laid her down on the couch. She hurried back to the car; the streets would fill up with kids in a short time. The neighbor was in the middle of the street now, talking to another woman. Azadeh opened the trunk and threw Hadji on her shoulder.

"What has she bought? Must be a rug or something."

"Hold on, let us help you."

Azadeh threw herself inside with two long strides and closed the door. Now, she couldn't even take one more step. She put Hadji down and fell on the ground. Goli was looking at her from the window and sighing in sorrow. Hadji, now conscious, was fighting and rolling on the ground. Azadeh took a deep breath in, got up and kicked him hard then pulled him into the hallway. She was breathing heavily, there wasn't much distance to the room. She bent over wishing for death. Then she straightened up and again pulled him into the room with the same effort. She locked the door and went to the kitchen and drank a few glasses of water. Then she lit a cigarette, took a few drags, then covered her face and head with the shawl to handcuff Hadji on the bed again. She brewed some chamomile tea and brought a cup for Goli. Goli was sipping on her tea and was trying to calm herself down. She prayed quietly. She had prayed the Prayer for Desperates in hopes of a miracle.

Azadeh, exhausted, had fallen on another couch and could see herself falling into a quicksand going deeper and deeper. She put a cigarette to her mouth and without lighting it, she was playing with her lighter. Goli looking at her helpless, desperate face said, "Don't worry dear, God is great."

"He doesn't seem so great at the moment. I think you'll get better in a couple of days and you can go back home. I'll surrender to the police. I should have done it earlier."

"Well, now I can't move. It's like my body is falling apart. But dear, I'm afraid they will put you in jail."

Azadeh ironically said, "I'll be happy with a jail sentence."

"Don't jinx it. God willing they'll let you go. Ahmad had a short life, but he knew what kind of disaster he had brought here. I could see it in his eyes. I swear to the prophet I think his spirit is in this room. I have a gut feeling. Oh great prophet, please have mercy on this woman."

In the other room, Hadji was confused and his eyes were looking around the room. It was the same room as before with the same dark curtains. He was confused as to why they took him out and brought him back to the same room again. He was dying with curiosity and was calling out to the woman. Azadeh got up. Goli said,

"Leave the skinny shit alone. Let him scream until he dies."

"I'm going to call my coworker at the hospital. I'm going to her house to tell her about the mess I'm in. She's the only one who can call my uncle tomorrow."

"Can't you wait for a couple more days? You said you went to see Ahmad at that Afghan man's house. Go see him, maybe he can help us."

"He's not as stupid as I am to get himself involved in this shit. I wish Ahmad had listened to him and forgotten about playing Robin Hood."

"Well dear, it won't harm to try. We tell him, maybe he will feel sorry for us."

Azadeh didn't stay to listen to Goli any longer. She went to her room and dialed Maryam's cell phone. Maryam answered her phone.

"I'm glad you called, I was going to call you. There was a guy here asking for you. He said his name was Mohammad. I wasn't going to give your number to him, but then I saw his family on his moped waiting for him. Are you in charity work now?" Maryam laughed at her own joke.

Azadeh's heart was beating fast by hearing Mohammad's name. What did he want from her? With a colorless face she went back to Goli and stayed with her.

"Well, did you call her?"

"No, but Mohammad had gone to the hospital asking for me. Strange, isn't it?"

"Who's Mohammad?"

"The same Afghan guy you were talking about. Maybe he's the fortune I was looking for."

When her phone rang again, she picked it up promptly. It was Mohammad. He said hi, and Azadeh, with shaky voice said, "Hello."

"Excuse me sister, I was thinking maybe you had heard from Ahmad. I went to the hospital, but you weren't there. God bless your coworker, she gave me your number."

"Ahmad has passed."

"He died? When?" Mohammad's voice was filled with deep sorrow, "Where is he resting?"

Azadeh cried, "Come here." Sobbingly, she gave him her address. "For God's sake, please come as fast as you can."

"What's going on?"

She couldn't talk anymore. She hung up and checked on Goli. She was resting. She kissed her. Goli opened her eyes.

"If you are seeing Ahmad, tell him Mohammad is worried and is coming here."

Goli sat up overwhelmed, "You mean that Afghan is coming?"

"Yes, he's coming." Goli, with eyes filled with tears of happiness said, "I heard the phone. So that was him? Thank God. It's Ahmad who sent him here to take care of this disaster."

"Well, I hope so but we'll see."

"Don't be so negative. Why do you think the guy has called you?"

"He was asking about Ahmad."

"No dear, you are Ahmad, my dear, dear, Ahmad. My life, Ahmad." Goli wiped her tears with her hand, brought out the prayer stone out of her pocket, put it on her lap, and prayed in the seated position. It felt like there was no end to this prayer. She wasn't asking for anything from God anymore, she had gotten her wish. Mohammad was rushing to them. This was the first time that she was worshipping God only for Him.

It was the middle of the day and there was a pale sunshine in the backyard. Azadeh opened the door to Mohammad and laughed so excitedly that it could be heard all over the house. Mohammad was surprised, he noticed Goli who was looking from the kitchen window.

"She is Ahmad's mom."

Mohammad's face grew sad, "God bless his soul, how long has it been?"

"Let's go inside."

Mohammad said, ya Allah, announcing his entrance, (a tradition of Muslims to announce that a man is entering so women would cover themselves). Azadeh followed him. He sat on the couch and with his head down he looked at Azadeh. She seemed prettier with scarf on her head.

Azadeh said, "I was going to the police when you called. You know, Ahmad kidnapped the Hadji. He's here. Mr. Ali never showed up and I think he took the money too. When I came back, I found Ahmad on the kitchen floor. The next day he died in the hospital."

Mohammad didn't quite comprehend what Azadeh had told him so quickly. Confused, he looked at Goli who was sitting in front of him.

Goli said, "Yes sir, my son passed away. Now the devil is sleeping at the end of the hallway. May God make him more miserable." Goli started crying and calling on Ahmad. Azadeh cried too.

Mohammad waited until they were done, then he said, "Now Ms. Azadeh, tell me the whole story."

Goli didn't let her, she started telling him the entire story from putting Hadji in the car and their trip to the hospital, and how it wasn't her time to die yet. She said it all with great details. Azadeh said of her anxieties and bad luck. Then she gave him some sheets to cover himself.

"Let's go and see Hadji." Azadeh covered her face and asked him to do so too. Mohammad was still confused and couldn't make sense of the situation. He put the sheets on the couch and looked at Azadeh questioningly.

"So you say, you saw Ali in my house the first time?"

Goli said, "That bastard must have gone under Ahmad's skin! May God punish him! I hope all the money turns into poison and kills him. This poor girl was thinking of me. Otherwise she wouldn't have believed this Afghan conman. You can't believe what hell we're going through sir. Please, for Saint Zahra's sake, take this man from here, may God repay you. It's a good thing to do. Good deeds will be rewarded for Ahmad's sake."

"Tell me, did this Ali have a scar under his eye?"

"Yes, a deep scar all the way to his nose." Ali's face was a face that Azadeh would never forget. His sad brown eyes, thick blue lips, a head with a full set of hair, narrow forehead, and a scar that would start from under his eys and all the way down to his mouth.

Mohammad whispered, "May God forgive us. He's at my home, I'm here, what a world, what a world!." "I can't believe this, where is this man, show him to me, the unthinkable is done, what have you done Osman?"

Azadeh said it's better to cover your face first, but Mohammad said that if the guy is the one he thinks who he is, then there is no need for him to cover his face, he wanted to look into his eye.

Goli said she wanted to go with them into the room. She wanted to hit the man in the face and pull each and every hair out of his dirty beard. Mohammad asked him to wait there, then he followed Azadeh into the room anxiously.

In the lamplight, Sadegh Jamal was lying on the bed with no color on his face. He was snoozing with his mouth open. For a second he opened his eyes, but as if he didn't see anything, closed them again and said something. Mohammad took a step forward, he stood by his bed, and tears rolled down his face. Bravo Ali, finally you jumped on Sadegh. Then he put his hands to his temples and sighed. It had been five years since his brother's death and now his killer was in his hands. A wish that he never thought would come true. Now he wasn't thinking about his own life on this earth. All he could think of was that day and the job he had to finish to take his brother's revenge from Sadegh to bring a smile to Shirin's face, his widow whom he had married two years ago. Now he was the real father to Maliheh. Mohammad was laughing from happiness and excitement. Azadeh noticed his tears. Mohammad looked at her and said, "I never even imagined this. What game fate is playing on us."

"Sister I have to put you on a big pedestal! Wow, what a big job you have done, you have no idea what a monster you have captured!"

Sadegh Jamal heard his voice. He turned his head and stared at him with eyes almost jumping out of his head. He mustered all his energy to rollover on his side. He heard a man's voice. He tried hard to open his eye lids and peer through the side of his eyes. In his confused state he wondered if he was awake or if he was still sleep?!!! Was Mohammad a nightmare or a reality? He was drowning in his fear. His shivering chin and quivering cheeks were a testamony of his fear of Mohammad and his fear of death. He turned his head and stared at him with eyes almost ready to jump out of his head. Mohammad smiled at him. "Sadegh, you have shit on your beard."

Sadegh Jamal touched his beard, which was knotted together from throw up and filth. He tried to say something, but his coughing didn't let him. Mohammad laughed and flicked his head. "Hey cousin, I see you're losing control all over your body."

Azadeh turned and with dropped jaw looked at him.

Sadegh Jamal coughing and with a weakened voice, said, "Mohammad forgive me. All my wealth is yours."

"You miserable shit, what wealth? It's all on fire. Don't you smell burned opium? Whatever is left of it Ali took, good for him. He really stuck it to you. Don't you want to ask about your aunt? Do you know she went blind after what you did to us? Can you give her back her eyesight? Sadegh, you must die. Your death will rid these people of your shame. Man, you have turned into something that does not deserve to be buried and should be chopped into pieces for the birds of prey. This is the price you pay for oppressing others, my dear cousin. I asked God to punish you, but the almighty had set some duties for us as well. We were not dutiful before." Mohammad turned to Azadeh and said, "You are a brave and respectable woman. You have no idea what kind of devil you have here."

Azadeh was still in shock and was looking at him with amazement. 'Cousin? What is he saying? Who is he anyway? God help us. Who am I dealing with?'

Sadegh Jamal was breathing with difficulty and was almost snoring. Mohammad said, "He is dying."

As Azadeh was locking the door, she asked, "Is he really your cousin?" Mohammad didn't answer. Azadeh said, "Do you have any idea what I've been through these past days?"

"God will give you strength. I never thought Sadegh would end up in your house. How did you allow this?"

"I was stupid and now I'm paying for it."

"No sister, you did a great deed. This man has killed so many people. If your heart wasn't with God, he wouldn't have ended up here. Isn't that right?"

"That's right. I wanted it. But I couldn't kill him. I couldn't press hard on his throat."

"You did press". Said Mohammad

It was true that killing him was my heart's desire. But I could not chock him. I did not want him to die like this" Azadeh sighed

"He ruined our lives but I feel he is dying on his own. He can't breathe any more. This is the pressure from your hands chocking him." Mohammad said trying to console her.

Don't you see death in his eyes? Tell your sister, she'll get happy."

Azadeh thought, never, it will kill my mom. Mohammad, deep in the couch and his head up towards the ceiling, as if his praying carpet was on it, was reciting Quoran out loud. Then he stroked his beard and his face was grim. He said slowly, "Does anyone other than you know about this?

"No, how could I tell anyone I have kidnapped a guy? What am I supposed to do with him now?"

"You? Nothing." Mohammad got up, pardoned himself and took out his cell phone from his gray overcoat and went into the backyard. Azadeh was surprised. She didn't think he was the type of guy to carry a cell phone. At that moment, the short answer, "You nothing" was dancing in her head. 'Did he mean that he was going to get rid of him, his dear cousin?'

Goli gave Mohammad a cup of tea. "Did you see the shithead? He's moaning day and night. At first he was screaming. If only you knew how much we have suffered. I don't wish it upon my enemies."

Mohammad asked, "Ma'am, how many sons do you have?"

"My two sons perished like an early flower." Goli, as if waiting for a chance to start talking about her life and bring out all her sorrows with her tears, talked to Mohammad for an hour. Azadeh looked at him. She was waiting for him to say something. But Mohammad's eyes were looking at the sky, the moon and the few stars shining. Goli signaled to Azadeh to prepare something for dinner. Azadeh asked, "Mohammad, what are you going to do with Hadji?" Mohammad came to the couch and sat down.

"At two o'clock in the morning, two of my countrymen will come here to take him away." A smile came to Azadeh's eyes. With a trembling voice she said, "You mean, this nightmare is going to end?" Happily she went to the kitchen to fix something for dinner. The hours of the night were passing slowly. Goli went to her room and Mohammad was sitting on the floor on his knees praying. Azadeh was sitting in the kitchen looking at the backyard and then at the wall clock. There was a pleasant excitement in her, an excitement that took away the fatigue and anxieties. Mohammad's cell phone rang. Azadeh jumped into the room. Mohammad said, "They're at the door. Go hide in another room. They shouldn't see you."

Azadeh said, "Okay." She was going into her room, but then changed her mind. She only had partial view of the backyard from there. She went upstairs to the roof and from above the oak tree looked at the gate. Mohammad was in the back yard and opened the gate. In the dim light of the moon the yard was slightly visible. Azadeh saw two men come in and pass through the yard with Mohammad. Azadeh went back to the stairs and listened. She heard their thick voices talking to each other. Then there was silence. She guessed they must be in Hadji's room by now. Then in a minute, she heard them again. She hurried back to the rooftop and saw the two men dragging Hadji towards the door, his head dangling down and his feet dragging on the ground. It looked like he was dead. They took Hadji. Azadeh was looking for Mohammad. Then she saw a man with a turban on his head in the middle of the yard looking up. Azadeh smiled and tried to hide, but it was too late. Mohammad waved at her and closed the door behind him.

Azadeh ran downstairs and went to the room to Goli. She found her looking out the window. She threw her arms around her. "Did you see them too?"

"Yes, I saw them all. I think there were four or five of them, two were mullahs. Azadeh laughed, "I thought you were sleeping."

"No dear, what sleep? I haven't slept in days."

That next day, Azadeh stayed in bed till noon. Her only wish was to sleep. Late afternoon, she woke up to Goli's voice. She was talking on the phone. Azadeh got up, and went to the kitchen. Goli asked, "You're up? It's Masoumeh. Do you want to talk her?" Azadeh took the phone.

Masoumeh said, "Hello Azadeh. I hope you are feeling better." Her voice reminded her of Sepideh. She wanted to talk to her more and ask about her life. When she hung up, she spent hours thinking about Sepideh and her mother. That day, her mother's neighbor, who had just come from pilgrimage to Kaaba, had a party and Azadeh had been invited too. But she sent Goli in her place. She was expecting her kids.

The next day, Azadeh accompanied Goli to Quom. She put a big flower arrangement on Ahmad and Hamid's graves. Ahmad's grave didn't have the stone yet. She sat down and touched the cold dirt, and told him the whole story with tears and laughter. Then she promised him to take care of his mom. She spent the night at Goli's house and spent time talking to her daughters, Sedigheh and Masoumeh. Goli had told them that she was going to Tehran to take care of Azadeh who was sick and lonely. Now when they were looking at her pale face and the dark circles under her eyes, they saw a huge difference between that face and the pictures Goli had shown them before. Sedigheh felt sorry for Azadeh and thought that she must have a really bad disease. Maybe Goli had convinced her to come to Quom to ask the saint for a cure. Sedigheh brewed her a pot of herbal medicine and made Azadeh drink it. It worked and made Azadeh so relaxed that she slept calmly and peacefully.

Azadeh felt that she was always right about her first impressions of people. She was studying these three little women carefully. The picture she had in her mind from Sedigheh was different from what she saw now. She was about forty, her black eyes were sad, and she looked at people with lowered eyes. Masoumeh, her daughter, had her long black hair gathered with a black ribbon. She seemed angry but, her independence was evident in her face. Azadeh felt that Masoumeh was not made to have an ordinary life. She had the capabilities to pull herself up in life later on. Fatima, Goli's daughter and Ahmad's sister, had been struggling with her husband. Ten years had passed since her marriage and still she couldn't give him a child. Now her husband was asking her to either get a divorce or give him permission to get another wife. Although she loved her husband, she figured that either way she would lose her husband so she was considering divorce.

The next day, it was early evening when Azadeh got back to her home, but as if being in fear had become her second nature, she didn't want to go inside. She got out of her car and started walking down the street. After an hour she got a cab and gave Hamed's address to the driver.

Zohreh greeted her warmly. She looked at her sickly face and she couldn't find traces of anxiety or sadness. Smiling, she said, "It's strange, you're both messed up and happy at the same time. You should name this condition. I have no idea what to call this."

"How about 'hell survivor'?'"

"That really suits you. Tell me, did you have fun? How was your vacation?" "As you know, I spent the first week with the boys, then I spent ten days in Mashad, and I spent ten days with Hadji, the same guy that Ahmad had kidnapped and brought to my house. Then I spent two days in Quom. Tomorrow I'm going back to work."

Zohreh started laughing. "I'm glad you finally sent Ahmad to the graveyard in your mind."

"Well, I had to get rid of him one way or another."

CHAPTER THIRTEEN

Finally, the smell of flowers and spring were starting to fill the air. But life for Goli was the darkest ever. They were poor and life had become difficult for them. Goli was spending most of her time at her two sons' graves. One day, when she was coming back to the house she was sharing with Sedigheh, she saw the neighbor with a fat man leaving. Goli asked, "Who is he?"

"Mashdi Hussein is my brother. We're here to see Ms. Sedigheh."

Goli said, "You'd better leave before I get mad."

The neighbor jumped inside promptly. Goli looked at Sedigheh with disbelief.

Sedigheh said, "I think she went inside to take the cake they brought." She was right. The neighbor came back with the cake box in her hand.

"Of course I'm taking it back. You're saying no to my

brother and you're expecting me to give you sweets too?"

Goli said, "Get the hell out! I don't want to see you around Sedigheh anymore." The neighbor pulled her brother and as they were leaving she said,

"You deserve whatever is happening to you guys. I hope your life gets worse than this."

"You can't even afford her. She is too big for your mouth."

Sedigheh said, "Thank you. The guy has five kids on his hands after his wife's death and now he wants me to take care of them."

"Low life! I shouldn't have trusted her with my secrets. What was she thinking bringing this bum here? Well, that's obvious. She wants a sex slave for her brother and at the same time, a free slave for his kids."

When Masoumeh came home from school, Goli told her, "You know, today the neighbor's wife had come here to ask for your mother's hand for her brother?"

Masoumeh looked into her mom's eyes and asked worriedly, "And what did you say?"

Goli said, "I took care of them. Your mom is only smart mouthed when it comes to me."

Masoumeh said, "Mama Goli, it's all your fault. You tell everyone about our lives."

"Well dear, people are not blind. They can see that week after week we don't set foot in the butcher shop. Well she must have thought we are very poor so she had brought her grave digger brother here."

Masoumeh started crying. Sedigheh said, "Don't cry, I'll find a cleaning job somewhere."

Goli said, "Don't you dare. You're going to disrespect Karbalai and Ahmad's name."

"Well, what am I supposed to do, just wait?"

Masoumeh said, "Mom, you don't need to clean people's houses. I'll quit school and I will get a job at the sewing factory. I heard they're hiring."

Goli started cursing her late husband. "I hope you're in hell burning, man. All day I was at the shop toiling and you were smoking it up at home. I hope your grave burns to hell. If only we had that shop, now we could hold our heads up and this poor kid wouldn't have to quit her school."

Sedigheh started crying. For the first time ever, Goli put her pride aside and kissed her on the head. She was more or less aware of the fact that she had no reason for hating Sedigheh. And now, she even liked the woman. In fact, after Ahmad's death she had a new feeling of responsibility towards this poor mother and daughter. Now they all shared the big stress of making ends meet. It wasn't important how they were living as long as they could pay for that month's rent. The rent was past due now and the landlord was at the door almost every day. The welfare money Goli was receiving could hardly put any food on the table. Often, Azadeh would hear Goli's sad voice on the phone. She wasn't complaining about Sedigheh anymore. She only spoke of them.

"Azadeh dear, what do you think we should do? How are we supposed to take care of this little girl? All the bums and nobodies are calling on her. They're asking for both mom and daughter. I'm afraid Sedigheh might give up and take her with herself to one of these lowlife's homes."

Azadeh wanted to help them out but how? Her salary was really low and even if she could help them out a little bit, it wasn't enough. Something must be done. She was thinking that if she could move them to Tehran, they could live in her mother's house and not have to worry about the rent. This was on her mind and she didn't think that Goli would accept it. Goli was accustomed to the Saint and her sons' gravesite in Quom. It was almost impossible to take her away from her daily talks with them, crying at the shrine, and the smell of burning candles. And then bring her to Tehran where everybody was a stranger and no one talked about their problems. On the other hand, she could foresee more problems coming up. Let's assume they accept to move, is it really possible to live with three different women with three totally different backgrounds in the same house? She was hoping to convince herself that these issues were not important, but she was always thinking about Masoumeh. She had talked to her on the phone several times, and had once sent her a gift of books and scarves. Just last night she talked to her for a long time and told her, "Stop thinking about quitting school. You are a good student. I'm sure you can get accepted to universities next year."

After a month Azadeh decided to go talk to Goli and also consult her mom and Sepideh about her idea too. Now they were living in a house in a London suburb temporarily and were happy with their lives. The only thing missing in there was Azadeh and her sons. Sepideh was taking English classes and her mom had found a few friends so she wasn't lonely anymore. She had said that the air was full of oxygen and it was easier to breathe. She told Azadeh that she didn't want to smoke anymore, plus the fact that they were not allowed to smoke inside the apartment. Azadeh took the pen, but what should she write about? How was she supposed to explain everything and tell them about the chain of events that had happened? It seemed like such a hard thing to do. It wasn't surprising that she couldn't tell her mother everything that had happened, even though it was over. But she knew if they found out from someone else, they would get so worried and their lives would turn dark. She wrote the story about going to Mohammad's house and everything about Sadegh Jamal from her memory, and then Ahmad's death and Goli's poor lifestyle. But what will her mom think? Why all of a sudden had she become so concerned about Goli and her family, and why would she let them in her own house? Azadeh thought, mom I know if one day you come back to your country and hear the whole story you will be happy to have them at your house too. I'll just wait until then.

One weekend, Azadeh just decided to go to Goli and tell them about what she had planned for them. Goli was wasiting for her. She took her inside and covered her face with kisses. Sedigheh brought her some herbal tea again.

Goli told her about her dream. It was Ahmad again, but with a happy face. Azadeh interpreted it as him giving her good news. Goli said, "Dear, if you see good news, tell me about it too. What good news?"

Masoumeh came in with fresh bread and got excited to see Azadeh there. "Thank you so much for the books and clothes. Whenever I become an attorney, I'll pay you back."

"I can picture you in your law office."

"I hope so."

Goli put the tea tray on the floor. "If she becomes a teacher like Fati, that's good too. By the way, she's getting divorced."

"But she wants to become a lawyer. She wants to protect women's rights.

Goli with a knowing laugh, said, "Dear, you can't defend people with paper. There should be bricks and sticks. Goddamn you Karbalai!"

Azadeh said, "If you don't mind, sit down. I have a proposition for you."

Masoumeh fixed her scarf on her head and sat in front of Azadeh looking at her with anticipation. Goli would have never imagined that Azadeh would make such a suggestion to them. Thinking about her routine life she said, "Dear Azadeh, how am I supposed to leave Ahmad and Hamid here? What about Fati? She is getting a divorce and is counting on me. And why do you want to make trouble for yourself? You know God is great, he will take care of us. It will all come together somehow."

Azadeh looked at Masoumeh who had a childish happiness in her eyes. "What do you think Masoumeh? Do you really believe a miracle is going to happen in your life?"

Masoumeh looked at Goli and said, "Mama Goli, you don't make sense. There's more to life than going to the graves. You have to think of me too. You told me yourself not to quit school, well how can I not if we stay here?" She couldn't continue because she had started crying.

Sedigheh said, "Masoumeh, stop it. Mama Goli is right. Even if we go to Tehran, we still belong here. Tehran is not close enough to be able to come back every Friday and wash your brothers' graves."

"That's enough mom! Just say no! Don't make up excuses! There's wind to clean up their graves and there's rain to wash them."

Goli looked at her angrily, "She's talking like there's potatoes buried under the graves!"

Sedigheh said, "Mama Goli, leave her alone. Don't make a fuss over nothing. She knows she shouldn't talk to you like that."

Masoumeh laughed and looking at Azadeh, shook her head and went into the kitchen to take care of lunch. Azadeh enjoyed the homemade soup by Goli and after a few hours returned to Tehran. But she knew Masoumeh would not let go of that idea and leave everything to fate. The truth was that Goli and Sedigheh wanted to keep their lives as it was and continue like that till their deaths. But Azadeh saw it clearly in Masoumeh that it wasn't what she wanted from life.

The second month of spring was gone. Azadeh had found a new purpose and energy in life. Now she wasn't thinking of her loneliness. She felt something in her had changed and she was changing her lifestyle. She wasn't thinking of her father as much. It was like the old sorrows were not as great to her as before. She wasn't thinking of her losses. She was thinking about Masoumeh and her future. Her dream was to make that girl's dreams reality. Now taking care of Masoumeh and her future was her responsibility.

Although all of her dreams had always been interpreted the opposite way, she felt that her dreams from the night before were intertwined with Masoumeh's life. She had seen her in a hall full of people listening to a lecture and today, Azadeh was preparing Sepideh's room for her since she was coming to live there permanently with her mother. Azadeh was not worried about Goli anymore. Since last week, Fati had moved in with her mom, now Goli had her daughter by her side. Fati had told her, "Mom, never even assume that I will leave you alone. You're mine. Whoever wants to marry me has to accept both of us."

As Azadeh was talking to Sedigheh and Masoumeh, her cigarette was burning in between her fingers. She had lit it by habit, but she didn't have any urge to smoke it anymore. She put it out in the ashtray. All these years I drowned my anger, hate, and sorrow with cigarettes. What a waste. She got up, picked a few bottles of wine, and started out towards Arezou's house. She missed her.

About the author:

"Nadereh Oweissi was born in Iran. She left Iran many years ago and have lived in and traveled to many different countries across Asia, Europe and United states. Her first published book, "The monkey and chain of life" has been originally written in Persian and recently translated to English. She lives in Sacramento, California along with her husband and is currently working on her second book."